Advance Praise
for Skull Fragments

"Tim L. Williams probes the darkness in human experience in penetrating detail, with an eye focused especially on those who are marginalized, lost, or desperate. His keen insights lay bare not only the inner drives that lead to violence but the small bright spaces that can be found in almost any life, in which there are glimmers of hope. He's a writer who never disappoints."
—Janet Hutchings, Editor-in-Chief, Ellery Queen's Mystery Magazine

"The ability to combine grit and darkness with a sensitive literary quality is no small thing, and Tim L. Williams can be mentioned in the same sentence as James Carlos Blake and Daniel Woodrell. It's about time that a book of his stories has been published."
—Otto Penzler, editor, Best American Mystery Stories of the Year

"In Tim Williams' splendidly written and noir-ish short stories, evil and love become indistinguishable and somehow fuse. When this happens to his characters, they're dealt a world that cuts to the bone. Everything a reader might ask is given generously in these tales of moments when the heart snaps. These are gruesomely wondrous love stories."
—Dale Ray Phillips, Pulitzer Prize nominated author of *My People's Waltz*

D1499181

Skull
Fragments:
Noir Stories

Skull
Fragments:
Noir Stories

Tim L. Williams

NEW PULP PRESS

Published by New Pulp Press, LLC, 926 Truman Avenue, Key West, Florida 33040, USA.

Skull Fragments: Noir Stories copyright © 2014 by Tim L. Williams. Electronic compilation/paperback edition copyright © 2014 by New Pulp Press, LLC. Cover art: Dahlia Woods

For information contact:
editor@newpulppress.com

ISBN-13: 978-0-9899323-8-7
ISBN-10: 0989932389

For Sherraine

Contents

I will not shoot you in the head, for I want to save it as a trophy.

—Moses Stegall to Big Harpe, America's first serial killer, at a crossroads in Western Kentucky that came to be known as Harpe's Head Road.

Where that Morning Sun Goes Down

Four days after we murder Tiny Gardner, Donny Ray decides he wants pancakes. It's closing in on three in the morning, still as black as a slag heap, so we head for the Huddle House out by the Western Kentucky Parkway and then Donny Ray pulls a thin, twisty joint from behind his ear before I can get out of the car.

"Hold on, Bubba," he says. "Let's fire this baby before we go in."

Normally I'd jump right on that idea, but it's early November, colder than it has any right to be, and the most the Pontiac's heater can manage is the occasional wheeze of frigid air. We've been on a wild one. We walked out of Tiny Gardner's trailer with a few bottles of Xanax, twice as many of Oxycontin, some not-bad Crystal Meth and four-hundred-and-thirty-six dollars in cash, and the first thing we did was stock up on beer. The second was score an ounce of head-busting weed from this old boy over in Dawson Springs. Now the last few days are fuzzy, blurred around the edges. I remember the bitter taste of pills on my tongue and the sharp tingle of cold beer and smudges of bare trees and dead fields glimpsed through the windshield, and that's about it.

"Let's smoke it after we eat," I say. "My ribs are about poking through my belly."

"Bubba?"

"Shit, Donny Ray. Stop calling me Bubba. I don't want to sit out here in the cold."

He fumbles around in his pocket for a lighter. "Nothing makes pancakes sweeter than a good old doobie buzz."

There isn't really any arguing with that, so while I wait for him to pass the number, I open a Keystone to rinse away the taste of old vomit. Of course instead of spitting it out the way I intend, I swallow, and of course that one swallow flips a switch in my brain, and I'm right back to feeling just enough fucked up to want more, more, more. I down the rest and reach for another. When Donny Ray passes the joint my way, I hit it hard and hold it long. Then I gulp my fresh beer while I listen to a little voice in my head telling me how we aren't kids anymore and how I have to stop living this way, get myself straight and be somebody respectable. I won't do it, but the fact that I know I should seems like proof I'm not the lost cause most people in Greenview think I am.

Donny Ray lets smoke roll out of his mouth towards the dome light. His long, greasy hair hangs over the seat. His jaws and throat are covered in reddish-blonde stubble that makes me think of the backlit portrait of Jesus that hung in my Grandma Nadine's living room - or not exactly of the portrait itself but of a copy that a clumsy-handed five year old might have made of that Jesus picture. Sometimes Donny Ray seems every bit as much of a mystery as the face in the painting. I've known him since we were in first grade, but sometimes the workings of his mind surprise me. Take Tiny Gardner. I never expected Donny Ray to come up with an idea like that since Tiny was his second cousin and had always been a good guy, fronting us pills or weed when we were low on cash and buying whatever crap we managed to steal from people's yards and unlocked garages without even dickering.

Now Donny Ray gives me a wall-eyed grin. "Blueberry fucking syrup," he says. He reaches beneath the seat, pulls out the .22 revolver he bought from a soldier down in Clarksville,

Tennessee. It's badly scratched and has electrical tape wrapped on the grips, but it looks dangerous anyway. "They ain't got no blueberry syrup, I'm going to raise nine and a half kinds of hell."

"You ever think maybe you ain't right in the head?"

"I'll tell you the truth, Frankie," he says. "Crazy or sane. One's about as good as the other."

* * *

The inside of the Huddle House smells like grilled onions and bacon and hamburger grease, and it makes my stomach rumble as soon as the door shuts behind us. The place is deserted except for an older guy in a sheepskin jacket slumped over his coffee cup, a fry cook leaning against the wall next to the grill and a red-headed waitress refilling ketchup bottles at the far end of the counter.

We sit in one of the rear booths, and I lick my fingers and do my best to smooth down my wild-ass hair. It's a week unwashed and bad tangled, so I don't accomplish much other than to make myself feel self-conscious. There's dirt on my face and my clothes reek of body odor and beer sweat and the gasoline that we've been syphoning from cars all over the county. Donny Ray is just as bad, with his eyes bulging and his flannel shirt caked with mud and dead leaves. We look to be the kind that make decent people vote for law and order and consider buying a gun.

When the waitress eases over to our table, coffee pot in hand, Donny Ray has his head tilted back, pouring sugar down his throat the way my grandma used to do with B.C. Headache Powder. I don't know why everything is reminding me of my grandma lately. She's a long time dead, buried under a piece of dirt that I haven't visited since her funeral. Now I keep wondering what she'd think of what we did to old Tiny Gardner. I don't figure she'd like it much. True, I didn't shoot him or cut his throat with a deer-skinning knife when the stubborn son of a bitch refused to die, but I knew what was going to happen before we ever knocked on his door, and I kicked his hand away when he grabbed my ankle and begged for help, saying, "Don't do this to me boys, why you all want to do me this way?"

"Coffee?"

Coming back to the here and now is like jerking awake after a fall in a dream, and I have to stifle the urge to cry out. I've been so deep inside my head that I haven't noticed anything about the waitress except for her red hair, but now I look up at a woman about our age, trim and built nice and with a face that would be magazine-cover-beautiful if not for the purplish scar that zigzags from just below her left cheek all the way down to her collarbone.

"You want coffee or not?" she asks. "You all can't be in here unless you order something. Ice water don't count."

It takes me a few seconds longer than it should to recognize her. Leanne Edwards. The girl of my dreams back in my high school days, which are barely five years gone but seem like a couple of eternities away.

"I do," I say, my voice as dry as ash. "Want coffee, I mean. We both do."

"Uh huh," she says.

Her daddy was a glorified maintenance man at a community college, so she wasn't one of the rich girls who belonged to the country club and wore jeans so expensive they looked cheap and got a new Mustang on her sixteenth birthday. But she was the most popular girl in the whole school anyway - captain of the cheerleading squad, prom queen in both her junior and senior years, the star of the drama club's annual play four seasons running. She dated Ross Franklin who everyone said was the best football player to ever come out of Harps County and whose daddy owned half a dozen mobile home dealerships scattered around west Kentucky. Ross accepted a scholarship to UK, and Leanne was supposed to go with him, and I figured that would be the last anyone saw of them until they showed up at the ten-year reunion as glamorous and exotic as Hollywood movie stars.

Then the spring before graduation they were coming back from a Dixie Chicks concert when Ross took a curve on old 431 at close to a hundred and ten miles an hour. He'd put away a few beers at the show, another six-pack on the ride home. His Navigator went off the road, clipped a beech tree, flipped and then rolled down a sandstone bank to an abandoned railroad track ten or fifteen feet below. Everyone said they were lucky to have survived, but that was before we heard about the aftermath. Leanne was shredded like a cabbage - they said from the neck down she looked like a corpse that had been stitched up after an autopsy - and Ross's brain was as hopelessly busted as a dropped egg.

They got married on the long-term-care ward at Greenview Community Hospital, and then Ross's daddy bought them a half-acre of land on Buck Gish Road and gave them a new doublewide. But word was that Don Franklin's business was faring about as well as everyone else's. When he stopped pumping money into their checking account, Leanne hired on for the nightshift at the Huddle House. I'd seen Ross from time to time, shuffling along like an old man or drooling over the candy bars at the checkout lane at Wal-Mart or standing on the post office steps with his face turned to the sun while piss ran down his leg. It shook me up pretty bad. You expected shit like that to happen to guys like Donny Ray and me, but you'd think for people like Ross and Leanne things would have worked out different.

"You got blueberry syrup?" Donny Ray asks.

She says no, and I steel myself for the moment he pulls the revolver and starts shooting. I don't really believe he'll do it, but I figure it's a possibility I ought to be prepared for.

"You ain't got blueberry syrup?"

"We got maple and just plain old syrup. You want blueberry you got to go someplace else."

"Where?"

"I don't know. An IHOP maybe. There's one in Nashville. You start driving now you'll be there by daylight."

"We're supposed to go that far for pancakes?" he asks.

"Or make do with maple like everyone else."

I sip my coffee and wait for what will come next. Then Donny Ray mumbles something under his breath and shrugs.

"Forget the fucking pancakes. We'll take steak and eggs. Medium rare, the eggs over easy. Not hard, but I don't want to see no slimy white shit on my plate neither. Hash browns all the way."

"Uh huh," she says. "Chili, too?"

"I said all the way didn't I?"

"It's extra."

Donny Ray snarls at her. "So fucking what? I didn't ask you was it extra did I?" Then he winks and pulls his hand back behind his ear like he's ready to throw a touchdown pass. "How's the quarterback doing? He still zipping those long bombs?"

She flinches, but she doesn't say anything, just nods at her little pad and walks off to put in our order. Donny Ray's grinning, pleased with himself.

"You didn't have to say that, man," I say.

"Hell, Bubba, I was just joking with her." He opens a sugar packet and dumps it in his coffee. "I never could stand that stuck-up bitch no ways."

"There were lots worse."

"She was bad enough." He dumps two more sugar packets into his coffee, sips, grimaces, reaches for another. "Don't tell me you're still caught up in that high school goddess bullshit. She ain't no different than the rest of the skanks around here, Bubba. You can take that to the bank."

"Quit calling me Bubba," I say although I know he isn't listening. "And you don't know nothing about her."

"I know I ain't beating my meat every night to visions of the pristine panties of the prom queen. I thought you were smarter than that, Frankie." Three more packets of sugar and he's finally ready to drink his coffee. "Tell you the truth, I figure her and the quarterback got what they deserved. I can't hardly stop myself from laughing every time I see him gurgling away while he pisses on himself."

"Sometimes I think you got a serious lack of normal human feeling. Like something was left out of you when you was born."

"Maybe," he says, slurping his coffee. "But the good Lord made up for it by throwing an extra three or four inches of dick my way."

He cackles and slaps the table and everyone - the fry cook, Leanne, the old man in the sheepskin coat - looks our way. That just makes him laugh louder until Leanne and the cook shake their heads, and the old man drops some money on the counter and slumps out the door. I laugh with him even though there's nothing particularly funny about us or this night or anything that has happened since we killed Tiny Gardner. It's always been that way with Donny Ray and me. No matter how bad things are, no matter how low I feel or what kind of low thing I've done, Donny Ray makes it seem like nothing more than a harmless joke that we're playing on the world instead of some bitter thing that we've done or, more often, that has been done to us.

Once the laughing is over, a lot of the mean goes out of his face, and he slumps in the booth. I stare out the plate glass window at headlights flickering through the bare branches that separate the town from the parkway. There are a lot of those lights cutting through the drizzle and the dark. It seems that everybody has somewhere to go except for me and Donny Ray. Then I realize that I don't know anything about those people. Maybe they are just driving for the sake of driving, chasing their tails around and around these chewed old hills the same way we've been doing for most of our lives.

I close my eyes and take a deep breath, trying to ignore my own stench and concentrate on the good smells around me. Brewing coffee, sizzling steak fat, toasting bread. Then yellowish light seeps into my head.

Donny Ray whispers, "Well ain't we the lucky ones."

I open my eyes just as headlights flick off, and my stomach shrivels. A KSP cruiser, as silvery and menacing as a shark, has pulled into the parking spot directly on the other side of the plate glass window.

"This could get interesting," Donny Ray says.

"Don't do nothing stupid."

He shrugs and winks and sits a little straighter. I watch as the driver's door opens and a short but broad-shouldered trooper pulls himself out and fits his hat on his head and then after a quick glance around the parking lot, comes inside, walking in that slow, cocky way that lawmen all seem to have. When the door shuts behind him, I glance down and see that my hands are shaking.

The trooper gives a quick nod in our direction, adjusts his gun belt and heads on over to the counter. Before he sits down, he places his hat on the stool next to him. He says something to Leanne that makes her smile and look down at the floor, and he laughs and leans forward, elbows planted on either side of a coffee cup.

After some time passes, the fry cook calls our order, and I watch Leanne stack plates on a carrying tray. I smile up at her when she sets a saucer of toast by my hand and mumble a thanks and feel warmed when she takes the trouble to smile back at me.

"You all need anything else?" she asks.

"You can warm my coffee when you get a chance. That won't put you out too much will it?" Donny Ray says.

"There's a pot brewing," she says. "It'll be done directly."

When she moves away, I watch her hips twitch and shift beneath her uniform. I remember her walking down the hall at the high school on a winter's afternoon. She was on her way to the gym for a pep rally, her little gold and black cheerleader's skirt kissing the back of her thighs. It makes my chest ache for that long ago before the scars and the drugs and the bad ideas got the better of us all.

"That wreck sure didn't hurt her ass none, did it?" Donny Ray says.

I look down at my plate. The food smells good, but the sight of those cataracted eggs and the smears of blood from the steak and the sheen of chili grease on the hash browns brings sour vomit to my throat. I want to run outside and take deep gulps of cold air, but I'm afraid to move with that trooper still watching us.

"He knows something's up," I say around a mouthful of egg that I can't really taste.

Donny Ray cuts off a hunk of steak and leans forward. "He don't know shit other than we look like the kind of guys he can give a hard time if the notion strikes him."

"Tiny ... "

"Don't matter at all," Donny Ray says quickly. "You think they give a damn about a fence and a drug dealer? They just figure someone wanted what he had and killed him to get it. Hell, they probably got a couple of hundred dope heads in Harps and Hopkins Counties they think could have done it."

"What about DNA? "

He tongues blood from his bottom lip. "What do you think this is, Frankie? CSI Greenview? They ain't no one shedding tears for Tiny Gardner, and they aren't going to any great trouble to find out who killed the son of a bitch either. All it means to them is one less asshole they got to feed and take care of a couple of times a year at the county jail." He points at me with his blood and yolk-smeared fork. "No one who matters around here gives a shit about me or you or Tiny Gardner. And that's our edge."

"Say what?"

"We're just cockroaches scurrying around in the shadows to those people. Sure when a roach fucks up and runs out into the middle of the room where you can't help but notice, you step on him and go about your business, but you don't ever get down on your hands and knees and waste your time trying to figure out what the roaches are up to, do you? If you don't see them, you forget they exist."

"Or else you set off a bug bomb and kill them all."

"Yeah," Donny Ray admits. "There's that, too."

He lowers his head and sets to eating, shoveling in forks of egg and hunks of steak and chili and cheese-covered potatoes, pausing now and then to slurp his coffee or mop yolk with a limp piece of buttered toast. I take small bites and chew until the food is rubbery and dry and swallowing it is like taking bitter medicine.

After a short time, Leanne comes to freshen our coffee, but Donny Ray's too busy chewing to goad her or do anything else but look up at her with his watery, bloodshot eyes. I try to smile, wanting her to know that I'm sorry for what happened to her and for the way Donny Ray has been acting and for all of us turning out the way we have, but I can barely manage a twitchy grimace that sends her hurrying back to the counter.

"You don't quit picking at your food we're going to be here until daybreak," Donny Ray says.

I cut a piece of steak and watch Leanne while I chew. The fry cook has disappeared behind swinging metal doors, and she's poured herself a cup of coffee and now sits at the counter with the trooper. He's talking and she's watching him, her chin tilted slightly, a small but warm smile on her lips. She's looking at him as if what he's saying matters, making it seem that there's no place on earth she had rather be than right here and right now. Seeing that brings on a sour longing that makes me want to run to the Pontiac, grab all of the pills we have left in the glove compartment and wash them down with a cold beer so the world and everything in it will fade to a sweet, sweet black.

"Let's get on out of here," I say to Donny Ray.

"You ain't eat nothing yet."

"Well I'm done with it," I say.

"Didn't your momma ever remind you

about them starving people in China?"

"There aren't any starving people in China," I say. "They got all the jobs."

He snorts laughter. "Hey, you reckon those Chinese parents come in from working at the sewing factory that moved over there and put my ma out of a job, sit down to dinner and then end up saying, 'Now little Wang, you better eat all your moo-goo-gai-pan cause there's a million rednecks starving in Kentucky?'"

Laughing makes it easy to not think about what's coming our way. When the drugs and the money run out we'll have a choice to make - either find someone else to do the same way we did Tiny Gardner or face a long, sober winter without a job or a place to stay or food to put in our bellies. We've run out of good luck and good will and good options. About a year ago, Donny Ray's daddy was killed when his pickup stalled on a railroad track. Not three weeks after the funeral, the sewing factory where Donny Ray's momma worked closed down and she moved into a low-income duplex in the projects. She doesn't mind feeding us from time to time or letting us crash on the floor once in a while, but the government won't let us stay long without cutting her benefits, so she gets antsy whenever we're around.

My family isn't any help at all. Sure my

momma will slip me a five if she happens to bump up against me in the Wal-Mart, but that's only by chance and only when she's alone. My daddy wouldn't piss on me if I was on fire. He's been running me off and letting me come home three or four times a year since my fifteenth birthday, citing the fact that I'm a drug addict and a liar and a goddamn disgrace as the reasons for sending me packing and my momma's heartache and natural maternal feeling as the reasons for letting me move back in. Then last April he got home early from a poker game and caught me in his garage. I had his new socket wrench set, his electric grinder, and his air compressor loaded into the back of a Nissan pickup I'd borrowed from Tiny Gardner. The old man set on me pretty good, and I was stoned, so it wasn't much of a fight. It ended with him whipping me raw with an inch-thick drop chord. He told me that if he ever caught me hanging around his door he'd shoot me dead and forget he ever had a son. When I dragged my bleeding, blistered ass out of there, I knew I'd never go back again.

Now, Donny Ray clears his throat and says we'll get out of here as soon as he finishes his coffee. Then he leans back in the booth and pulls a crumpled pack of Camels from his pocket and lights one the way you will without really thinking about it.

"You ought to get a box to put this in," he says. "We'll get damn hungry when we smoke the rest of that weed."

Suddenly, Leanne Edwards is right at our elbows, looking a little scared but more shocked and angry than anything else. "You can't smoke that in here," she says.

"Huh?" Donny Ray says.

"You can't smoke that in here. You can't smoke in restaurants no more." She points to a No Smoking by City Ordinance sign mounted over the grill. "You get out of here with that thing."

Donny Ray looks genuinely perplexed. "Say what?"

"Put that damn cigarette out."

His brow furrows and his eyes darken. "You don't got to cuss at me," he says, his voice low and serious. "I don't take being cussed at from nobody."

"Get out of here," she says, her voice shaky. "Or put it out. One or the other."

"Make me," he says like a kid on a playground.

"We're going," I say. "We were just about to head out."

"But you need to bring us a box first," Donny Ray says. "We ain't going to leave all this food on the table so you can take home scraps for your retard."

Her face blanches and her eyes water. Then I hear the soft steps of rubber-souled shoes and the creak of a gun belt. The trooper puts his left hand on her shoulder, but his right never strays farther than an inch from his holster.

"Watch your mouth," he says. "You're smoking in a public place and that's against the law."

"We're leaving," I tell him.

"I know you are," he says. "Either quickly and quietly or with your hands cuffed behind your backs. It's your call."

Being spoken to like that rankles me; I won't say that it doesn't. But I know there's nothing I can do about it, so I just hang my head the way people like me always do when the law has decided to walk over us for driving to work without the insurance we can't afford or for getting a little too rambunctious on a Saturday night or maybe for just forgetting and lighting up with our coffee the way we've done a thousand times before. But Donny Ray's a different case altogether. For as long as I've known him, he's been bucking up against somebody - his daddy, teachers and principals, anybody with the word "officer" on his uniform. He usually pays a price for it, but paying it has never taught him to behave any different. Now, his eyes are narrow and his nostrils are white, and his right hand sort of wanders towards his pocket. I'm not the only one who sees it either. The trooper's thumb flicks at the trigger guard on his holster. I figure he'll kill both of us, but I'm so tired and so sick of being scared and of being high and of being sober and most of all of just being me that I don't care one way or the other.

Maybe that's what does it. Maybe Donny Ray sees the hopelessness and resignation in my face, and that's why he changes his mind. I can't say for sure. All I know is that he moves his hand back to the table.

"We're going," he says.

"Good," the trooper says but his jaw is clenched so hard the word comes out like a curse.

Then Leanne speaks up in a tiny, frightened voice. "What about your food?" she asks, and I figure she's so scared she doesn't know what she's saying.

"Take it home to your husband. I got a feeling he's used to sloppy seconds," Donny Ray says.

But he mumbles it under his breath the way a scared but not wanting to be scared kid might backtalk his daddy. Then the two of us slide out of the booth and head for the door. We're almost there when the trooper's hand closes around Donny Ray's arm.

"You're forgetting something aren't you?" the trooper asks.

I hate him then, hate the mocking, bullying tone of his voice and the pigheaded stupidity that won't let him leave well enough alone. I think if Donny Ray doesn't shoot this asshole, I reckon I will. But those are just empty thoughts, and I know it.

"The check," Donny Ray says.

"Well, you didn't think I was going to pay for your dinner, did you?"

"It was eighteen sixty," Leanne says in a weak, about-to-be-sick voice.

Donny Ray pulls his arm free from the trooper's grip and then takes out his wallet. He finds a couple of tens and drops them on the counter near where the trooper's hat is still sitting. Then he looks back at Leanne for a long, long minute. When I hear the toilet flush in the men's room, I figure that's as good a cue for an exit as any other, so the two of us slither out the door.

* * *

A half hour later, Donny Ray parks at the top of a mud-and-gravel-covered hill just off

Buck Gish Road. Through the bare branches of scrub timber, I see a feeble yellow porch light burning at a doublewide trailer. I'm not surprised. I've known where we were going all along.

"Give me a couple of those Oxy and pass me a beer," he says. "Her shift probably won't end until six so we got some time to burn."

I hand him a Keystone and he turns it up, letting the foam run down his chin. When I pass him the Oxy, he shakes two or three in his mouth and washes them down.

"You ought to help yourself," he says. "Scared as you look, you're going to need it."

"For what?"

"Don't ask stupid questions. Just open a beer and relax."

I start to tell him that I don't need a beer and that I'm fed up with this bullshit. But of course while the later part is true, the first is pure hot air. I need a beer right now as much as I ever have, so I fire up a joint to go along with it.

"That's the spirit," he says.

"Whatever you got in mind, you can forget it," I say. "All we're going to do is finish these beers, smoke this number and then drive our asses right on out of here."

"You saw the way she was smirking at me,

laughing her ass off when that trooper put on his show."

"She wasn't making a sound," I say.

"With her eyes, Bubba," he says. "She was laughing with her eyes."

"Come on, man," I say. "You're just fucked up is all. Let's get out of there, find some place to crash and everything will ... "

"That trooper made me eat shit and I just hung my head, lapped it up and pretended it was good. You think I can live with that?"

"What were you supposed to do? Go for your gun and let him shoot you dead right in the middle of the fucking Huddle House?"

"I might have drawn before he could."

I know it's a lie but there's no point in saying it. "Then what? You kill the state trooper, Leanne and the fry cook, too? How long you think it would be before the cops run us down?"

"Dying with your head held up is better than living with your tail tucked between your legs."

"Who told you that? This ain't a movie. We don't go down with guns blazing and then get up and hang by the pool and drink imported beer and sign autographs after the director yells cut. This is our life, man."

"That don't mean we got to live it by

somebody else's rules." He lights a Camel, tilts his head and blows smoke at the car's ceiling. "You're probably right. It's better this way. We settle the score and keep on keeping on."

"That ain't what I'm saying," I say. "We just need some sleep. Maybe ... "

"She was laughing at us. From the moment we came in. All this stuff happens to her and she still thinks her shit don't stink." He hits his cigarette again and then flicks it out the cracked door. "I'll tell you this, too. That trooper wouldn't have pulled that crap if it hadn't been for her goading him on."

"Sure," I say. "State troopers are never known to be pricks on their own. It must have been her that corrupted his usually sweet nature."

"Don't take up for her, man. That cunt was mocking us. She always was."

But I know that to be a lie. When we were in our sophomore year I wrote her a love note. It was long and rambling, but the gist was that she was the most beautiful girl I'd ever seen and even though I knew she'd never be interested in somebody like me, I loved her and promised that should she ever need me I'd be there. I imagined her reading that note and understanding the extent of my feelings and realizing that Ross Franklin was wrong for her and that I was the only one special enough to deserve her. I was special all right. So special I should have been riding the short bus. I realized that as soon I saw her take the note from where I'd wedged it in her locker door. I knew exactly what was about to happen. She'd read the note and then pass it to one of her girlfriends and then that girlfriend would read it to everyone else. They'd laugh and point and blow kisses at me. I could hear words like pathetic and loser and freak echoing in my head.

But none of that happened. She took her time reading the note while I stood helpless in the hallway, my face burning hotter and hotter. When she finished it, she looked squarely in my direction and smiled. It wasn't a my-God-now-I-know-I-love-you smile but it wasn't a mocking, what-a-fucking-loser-you-are smile either. I couldn't think of a way to describe it to myself at the time, but later I realized that respectful was the word I wanted. She held onto my note as she gathered her books and then neatly shredded it into the garbage can outside the lunchroom before she went on to her next class.

Now Donny Ray opens his door. "What are you doing?" I ask.

"Taking a piss if you got to know."

"That's not what I meant."

"You really want me to spell it out? We're going to sit here a few more minutes, drink another beer, snort a little of the crank we got left. Then we're going to the trailer. I'm going to knock on the door and when the zombie answers it, I'm going to put a bullet in his head. And don't look at me like that. It'll be a mercy killing. Somebody should have done it when they pulled him out of that wrecked SUV." He lights a fresh cigarette, exhales, licks his lips. "Then we're going to help ourselves to what there is to find. Pills or cash or booze, whatever they got lying around. And when the Prom Queen walks in?" He winks and tips his beer in my direction. "You can do whatever you want, but me, I'm going to plow that ass and find out if it's as sweet as that bitch thinks it is."

"I don't want ... "

"Then you can sit on the couch and listen for all I care. " He looks at me with the kind of hard disappointment I'm used to seeing from my old man. "Listen Frankie. Back at the Huddle House? I'd have gone for my gun if it hadn't have been for you, the way you were sitting there looking scared and whipped and shaky. That's what stopped me."

"Bullshit," I say although it's exactly what I thought when it happened.

27

He leans closer and his voice isn't much more than a raspy whisper. "You made me a coward, Frankie. You've always been mealy-mouthed and cringing, a chickenshit at heart. I ... "

"No," I say, bitterly. "I'm just not crazy."

"Call it what you want. But I've seen it in you since we were kids, the way you let the older boys push you around and turned red and stammered whenever a teacher called on you and about piddled yourself whenever your old man was around. But I love you anyway."

"Donny Ray ... "

"No, I got to say it. I love you like a brother. But I got humiliated tonight because of it. That can't happen again. You want to go on cringing and eating shit, that's cool. Take a beer with you for the walk back to town."

"Jesus Christ, Donny. You're not talking about robbing banks like John Dillinger or starting a revolution. You're talking about murdering a guy who doesn't know when he pees himself and then raping a Huddle House waitress."

"You don't like it? Start walking. But we're through, Bubba. You head down that road, I got to think you're exactly what your daddy always said you were, and I don't want no part of it."

I want to hit him, want to tell him that he's a psychopath, no different from a rabid dog. More than anything else I just want the world to go black, so I can forget this night ever happened.

"That's the way it is?" I finally say, hating myself for how scared and lost I sound. "You mean what you're saying?"

"Yeah."

I look at him a moment, thinking about how he's always been my friend. Then I think about what my life will be like without him and that's a hard, hard thing to think about.

"Fine," I say. "Give me the gun."

"What?"

"You want me to prove something? Give me the gun and I'll do it."

"Don't try to pull no shit on me," he says.

I look him in the eye. "If this is the price that has to be paid, I'll pay it. Like you said, it's just a mercy killing."

"All right," he says. "You sure?"

"Yeah."

He stretches back in the seat to work the gun from his coat pocket. "I always knew deep down you had something extra in you," he says. "We'll be careful to clean everything up. Maybe set the place on fire to burn up whatever we miss. What do you think?"

"It's your show."

"Our show," he says. "I tell you what else, Bubba. We're going to settle with that trooper, too. I know the son of a bitch. Tom Harvey's his name. He lives up in Gishton, got a wife and a couple of kids. Maybe we'll pay them a visit. Or maybe we'll just happen to catch him sitting in his car drinking his coffee." He slaps his hands together hard enough to make my ears ring. "Blam!" he says. "He'll never know what hit him." He punches my shoulder and grins. "Get the crank ready while I'm taking a piss. We'll do a couple of lines and then get on down to business."

He steps from the car and leaves the door open. I sit there a second, looking at the gun in my hand. Then when I hear him splashing the ground, I force myself to get out.

"God that feels good," he says without looking around at me. "I was about to bust a kidney I had to pee so bad."

I close my eyes and take a deep breath, trying to hold onto this moment as long as I can. But what comes next always happens no matter what you do, so I let out my breath in a rush and open my eyes and aim the gun at the back of his head.

Donny Ray's zipping up, saying how he sure wished they would have had blueberry syrup. I kill him before he can turn around.

* * *

As the last of the darkness seeps from the sky, I stand on the banks of the Green River and watch all that black water move on to somewhere else. I think about this girl who washed up in the crook of a beech tree when I was fourteen, how the flood water played a trick on her or maybe on whoever had killed her and brought her right back home, but that was a lifetime ago. Today, the river's running straight and true. This very water I'm looking at right now will be somewhere different tomorrow and then somewhere else entirely the day after that, and somehow it makes me feel better, stronger, and I roll Donny Ray's body off into the river. While I watch him sink and rise and bob and finally catch the current, I say my goodbye, open a beer in his honor. Nobody can go on fighting the world as hard as Donny Ray did and not be ruined by it, but a man can't spread his hurt and his ruination to everyone else. And deep down I know the Donny Ray that had once been would have wanted me to do what I did.

When the threat of the morning is too strong to ignore, I drive back to town. It seems wrong to be behind the wheel, wrong for everything to be so quiet, and it's then that I begin thinking about the time that's going to stretch out before me. When I pass the Huddle House, I'm tempted to pull in on the chance that Leanne Edwards might still be there, hoping that seeing her might go a long way towards easing the loneliness that's setting in. But I keep driving. Even if she is there she won't see me as anything other than what I am.

Now the sun has broken through clouds the color of rotting meat, and I squint into its brightness, my hands tight on the steering wheel. Just ahead I see the entranceways to the Western Kentucky Parkway and know I have a decision to make. East or West? I think about California, how it always looks so clean and hopeful in all those movies and television shows. I tap my brake and put on my signal. Then it occurs to me that heading west means the sun will always be chasing me and that every mile I travel will take me deeper into the morning's lie. What I need is a place where that morning sun will soon go down. I head east and merge into sparse traffic, moving in the opposite direction from which the rest of the world seems to be traveling. I settle behind the wheel, comfortable in the fact that I'm doing what I've always done - stumbling blindly into

morning in the hope that I might find darkness
as quickly as I can.

And Ivy Leaves the Door Unlocked

Shepherd's life had become unhinged ten years ago, but he was certain that the girl could help him put it back together. Still, he hesitated. The first night he saw the girl and the man huddled in the corner of the Copper Penny Lounge, he vowed to visit his own daughter's grave. The second time he saw them, he cut through McAllen Park on his way home, spotted a bum passed out beneath a dilapidated bandstand and spent five minutes watching him sleep, fingering the bone-handled hunting knife in his pocket and imagining slitting the old drunk's throat. On the third night the girl and her "father" came into the Copper Penny, Shepherd decided to buy them a drink.

There was something about her darting eyes or the tilt of her chin or the way she lifted her mousy brown hair from her shoulders that drew him. The grief counselor he'd seen in the aftermath of Miranda's suicide would have had an answer. He would have tapped his acne-scarred jaw with a fingertip and said in his reasonable voice, "Your daughter, Alan. You're projecting your feelings for Miranda onto a stranger. It's perfectly understandable if not terribly healthy." Everything Shepherd did after his daughter's death was perfectly understandable if not terribly healthy in the eyes of Gregory K. Lambert, PhD. Odd that he should be thinking of him now as he listed his way across the bar. It was the gin and grapefruit, of course. He'd put away a baker's dozen. Shepherd thought of an old joke. He was no longer a practicing alcoholic; he was a goddamn professional.

"Did you say something?" the man with the girl asked.

Shepherd stood a little straighter, tucked in the tail of his ash-smeared shirt. If he'd spoken aloud he was drunker than he'd thought.

"A drink," he said, relieved that at least his voice was steady. "I thought you two could use one."

The man was both shorter and rounder than he'd appeared from across the bar, his face red and jowly and somehow innocent in the muted light. His smile was as wide and phony as Shepherd's own. Still, drunk as he was, Shepherd didn't miss the quick shift of his eyes or the disdainful smirk that lurked beneath the smile. To hell with him. It was the girl he was interested in. She barely glanced Shepherd's way before shifting in her seat to stare out the plate glass window. Up close he saw that she was at least eighteen or nineteen. She wore a stained plaid skirt, a sweater with a pale blue teddy bear over the bump of her left breast, a pair of worn, pink, canvas sneakers. The outfit, the loose ponytail, the bangs and the smear of bubblegum lipstick were designed to make her look younger, like a careless adolescent whose clothes came from a Goodwill.

"Christian," the man said.

Shepherd squinted, certain he'd been accused of something, but then the guy's eyes twinkled and he said, "It's good to know that Christian charity still exists."

He invited Shepherd to sit down. It was as easy as that.

* * *

It was a game, a lie, a con. Shepherd played along, but the high school English and drama teacher he'd once been remained beneath the booze and anger, and he longed to interrupt and explain that they had it all wrong. The girl was supposed to be fifteen, but she was playing too young. At fifteen, Miranda had been desperate to appear grown up, sophisticated, mature. This girl's act was a caricature of a teenager, every bit as phony and exaggerated as the man's southern accent.

He claimed his name was Buck, his "stepdaughter's" Ivy. As soon as he had his second bourbon under his belt, he began to skirt the edges of a spiel that would end with an offer of an hour of Ivy's time in a motel or in the backseat of a car. Meanwhile, she drank Diet Coke, fidgeted, stole glances that were supposed to be both shy and provocative, chewed her plastic straw and made sure that Shepherd noticed the way she caressed it with her bottom lip. They were in a booth, and with each fidget, she moved closer to Shepherd until he felt the cool skin of her bare leg against his thigh. It was tiresome. Shepherd flagged a waitress, hoping that another round would move things along.

This time, when the waitress brought their drinks, she bent to Shepherd's ear and whispered, "Street trash." It was funny, Shepherd thought, that even the damned believe in social hierarchies. The waitress, Rose, watched him drink himself into paralysis six nights a week, and yet she carried the illusion that because he was a regular he was respectable. She seemed as shocked and disappointed that he would choose to sit with a pair of street hustlers as one of his students at Harps County High would have been to catch him coming out of a dirty bookstore a decade ago.

It struck him then that his life had constricted and hardened like the arteries of a man days away from a heart attack. He glanced out the streaked glass window at the dirty sidewalks of the Greenview strip. This was now the extent of his world. He lived in a small, roach-ridden efficiency two blocks away on the west end of McAllen Park. Every morning began with breakfast at the Excellent Café and every night ended with him stumbling from the Copper Penny. The hours between rarely took him off these streets. He ate his lunch at Winnie's Grill or Ella's Diner. He bought his cigarettes, his lottery tickets and his occasional take-home bottle at 4th Street Liquors. Each day he worked his way from north to south and then back again, stopping at the Coyote Lounge, the Sunset, the Bunker, Bobbie's Bar, and finally the Copper Penny, chasing drink specials, happy hour snacks and his own boredom like a stupid dog snipping at its tail. Thinking about it made his chest ache and his throat close until he gasped for air.

"Hey, buddy, are you okay?" Buck asked, the phony southern accent disappearing in his surprise. "You having a heart attack or something?"

Shepherd cleared his throat, managed a weak smile. "I'm fine. Just a touch of asthma. Smoke irritates it." He glanced at his pack of Marlboros on the table and gave an embarrassed shrug. "Yeah, I know. But I can't seem to kick the habit."

"We all choose our own poisons, I guess."

Shepherd couldn't miss the nasal Chicago bite in the guy's accent. He'd pegged the pair for what they were. Chi-town hustlers working their way south. Just off the Western Kentucky Parkway and located on a Greyhound route, Greenview saw its share.

"You have no idea how much your generosity is appreciated," Buck said, lifting his third bourbon in a toast and donning his phony accent again like a kid trying on his father's hats. "There's still kindness in the world. Genuine kindness. I tell Ivy that all the time, don 't I sweetheart?"

"Yes, Daddy."

"I know it's hard for her to believe given the circumstances we're in, but it's true. I know it in my heart of hearts. When you're in my position, when you've had to do the things I've been forced to do, sometimes holding onto the idea of kindness is all you have."

"Oh Daddy, stop," Ivy said, reaching across the table to touch his hand and giving Shepherd an embarrassed teenager's grin. "It doesn't do any good to talk about it."

Buck cleared his throat, brushed his eyes with the heel of his hand. "You're right, sweetheart. I get lost in my problems sometimes and forget other people have got worries of their own."

"No, go ahead," Shepherd said, biting back his laughter. "I'd like to know."

Buck's story was as detailed as it was melodramatic. Once or twice, Shepherd was tempted to interrupt to ask if he'd cadged the entire plot from a made-for-television-movie. It went like this. At one time Buck had had it all, a wife, a loving stepdaughter, a home, a job as a welder at a tool and die company in Cicero, Illinois. He and Ivy's mother, Dianna, had followed the American dream north from Jackson, Mississippi, and they had thought they found it. Then breast cancer struck Dianna in her prime. She had "lingered." Dutiful and loving husband that he was, Buck wanted to spend as much time with her as he could, and that had cost him his job. By the time Dianna passed on, Buck had lost everything. He and Ivy lived in homeless shelters for a while, but those were no good for a child, and so he'd pawned what little he had left and bought a bus ticket, hoping to get them back to Jackson where he had relatives.

"The things I've had to do make me ashamed," Buck said.

He seemed on the verge of weeping. Ivy reached across the table, squeezed his hand again.

"We have to do what we have to do," she said. A look at Shepherd that was supposed to be both anxious and lascivious, but only succeeded in seeming hostile. "And sometimes I don't mind. Not if the man is nice and promises not to hurt me."

"You see?" Buck said. "God forgive me."

Shepherd thought of telling him the truth. God was a mild psychotic with the sense of humor of a disturbed, twelve-year-old boy. He forgave no one. But before he could speak, he felt Ivy's hand on his inner thigh.

"You like me, don't you, Mr. Shepherd? I can feel that you do."

It was a lie like everything else. It had been

a couple of years since he'd been capable of having an erection.

"A hundred dollars," Buck said. "That would get us a warm place to sleep tonight and a little further down the line." He crossed himself and mumbled another Lord forgive me. "I know you must think I'm an awful man."

"A hundred you say?"

The girl rubbed her palm on Shepherd's lifeless crotch. "It's what we have to have."

Shepherd smiled, relieved that most of the charade was over. "There's an ATM a couple of doors down."

* * *

With Buck paid and left behind at the Copper Penny, the girl grew more animated. Her step quickened; her voice came alive. She talked nonsense about her "stepfather," spinning a history that was as false and ludicrous as the story Buck had told at the bar. As they passed 4th Street Liquors, she took Shepherd's hand, gave him a mischievous smile and asked him to buy a bottle.

"Buck hates it when I drink. But what he don't know won't hurt him."

He thought of Miranda clandestinely asking for an advance on her allowance or permission to go to a concert when her mother stepped out of the room. Now he touched Ivy's cheek with his fingertips and asked what she wanted. He expected her to ask for wine or some sweet and girlish liquor.

"Bourbon," she said. "It doesn't matter what kind but get at least a pint."

Shepherd left her outside. The Copper Penny and the rest of the bars on the strip got around the No One Under 21 law by serving food until nine o'clock, but the liquor stores were as severe and impatient with minors as the railroad police were with hoboes.

As he waited in line behind a hunchbacked man buying cheap wine and lotto tickets, Shepherd alternated between worrying that the girl would ditch him and about the money he was spending. When he and teaching came to a mutual parting of the ways - no one spoke the words aloud but Shepherd could see the question that lurked behind their eyes: how can this man who could not save his own child be trusted with ours? - he'd cashed in his retirement and banked it along with half of the profit from the sale of his house. He thought if he were careful the money would last, but of course it hadn't. The life of a drunk who prefers to drink with company gets expensive. But his dwindling bank account didn't really matter right now. There was something he needed from the girl. He would have emptied his wallet, his checking, and the pennies he kept in a chipped fruit jar to get it.

When he stepped from the liquor store and found Ivy leaning against the building's brick wall, smoking a long, slim cigarette, he shivered with relief. He offered her the pint of Jack Daniels like a father bringing a belated birthday gift, anxious for her approval. She shrugged, dropped her cigarette and ground it beneath her heel.

"How far is the motel?" she asked.

"A couple of blocks."

She took his hand. "Let's hurry. I'm freezing."

"My daughter," he said or thought he did as he spotted the Sundowner in the distance.

"What?"

"Nothing."

She paused to light another cigarette, cupping her small hands around it against the wind. When she had it going, she took a deep drag, looked around and then passed judgment.

"This is an ugly fucking town."

He opened his mouth to tell her not to use that kind of language and then bit the words back when he realized how ridiculous they would sound. Besides, looking at the wind-blown, trash-littered streets, the splash of neon that seeped from the bars, the smoke-stained buildings, the sagging Christmas tinsel that no one had bothered to remove even though March was only a few days away, made it hard to argue.

"It's an ugly fucking world," he said.

Ivy looked at him as if he were simple-minded. "And that's supposed to be a surprise to me?"

Before he could think of an answer, they reached the motel.

* * *

The room was warm and smelled of mothballs. Shepherd sagged on a creaky bed, perspiring, aware of his gut drooping over his belt, and the raspy sound of his breathing. He swallowed back a mouthful of vomit and wiped his lips on the palm of his hand. He hadn't really been able to smell the girl before, but now he gagged on cherry-scented perfume that couldn't quite hide the fact that it had been awhile since she'd had a shower. He wondered what he was doing here with this girl. Did he want to save her or did he expect her to save him? God knew he didn't want to fuck her. It had been ten years since he'd really wanted to fuck, two years since he'd been able to keep an erection. That had been here at the Sundowner Motel with a woman named Audra whose husband was dying of prostate cancer. When they finished, she turned her back and wept. He'd wanted to kill her, longed to wrap his hands around her scrawny, wrinkled neck and choke until his fingers cramped and her eyes set in her head. He hadn't done it. But God, he'd wanted to.

"So what do you have in mind?" Ivy asked, pouring a glass of bourbon. "I'm up for anything." She bit her bottom lip as if reconsidering. "Well almost anything. If you want to spank me or do my ass, it's going to cost extra."

The way she bit her bottom lip. That's what had drawn him to her. Miranda had the same habit when she was concentrating on her homework or summoning courage to ask for something she knew she wasn't going to get. Ten years. It seemed impossible that it had been that long, unbelievable that if she'd lived she would have been twenty-six now, out of college, married, probably with kids of her own. The sheer unreasonableness of it all made him want to ram his head through the motel room's plaster wall. Miranda's friends, the girls who'd been like second daughters to him, had lived their lives. The boys she'd dated had found other girls. Even Sharon had moved on. She still grieved, of course, but she was remarried and living in a ranch house with a stepfamily she seemed to think of as her own.

"My daughter," he said.

Ivy set her whiskey on the dresser, went to her knees in front of him and nuzzled her head between his thighs. Off balance and confused, Shepherd glanced down, saw her small, pale hand tugging at his zipper.

"Don't," he said.

She blew her bangs from her eyes, looked up, arching her thin eyebrows in a question. Then she shrugged and pulled herself to her feet.

"It's your hundred."

"Can I have a drink?"

"You paid for it."

Then her expression softened, and she filled the room's only other cup with bourbon and handed it to him. He hated whiskey, always had. It made his stomach churn. But it felt good, very good, when it rushed to his head.

"My daughter," he said again, the words a little stronger this time.

She sat beside him on the bed, dropped her

hand to the inside of his thigh. "How old is she?"

"She was sixteen."

"You got a thing for her? Hey, it's okay. I hear that from a lot of guys. What happened, you see her getting out of the shower and get a hard-on? Maybe you caught her making it with a guy and started thinking about it?"

"No," Shepherd said. "Stop."

"Hey, it's cool." Her voice was as cold and ugly as the streets outside. "I'm close to her age, right? You want me to pretend to be her?"

"No."

"Tell me her name."

"Miranda." Speaking it felt like a blasphemy.

"Pretty name." She grabbed his crotch, squeezed. "I love my daddy. I want to be a good girl and make him happy."

"Don't."

"And I've thought about it. All girls do, you know that, Daddy?"

She kept talking. He didn't respond, but still, she wouldn't stop. Shepherd thought of a desperate salesman fumbling for the right pitch to close a deal. Finally, she ran out of words. She lifted her sweater over her head, pulled it free, and shook her hair. She wore a dingy white bra that was frayed at the straps and completely unnecessary. Her shoulders were narrow and kissed with freckles, her stomach flat and pale. Shepherd spotted a piece of sweater fuzz in her belly button and pulled it away.

"That's right," she said, her voice a grating falsetto that was like broken glass in his head. "Down there. Come on, Daddy. I won't tell."

He shoved her away from him before he realized what he was doing, and she tumbled from the bed, landed hard on the floor. "Stop it, goddamn it," he said, clutching at his pants leg to keep his hand from curling into a fist.

She met his eyes, her expression changing from surprise to anger. Without speaking, she pulled herself from the floor, paused to straighten her crumpled skirt and turned her back on him. He thought she would run for the door. Instead, she dug a pack of Marlboro Light 100's from her purse and rummaged for a book of matches.

"Hey, man, you'd better listen," she said, blowing smoke in his direction. "No rough stuff, okay? Don't even think it. I don't play that shit. You want to spank me, pretend I'm a bad girl who needs to be punished, that's fine. But it'll cost you another hundred up front. You don't hit anywhere near hard enough to leave bruises and you don't touch me above the waist. Those are the rules. You don't follow them or you get out of line again, I'll use the straight razor I got in my purse to carve your ass like a Christmas turkey."

"I don't want to hit you," he said.

"I'm not a mind reader, okay? You want me to play with my pussy while you watch or you want me to get in the tub so you can wash my back or braid my hair or what the fuck ever, you got to tell me."

She talked tough, her voice edgy and impatient, but standing there in her worn out bra, she looked pale, wasted and vulnerable. Had he brought her here to kill her? After years of venting his anger by imagining murder, was tonight the night that he would cross the line into action, and if he did, would it exorcise his daughter's ghost? He licked his lips, tried to smile at her, and flinched from something hard and calculating he saw in her eyes. Was she lying about the straight razor? And if she wasn't, would she use it? Perhaps that's why he'd been drawn to her. She would kill him, slit his throat in this dim motel room with its mismatched furniture and put an end to his suffering.

"Talk to me," she said, on the verge of shouting.

Shepherd put his head in his hands. "My

daughter died."

A pause and then, "What happened?"

He told himself that he heard a genuine interest in her voice. He knew it was another lie, but he forced himself to believe it. He wanted to tell her. But how could he say that his daughter, the baby whose umbilical cord he'd cut after her delivery, the child with whom he'd played patty cake and Chutes and Ladders, the girl who'd been the brightest in her class and the captain of the soccer team and who had cost him a fortune in dental work, had run a bathtub full of water and cut both wrists with the bone-handled hunting knife that he now carried in his pocket?

He'd found her. Sharon was working late, and he'd been drinking beer and watching Sports Center when he realized that Miranda had been in the bathroom a long time. The door was not locked. He'd turned the knob and stepped inside and saw his daughter floating in blood-skimmed water. He stood there for a second, breathing hard through his nose, looking at her. What he remembered most clearly was the way her pubic hair swayed beneath the water like seaweed. It was long and jet-black, and what went through his head was both absurd and profane. Randi's bush is even thicker than her mother's. That was what he'd been capable of thinking while he stood in his clean, pine-scented bathroom and stared at the corpse of his only child. He'd told his dear friend Dr. Lambert that, and Lambert had grunted in sympathy and told him that at times of stress the brain was a frightened monkey on a chain, likely to jump in all different directions. Shepherd should forget it. When Lambert had said that, Shepherd had imagined himself picking up a pencil and jamming it through the doctor's razor-burned neck and twisting and twisting.

"Leukemia," he said. "My daughter had leukemia."

"That sucks."

Shepherd laughed a deep belly laugh that was as genuine as the ache in his temples. "Yeah, it's a bummer. It's totally random. It's gay as hell," he said, spitting out the clichés he dimly remembered his daughter and her friends using. "It's totally lame."

Miranda had stopped talking. At least to him and Sharon. In the months before he found her in the bathtub, she dragged herself home from school and then slunk off to her room and hid behind a locked door. On the weekends, she slept until noon, rarely ate anything other than the occasional cup of yogurt, hung on the edges of Shepherd's awareness like a ghost that was too tired to bother with a haunting, and then retreated back to her bed. Even when she was awake, the lights in her room were never on, and Shepherd wouldn't have known she was conscious if not for the constant blare of her stereo. She decorated her room with posters of an eclectic mix of dead rocks stars - Hendrix, Morrison, Joplin, Lennon, Sid Vicious, Ronnie Van Zandt. Somehow, someway she'd discovered the Beatles. At first Shepherd had kidded her about it, telling her that she was listening to old folks' music and threatening to buy her *Lawrence Welk's Greatest Hits* for Christmas, but after awhile it wasn't funny. Ten years later, he could still hear John Lennon promising that Strawberry Fields were forever. It was yet another lie. Nothing was forever, not Strawberry Fields or John Lennon or Miranda. Shepherd should have known. After all the professional development seminars on depression and at-risk-teens, he should have sensed that Randi was in trouble, but he hadn't. The truth was he'd always been a careless caretaker of the most important things in his life.

Now, Ivy sneaked a glance at her watch and then stubbed her cigarette in a tin ashtray. "So like what do you want to do? I got to get back to

Buck before long."

Shepherd pressed his palms to his eyes. This was crazy. Why had he come here with this child who was not a child? He gasped for air and only got a mouthful of cherry perfume and cigarette smoke.

"Take a shower."

"That's what you want, huh?" She sounded relieved to be back on familiar ground. "You want to watch me undress?"

"No."

"I'll leave the bathroom door open in case you want to accidentally come in on me."

Shepherd lay back on the bed and tried to focus on the ceiling to stop the swimming in his head. He thought about killing himself. He could take either the knife from his pocket or the straight razor Ivy claimed to have in her purse and slit his throat. But he knew that he wasn't going to do that. He was going to keep on living for the most absurd of reasons. Killing himself here would cause the girl too many problems.

"Shit," he said, swallowing back a belch that brought vomit to his mouth.

The shower creaked, groaned and then rumbled to life. A moment later, she invited him in and seemed irritated when he didn't answer, asking why he'd wanted her to take a shower in the first place.

"Because you stink."

"What?" she shouted over the roar of the water.

Shepherd didn't bother to answer. It was the note. Perhaps just perhaps, he could have recovered from finding his teenage daughter dead in the bathtub, but it was her suicide note that was a jagged piece of glass in his mind. If she'd blamed him and Sharon for being bad parents, ignoring her or not understanding who she was, if she'd complained about the pressure of being a straight-A student and an athlete, if she'd lamented a failed love affair, confessed to a drug problem or revealed that she was pregnant and scared, his life wouldn't have tilted off its axis. If she'd given a single goddamn reason for what she'd done, he might have been able to live with it. All she'd left by way of an explanation was a series of nonsense phrases. *Jesus Saves. Save the Wales. Abortion is Murder! Don't Blame Me I Voted Democratic! Throw the Bums Out! Wal-Mart Sucks! Spay and Neuter Your Pets. It Takes a Village. My Honor Student Can Beat Up Your Honor Student. My Wife Got the Good CAR! I'm Going to Disney World. Meat Is Murder! God Bless the U.S.A.*

Was it the nonsense, the lack of meaning,

the pure randomness of life that had killed his daughter? Or was it something else, a reason that he would never know? And if he couldn't hope to understand what killed his daughter, how could he believe he had ever known anything important at all? In the end, the chaos, the nonsense, the babble of voices came tumbling down and wiped away even a trace of reason. There was nothing to know, nothing to understand but that understanding itself was futile and impossible. In this matter, his child had been his teacher. Life was ugly and scarred and every bit as logical as a madman's nightmares. That realization had destroyed his career and his marriage, but Shepherd was glad to be shed of both.

"Are you asleep?"

Ivy stood at the edge of the bed, a towel draped over her shoulders, her hair flat and dripping water on her white skin. She was even thinner than he'd thought. Her breasts were small bumps capped with tiny pink nipples, her stomach so flat that it bordered upon emaciated, her legs as slim and white as a straw still wrapped in paper. Stripped naked and free of the costume of a child, she finally succeeded in looking the part that she tried so desperately to play.

"Goddamn," Ivy said. "You're the weirdest

trick I've ever met." Exasperated, she dropped the towel to the floor. "So what now?"

"Come here." He patted the bed. "Lie down with me."

They lay side by side, not touching, not talking. He felt her tenseness, the way her muscles thrummed with electricity. Then she rolled onto her side, and Shepherd rolled with her, put an arm around her thin upper body, pulled her close and held on.

"What now?" she whispered, her voice soft and small.

"Talk to me."

He buried his face in her damp hair and drifted to sleep breathing in the clean smell of motel shampoo. Her words were like a lullaby he dimly remembered from a long time ago.

* * *

Three days later, Shepherd caught up with them at a truck stop in West Memphis. He parked his rattletrap Oldsmobile at the edge of the lot, lit a cigarette with a hand that shook so hard it took him three tries to get it going. He hadn't had a drink since he'd woken sweaty and ill at the Sundowner Motel. Ivy had skipped out while he was sleeping and had taken his wallet with her. No big deal. The credit cards were maxed and delinquent, and what did losing fifty-three dollars in cash mean in the grand scheme of things?

He'd started his search for Buck and Ivy as soon as he'd dressed, swallowed a cup of black coffee, vomited it up and then forced down another. He hit the bars, the liquor stores, diners and pizza places on Greenview's strip. In the end Greenview was a small town. Hustlers like Buck and Ivy did not pass without notice. By lunchtime he'd learned that they'd been staying at a tent city off Westmoreland Avenue. A ten-minute conversation with a fat, saggy-breasted blonde had given him the make and model of their car.

Now, he was staring at a red Buick LeSabre with Illinois tags parked in a handicap space outside the Iron Kettle Truck Stop and Diner. Buck was behind the wheel. Ten, fifteen minutes earlier, Ivy had hurried into the restaurant. Today she'd done her hair in pigtails and dressed in a short, red skirt and plain white blouse. Watching her rush into the restaurant, her skirt rustling against the back of her thighs, was like breaking the seal on a chilled bottle of vodka.

When he'd left Harps County, he told himself he was on a fool's quest. He cleaned out his bank account, bought a .22 automatic and a roadmap and decided to follow a hunch south though he suspected it was hopeless. In the end he'd drive the interstates until his money ran out. But it didn't matter. Choice was not an issue. The twenty or thirty minutes that he lay with the girl, feeling her fluttering, fragile body against his, listening to her sing-song voice spinning the lie that she claimed was her life had been the only peace he'd known since Miranda's death. He couldn't let that go. As he drove the flat, hopeless stretch of interstate past the dead fields and the fast food sprawl of Kentucky, Missouri and Arkansas, he imagined a life spent with Ivy, not as lovers, not even as father and daughter but as something else, something that he couldn't quite comprehend. He had followed his hunches, stopping at the larger truck stops where he figured Ivy would ply her trade. His hope had surged each time he spotted a red Buick in the distance and then collapsed as he drew closer and saw a face that was not hers. Still, he kept driving, kept searching. Now he was here, and his future waited less than fifty feet away.

He stubbed his cigarette and willed himself to act. He'd imagined this moment a thousand times in the last three days. All he had to do was to move forward without thinking.

He lifted the .22 automatic from the

passenger seat and pulled a square piece of foam from the glove compartment. Shepherd had read somewhere that foam could act as an effective and legal silencer. Now he was only seconds away from finding out if the effective part was true. He worked the .22 into the waistband of his Dockers, zipped his jacket, and put the foam in the jacket pocket just as Ivy stepped from the truck stop with a grease-soaked paper bag in her hand.

Shepherd headed across the lot, taking deep breaths of diesel and exhaust fumes, his head spinning. He scurried around the back of the Buick to the driver's side, grabbed the handle on the rear door, certain that it would be locked. It wasn't. The door opened. A bell dinged. Shepherd slid into the backseat, slammed the door behind him. Buck spun around, a half-eaten chicken wing in his hand.

"Hey, buddy, what the fuck you think you're doing?" Then his eyes widened and he dropped the wing. "You're that freak from Kentucky."

Shepherd pulled the pistol, fumbled for the foam. In his head it took forever. He could hear his and Buck's breathing, smell the cigar smoke and chicken grease in the car. He placed the barrel to the back of Buck's head and tightened his finger on the trigger. There was a flat whap, a thin spray of blood across the windshield, and torn pieces of foam floated in the car like tiny balloons. Buck jerked in his seat, a marionette with a severed string, and fell forward, his head slamming the steering wheel.

In all of Shepherd's imaginings blood and brains had fallen like April rain, and Ivy had screamed until he consoled her, assured her that he meant her no harm. But there was just that one sprinkle of blood, and a clumsy jerk forward as if Buck had sat on his car keys. Ivy wasn't screaming, wasn't moving, and wasn't even breathing as far as Shepherd could tell. She simply stared at him, pupils narrowed, small flecks of gold floating beneath the hazel of her eyes until he felt as if he were trapped there, shrunken and hopelessly spinning. Then she took a breath, and Shepherd's head cleared a little. He saw her face, saw that her lips were trembling, but the rest of her was corpse-still. He thought of a frightened rabbit caught in headlights and unsure of which way to run.

"Listen," he said.

She didn't move, but her eyes hardened, and he realized how wrong he'd been to think of her as a rabbit. Her posture, her eyes, the nervous way she licked her lips didn't remind him of a rabbit at all. It was a rattlesnake he was looking at, cornered, frightened, trying to decide whether to strike or slither away.

"I'm not going to hurt you," he said.

She panicked then. She screamed once and then lunged at the door, snatching at the handle, not finding a grip and then clawing at the window.

Shepherd reached over the seat, hit the automatic locks. "Stop it."

She clawed at the window once more and then slumped against the seat, her head lowered. "What do you want?"

Shepherd couldn't believe she'd asked the question. "You," he said, as if explaining simple cause and effect to a child. "I want you."

She stated the obvious. "You killed Buck."

"Yes."

She turned in her seat, struggling to make her expression provocative. "Don't hurt me, okay? Don't hurt me and I'll do anything you want. No charge."

Shepherd punched the seat in his frustration. "No. I don't ... "

"I'll be your walking, talking love doll if you don't kill me."

Shepherd felt himself shriveling and squeezed the gun butt in his hand. "This isn't what I wanted."

She wiped her lips on the back of her hand, looked at him with desperate eyes. "What do you want from me?"

"I want to help," he said and realized how foolish it sounded. "I want you."

She licked her lips, took a deep breath, brushed her sweaty bangs from her eyes with her fingertips. "Like partners?"

It wasn't what he wanted, what he needed, but it was closer than the other, so he nodded. "Something like that."

"A 50/50 split," she said, her voice hard and sharp. "None of that 40/60 shit like I had with Buck."

Shepherd sagged against the seat. This was all wrong. Still, what were his options? Kill her? Kill himself? Walk away without her?

"Partners," he said and opened the car door.

* * *

The third night they worked Des Moines, Iowa, Shepherd followed the plan and walked through an unlocked door. Room 114 at the Conquistador. Ivy had marked it with a dropped pack of cigarettes.

Shepherd had waited too long, had one too many gin and tonics at the Bulldog Lounge. When he stepped into the room, .22 in hand, the john had already mounted Ivy. He rode her from behind. Her face was pushed into a pillow, and his pimpled white ass jiggled like Jell-O someone had taken out of the refrigerator too soon.

"Get away from my daughter," Shepherd said. The words were wooden and hollow on his tongue.

The man raised his hands, and Shepherd almost giggled - this pudgy, middle-aged guy holding his hands over his head but rotating his hips anyway, greedy for one last thrust. Sometimes, Shepherd despaired of the entire human race. Then the man pulled out of her and pushed himself off the bed.

"Don't hurt me," the guy said, jowls and prick bobbing with his words.

"Get away from her. You don't, I'll shoot you in the head."

He'd practiced the lines a dozen times in rest stop mirrors, but they still sounded false. He thought about Buck, about the way he'd laughed at his story. Maybe he'd been unfair. Even the best of actors can occasionally get trapped in a lousy role.

"It took you long enough," Ivy said, rolling off the bed and scrambling for her clothes. "You think you're going to touch any of this money, you're crazy.

The scam had been her idea. She'd laid it

out for him after they dumped Buck's body in a drainage ditch outside of Wynne, Arkansas. She was tired, tired of sucking dicks until her jaw ached, tired of diddling herself for greasy-mouthed perverts, fed up with having wrinkled, old pricks stuffed inside her and being sweated on by fat men who smelled like Cheetos and cheap cologne. She'd had the idea for a long time, but Buck - who wasn't her father but a part-time maintenance man and a nickel and dime shill artist she'd met in Milwaukee - had been a coward who was scared shitless of cops and angry johns and guns.

"A hundred and twenty-seven dollars," Ivy said now, rifling through the guy's wallet. "Don't even think you're going to take a cut."

Shepherd licked his lips, kept the gun pointed at the john. The man had found his way to a wall and stood there, his hands still raised, his prick shrinking like a balloon with a pinhole. There was something about his eyes that bothered Shepherd. They were gray, flecked with blood, familiar.

"Please," the man said. "Take my money."

"Oh, we intend to," Ivy chirped.

Shepherd cut his eyes in her direction. With her new outfit and new haircut, she looked enough like Miranda that there were nights that he dreamed his daughter had come back to him.

"Look," the man said. "I thought it was okay. I thought this was what you wanted."

Shepherd's legs tried to buckle, but he wouldn't let them. "What's your name?"

"Kevin," he said, crossing his arms over his sagging pectorals. "Kevin Henderson. I told you that. Remember?"

"That's what his driver's license says," Ivy said and pitched the wallet to the floor.

Shepherd glanced at the grinning clown portrait over the bed. He'd taken Miranda to the circus when she was seven. She'd been terrified of the elephants.

"Take what you want. I won't tell anyone. I swear to God."

And he wouldn't. That was what Ivy was counting on. Johns didn't go to the police, especially not when they thought that the whore who'd robbed them was underage. This man was not a threat. Except that he was sweating, embarrassed, ashamed and familiar. Looking at him was like looking at a blurred snapshot of a distant relative in a family album.

"The bathroom," Shepherd said, thinking of the way the guy's ass had jiggled as he'd thrust in and out of Ivy. "Get in there, right now."

She paused in the middle of stuffing cash

into the pockets of her blue jeans. "What are you doing?"

Shepherd silenced her with a raised finger. The man shuffled his way into the bathroom, shoulders slumped, eyes on the floor. Shepherd followed him, closed the door.

"Sit on the toilet," he said, noticed that the cleaned-for-your-protection seal hadn't been broken and changed his mind. "Forget it. Just sit on the side of the tub."

"I got a wife and family," the man said.

"Lucky you."

"What do you want from me?" he asked, his voice breaking. "Just tell me what you want."

It was his eyes. Shepherd felt as if he'd seen them a thousand times before, staring back at him from toothpaste-splattered mirrors. Bloodshot, frightened, ashamed. One second Shepherd was looking into them, and the next his finger was tightening on the trigger. Six times. When he finished the guy tumbled into the bathtub and lay there, his eyes just glass now, blood blossoms on his chest like spring flowers.

"What are you doing?" Ivy shouted.

Even though his ears rang from the shots, Shepherd was sure he heard her footsteps whispering on the worn carpet. She glanced inside, swallowed hard, and then stepped back, slamming the door. She spent the next two minutes calling him a stupid shit and cursing his incompetence. Shepherd didn't listen. He stared into the mirror over the sink until his breath fogged it and obscured his own eyes. Then he wrote his name in the condensation. Ivy yanked open the bathroom door, huffed past him, her hip knocking him against the sink. She tore open the shower curtain, leaned over the tub and glared at Henderson's corpse.

"Fucking asshole," she said.

Shepherd thought of apologizing but then realized that she wasn't talking to him. She walked back to the other room. Then he heard the bed squeak.

"No," Ivy yelled to him. "You're right. This is better."

When he came out, she stepped to him and patted his head the way she might a kindly old grandfather or a loyal but stupid dog. As she gathered her things, she kept talking, and his future unrolled in front of him like an endless ribbon of interstate. Now that he'd done this, he'd have to do it again and again. Leaving a witness behind to give their descriptions to the state police or FBI wouldn't be an option. He glanced at a cracked mirror over a burn-scarred dresser. What he saw there made him sick to his stomach. But it didn't have to be that way. Maybe he would take a detour off the road they were traveling. The cops might find them or maybe one of these nights, he'd turn the gun on Ivy and then himself when he finished with the john.

"Are you coming?" Ivy shouted.

One of these days it would end. But not tonight. Tonight he still preferred this, whatever it was, to being alone.

"I'm coming," he said.

Then he gave one last look at the bathroom and followed Ivy through another open door.

Promissory Notes

When the old man shows up just after dawn with a stolen .22 automatic, a box of hollow point shells and three hundred and seventy-five dollars, I understand that this is a serious situation. He wants his soon-to-be-son-in-law dead and expects me to do it.

"I ain't trying to rush you," he says, winded from the three small steps to my trailer's front door. "But I don't think I got much past Thanksgiving."

I figure he's being overly optimistic. This morning his skin is the color of a nicotine stain, his face bloated and twitching, his breath heavy with rot. A gurgle rises from his fluid-filled lungs. He's suffering from what he likes to call the big three, prostate cancer, heart failure and COPD - a disease I'd never even heard of until they made a commercial about it. The poor man can't die in peace thanks to his love-stupid daughter and the ex-con, drug dealing woman-beater she plans to marry. I've got nothing but sympathy for him even though I'm sure had my own daughter lived she would have never ended up in this kind of predicament. But this whole thing makes me uneasy. I'm a temporarily unemployed salesman, not a professional killer. Forty-four is too old to seriously contemplate a change of careers even if I didn't have an aversion to guns, violence and long stretches in prison. Still, I feel bad for the old guy standing there on his trembling legs, soggy grocery bag in hand, cold November drizzle dripping from his liver-spotted head. Instead of slamming the door in his face and going back to bed like I should, I invite him in for a cup a coffee.

"You think it's smart?" His milky blue eyes dart around as if he thinks the FBI might be lurking just behind the junk pickup or the rotting doghouse in my neighbor's yard. "For the two of us to be seen together is what I mean."

"You're already here, aren't you? You might as well come in and get warm."

He wipes his feet on a worn Kentucky Wildcats welcome mat that the last tenant left me and takes everything in: the ratty secondhand furniture, the empty beer bottles, pizza boxes and overflowing ashtrays on the coffee table, the clothes strewn across the living room floor. I wait for him to remind me that cleanliness is next to godliness or to ask if it's the maid's day off, but instead he says,

"I bought a car from you once, must have been ten, twelve years ago? A used Impala with just thirty-three-thousand miles."

"Is that so?" I say. "I bet it was a good one."

"Wasn't a bad one." He pulls up a chair at the kitchen table and scrapes dried ketchup from the table top with a long, yellow fingernail. "Had a hitch in the transmission though."

"Oh yeah?"

He squints at his fingernail, frowns, wipes it on his pants and then scrapes some more. "Just a little one, but the damned thing about drove me crazy."

While the coffee percolates, I lean against the kitchen sink and listen to him tell me all about the hitch, the way it would catch on a hill but never really slip a gear and how he brought it back to the dealership a half dozen times and had three independent mechanics take a look at it but no one could ever quite put a finger on the problem. Eventually, he gave up and traded it on a new Toyota. I don't bother to say "you and everybody else, brother, which is why I'm out of a job." It's too early and I'm too sober to lie to myself anyway. Thanks to a taste for afternoon whiskey and a six month tornado-like affair with a large-breasted, doe-eyed, recently divorced accounts payable clerk named Ashley, I'd barely been hanging onto my job as assistant sales manager at Dobbs Brothers GM even before the economy went belly up and the dealership shut down. At the time I thought the sweet burn of a double Makers Mark and Ashley's smile were worth whatever price I might have to pay in the future. But when that bill came due it was more expensive than I could have imagined. It cost me my professional reputation, my three-bedroom ranch house in the Oak Dale subdivision and my marriage.

"Black." For a second I think the old man's talking about the stretch of luck that landed me here, but I see he's nodding at the coffee pot in my hand. "Used to take cream, but some of these medicines I'm on make me lactose intolerant." He blows at his coffee to cool it, and the effort seems to take most of the breath he has left. Then he says, "You ain't never done nothing like this, have you?"

It's time to tell him that yesterday it was just whiskey and outrage talking. Hell, I want to say, I agree that this Ronny Wayne Curtis deserves to be shot. Any man who'd beat a woman and cost her her children does, but I'm not the one to do it. I need to say I'm a car salesman not a killer.

"You got kids, Kincaid?" the old man asks before I get the chance. "I don't remember you saying one way or the other."

It was nineteen years ago, and I don't want to think about, let alone explain, those last days of the pregnancy when we knew it had soured and the baby was dying in the womb. Sometimes, late at night when the world is still and I'm sober enough to feel the silence, I can hear Laura's endless, choking sobs after they induced labor and sucked the shriveled, hopeless thing that would have been our baby from her womb. Alicia. That's the name Laura had inscribed on the tombstone at Rose Hill Cemetery.

"No," I say. "It just never happened."

He tongues a blood blister on his lip. "She came along late in life, you know? Patricia and I had just about given up on trying when we found out she was pregnant. Deanna was my princess, just the cutest and sweetest thing you could imagine. I know all daddies think that about their little girls but it was true. She was my little princess and smart as a whip, too, boy. But things went wrong for her somewhere, I guess. I'll be damned if I know why." He wipes his mouth on the back of his hand, grimaces.

"This doesn't give me pleasure. I never thought I'd want a man dead, let alone pay someone ... I managed a grocery store for thirty years!" He slaps his fist off the table so hard it sends empty beer bottles rattling. "But I ain't got no choice. I got to do what I can to save my daughter and my grandchildren, don't I?"

I heard it all yesterday but he tells me again anyway. He says Deanna was never "loose," and he doesn't want me to get the wrong impression. She made good grades, dated nice boys, didn't get pregnant in high school like a lot of girls did. She waited until her junior year in college. It was just her bad luck that it wasn't by a bright and honorable would-be accountant but by a part-time bouncer at a campus bar. He took off when the baby, a girl, was three weeks old and that was the last anyone heard of him. Deanna dropped out of Murray State, came back to Greenview and took a job in the office at the Super Value Foods warehouse. Then she fell hard for a long-haul trucker with a fast line and a wife somewhere up in Michigan or maybe it was Minnesota, the old man couldn't remember. A week after he told her that he was going back to his wife for good, she found out she was pregnant - another daughter.

"It hurt Patricia even more than me because she had the pancreatic cancer then and knew she wasn't long for the world," the old man says, staring into his coffee. "But Deanna turned around after that. You better believe she did."

There were calm waters for a long while, the old man says. She worked her way up to office manager, had two beautiful little girls, played organ every other Sunday at West Bank Baptist. Then, one night three years ago, she went to the Yellow Rose to blow off steam after work and met Ronny Wayne Curtis. He was an ex-con who was quick with his fists, especially when it came to his woman. The last three years had passed in drunken quarrels, black eyes, broken bones, mumbled excuses. A year ago, Curtis took a fall for possession with intent and since Deanna was in the car with him and holding a half-ounce of marijuana, she wound up on six months' probation. Her daughters, eight and eleven now, ended up in foster care. Super Value gave her a chance, tried to keep her after everything that had happened, but the missed days ran one into another and finally they'd let her go.

"She didn't care," the old man says. "All she could do was stay in bed and cry." His lip curls into a sneer I'm not sure he's even aware of. "I thought it was for the girls, tried to talk to her about it, told her I'd do all I could to get them back. But it was him she was crying for - that piece of crap who caused all this in the first place. Now, he's out of prison and she's moved him right back in with her even though her lawyer's warned her that it's going to mean she loses the girls for good. It's like she don't even hear him."

Yesterday, fueled by whiskey and weepy empathy, I'd been outraged by the story. When the old man had said, "I'd give the last two-thousand dollars in my savings account and my grandfather's gold watch if someone would kill that son of a buck." I slapped the bar, winked at him and said, "I'll do it and you can keep the gold watch." He asked if I was kidding, and drunk as I was, I told him "Hell, someone has to do it." We worked out the details: the old man would buy an unregistered gun from this guy he knew who ran a de facto pawnshop out of the back of his SUV, pay me fifteen percent of the money up front and deliver a picture, an address and whatever details he knew about the target. It felt like playing make believe when you're a kid. But now that there's a paper sack with a gun, bullets and three hundred and seventy-five dollars sitting on my kitchen table, this thing has taken on an entirely different hue.

As if he's read my mind, the old man taps

the bag with a long, thin finger. "The gun, the bullets, the money and the pictures are in there," he says. "I wasn't sure what details I should give you other than he likes to beat my little girl."

Reluctantly, I open the bag, pull out the pictures. This Ronny Wayne Curtis is sandy blonde, mid-thirties, short and chubby, not the kind of man, you'd think, who could inspire enough passion to cause a woman to take a beating twice a week and throw away her children. But then again Ashley in accounts payable had a mule's overbite and a habit of arching her eyebrows like Spock in the original *Star Trek* series, and I'd given up most everything I had for her.

"You'll want to burn them," the old man says, fighting back a cough. "When you finish the job."

If there's anything a salesman hates it's to tell a customer no or give back money, but I'm right there on the verge of saying that I can't do it when he surrenders to a coughing fit. He grabs a balled up paper towel from his pocket and spits up a glob of blood and then sits there pale and shaking. He's worse off than he wants to acknowledge. The way it looks he'll be lucky to see the weekend. That's when I realize that there's a way to keep the three-hundred and seventy-five bucks I need - I've got eleven dollars in my wallet and eighty-six fifty in checking - and let the old man die happy.

"You don't worry about a thing," I tell him. "But you can't rush into something like this. It might take a little time."

* * *

That afternoon I park across the street from my ex-wife's house and watch the rain beat on her empty concrete drive. This isn't the ranch house that was ours for the last seven and a half years of our marriage, but a two-bedroom country cottage near the library that she bought after our divorce. It's a nice place, small but neat, ordered and peaceful, and I come by here from time to time when I know she's working. I'm not sure why other than it's like looking at a snapshot of normal - a place I've long since left behind.

I take a quick nip from a half pint of bourbon and think about maybes and only ifs and what could have beens. We should have tried again after we lost the baby. The doctors swore that the next pregnancy would probably have been normal, but neither of us wanted to risk probably, at least not at first. Then it just got easier not to try. The yearly vacations in

Myrtle Beach or Clearwater, the weekend getaways to a cabin on Lake Barkley, the new cars, and the three bedroom ranch in the subdivision wouldn't be possible if we'd had to pay for diapers or buy school clothes every fall or put away money for college. We were spoiled; that was the problem, and if we'd tried again, everything could have been different. Having a child might have saved me from a lot of bad decisions.

I'm still thinking about it, trying to imagine my make-believe child's future when Laura's Toyota Four Runner pulls into the drive. On instinct, I reach to start the ignition, but it's too late to make an escape.

"What are you doing here, Kincaid?" she asks before I even get the window half way down. "Old lady Crenshaw said she saw you sitting out here, but I thought she was crazy."

Even soaking wet and angry, she looks better than she has in five, maybe ten years. It's not just the new, short haircut or the twenty pounds she's lost. She looks like someone who just found out that a terminal diagnosis had been an error.

"Well," she says. "Explain yourself, Kincaid."

There's no point in telling her she's beautiful or I still love her - both of which are true and totally useless to me now. I can't say that I'd come by to take a long look at a life I should be living. She'd think I was crazy. Telling her about the old man, the three-hundred and seventy-five dollars and the stolen .22 automatic I have stuffed beneath the front seat of my rusting Monte Carlo isn't an option either, so I say the first thing I can think of.

"I've been thinking about Alicia. You ever wonder what kind of life she might have lived?"

She flinches just like she always has when you mention Alicia. Maybe she doesn't even know she's doing it after all this time. "Don' ... " she says. "What's the point, Kincaid?"

"You ever wonder how things would have been if ... well, you know. Or maybe if we'd tried again."

She closes her eyes and raindrops curl down her cheeks. "We'd be divorced, Kincaid. That's what would have happened."

"I don't know," I say but my voice sounds weak and shameful to my own ears. "It might have made a difference."

"Why would you have thought about your child? You didn't think of me. Not when you were with your little girlfriend. I never even crossed your mind until she got remarried and moved to Indiana, did I?"

"Ohio," I say, although I'm not sure why I

correct her. "She works in medical billing."

"You know what? I don't care anymore, Kincaid. I haven't *really* cared since I caught the two of you together, but I'm not even mad now. I'm really not. I'm just glad to be done with you. I feel like I've had a tumor removed." She takes a deep breath and blinks away the rain. "Maybe I'm still angrier than I thought. But I really want to know what in the hell you're doing here."

"I've got money," I say. "I owe you on that old credit card."

"You didn't come here to pay me," she says, chewing her bottom lip the way she does when she's being thoughtful. "And it's a little late in the game to be wondering about what might have been."

"Last weekend," I say. "Saturday was Alicia's un-birthday. I guess it got me thinking."

Her brow is furrowed, her lips tight. "What did you say?"

"It got me thinking, you know. Maybe things ... "

"Her un-birthday? Was that what you said?"

I shrug and wish I'd drank more of the whiskey. "That's the way I've always thought about it," I admit. "It's from *Alice in*

Wonderland."

"I saw the damn cartoon, Kincaid."

"Since she wasn't really born ... I mean, I just always called it her un-birthday in my head."

She tucks in her chin and her brow furrows even deeper, and she steps away from my car as if she's brushed against something repulsive. "Your half of that Visa you never paid off was nine hundred and sixty dollars."

"Listen," I say but can't think of how to go on.

"Forget about it, Kincaid. Just forget the money. Then you've got no excuse for coming around here. If you do I'll call the cops and go to court to file a restraining order."

"Laura," I say. "I can give you part ... "

She turns on her heels like a well-drilled soldier, takes a couple of stiff steps across the street before she loses her composure and runs for her front door. I lean forward, turn the key in the ignition.

I'm at the end of the street, waiting to pull onto the main highway when I realize that I'm not sure where it is I should go.

Buck Gish Road is a narrow, pot-holed strip of blacktop that cuts through acres of scrub brush, thickets, and overgrown fields on the edge of the Sugar Creek Mines. Every few hundred yards an old Fleetwood trailer or a small, weatherboard house pops from the weed fields, and I pass a lot of pickup trucks, rusted swing sets and mangy dogs before I cut off onto a gravel and mud farm road that winds up a steep hill. The old man forgot to give me the address or maybe I just forgot that he had, but Greenview, Kentucky, isn't exactly a metropolis. It took less than a minute to find the address in the phonebook, another thirty seconds to remember that I knew the area pretty well. It's a quiet spot, partially hidden by dead weeds and a blighted birch tree, the kind of place where teenagers gather to drink beer and where married sales managers bring their girlfriends in the early, recklessly giddy days of their affairs.

I park at the top of the hill, pull a can of Old Milwaukee from the 12-pack I picked up to keep me company and look out at the box-shaped farmhouse below me. The view is a little less than impressive. There's a '86 or '87 Ford F150 painted the yellow and black of a bumble bee parked in a gravel drive, fifty gallon drums crammed with garbage beside the crumbling front porch, lots of empty beer and soda cans strewn across the yard. I'm not sure why I'm here or what I expect to find, but it seems as good of a place for me to be as any. I figure I can at least tell the old man I've been checking things out, keeping an eye on his daughter. Maybe it isn't a lot, but at least I feel like I'm doing something to earn the old man's three hundred and seventy-five dollars.

Not long before sunset as the last of the feeble gray light seeps from an even grayer sky, Deanna Browning lugs a trash bag to one of the fifty gallon drums, pauses to scratch her stomach and then lights a cigarette. She's plump with frizzy dyed-blonde hair, dressed in Dollar Store sweatpants and a UK bubble coat - not exactly the princess the old man made her out to be.

Before she finishes her cigarette, Ronny Wayne Curtis steps onto the porch. He's barefooted and a cigarette dangles from the corner of his mouth. I've heard that prison hardens a man, but Curtis just looks older and fatter and smaller than he had in the old man's pictures. Now he drains the can of beer he's holding, pitches the empty at one of the barrels and doesn't seem surprised or worried when he misses. She says something to him, but he just shrugs, flicks his cigarette off the porch and walks back inside. She raises her middle finger slowly and with great relish at the front door and picks up the empty can and drops it in the trash. Given the dozens of others scattered around the yard, I'm not sure why she bothers. Then she grinds her cigarette out beneath her heel, clumps up the steps and back inside.

A few minutes later, a light flares on in the house, and I start my ignition. I change my mind and open another beer. There's nothing to see, no real reason to be here, but it feels comforting somehow, so I turn off the car and watch that feeble light in their window. I wonder what they're doing in there - fixing dinner or shooting crystal meth or arguing over that beer can or making love. Anything seems possible. I wonder what Laura would think about me keeping vigil outside of a stranger's house, but I know that it doesn't matter, not anymore. For the first time, she seemed serious when she said she didn't want to see me again, and I know all the roles I've played in her life, lover, husband, friend, adversary, are over.

Now silhouettes step in front of the window. They're close together, moving in an imperfect rhythm, but I can't tell if they're fighting or dancing, and it doesn't really matter. There's nothing I can do about it anyway. Still, it feels right for me to be here, so I slump down in the seat and settle in for a long night while shadows swallow everything but the dim, yellow light in that distant window.

* * *

Four nights later, I walk into the Coyote Lounge, ready to tell Old Man Browning that I've done all I can and that I'm keeping the down payment. After hours spent watching his daughter and Ronny Wayne Curtis carry out trash, drink beer, smoke cigarettes, bring home buckets of takeout chicken, order pizzas, throw scraps to a legion of stray cats, argue, make up and then make out in their front yard, I've earned the money. But tonight the old man's seat at the end of the bar is empty.

Danny or Donny, I can never quite remember his name, drops his dingy rag in the sink below the bar and takes his time sauntering over. "Getcha?"

"This still happy hour?" I ask.

"That's what they call it."

I order a double bourbon with a Bud draft chaser. "The old man been in today?" I ask, hooking my thumb at the empty stool.

"Huh?"

"Browning. Real thin, sick looking guy."

Danny or Donny, or maybe it's Dave, nods. "You were a friend of his, I guess. I remember you all talking." He grimaces and tugs at the collar of his sweater. "I reckon you ain't heard, huh? He passed on last night." He picks up a dirty towel like a devout Catholic reaching for a rosary. "My momma goes to West Bank Baptist and I reckon the old man was a member because that's the way I heard about it. She's on what they call the grief committee, a group of ladies who bake cakes and make casseroles and such when something like this happens. I went by there this afternoon, and she was baking a pineapple upside down cake so I knew someone was dead. She told me it was Mr. Browning that had passed."

"You're sure?"

He frowns as if I've accused his mother of an inaccuracy, but then his features soften. "Yeah, I'm sure," he says. "He went in his sleep, so I guess that's some kind of comfort." He shrugs as if there's nothing left to say, and maybe he's right; maybe there isn't. Then he points a finger at my empty glass. "What about it? You ready for another?"

* * *

The next day a manila envelope crammed with seventeen hundred dollars in cash arrives in the mail. There's a scrawled note on a piece of yellow legal pad. "I wasn't feeling well so I thought I'd better get you the rest of your money. Thank you for giving me peace of mind."

The day after that I stand by a freshly dug grave, silently explaining myself to the old man's flag-draped coffin while a harelip preacher reads from Psalms. In my head, I tell him that this whole situation was something akin to divine providence. He was like an angel in disguise who'd turned up at the Coyote Lounge searching for a decent man. Of everyone there I was the one who listened, sympathized, gave him comfort in the last days of his life by letting him believe he'd done something about his daughter's predicament. Anyone else might have a) called the police and then he would have spent his final hours in jail, or b) actually committed a murder. To my way of thinking I've done the only decent thing possible under this particular set of circumstances.

The minister concludes another psalm, and there's a weary and shivering echo of amen. It's a larger crowd than I'd expected. Every folding chair beneath the worn, Tucker Funeral Home canopy is occupied, and a half dozen almost-teenagers stand around behind the last row of chairs, kicking at the dirt and fidgeting. I peg them as about a third of the congregation from West Bank Baptist. Deanna Browning and

Ronny Wayne Curtis sit in the front row. They're holding hands and shifting in their seats, uncomfortable in their cheap coats and Wal-Mart clothes. They're the only ones here besides me who don't seem to be on a first name basis with the Lord.

Finally, the minister instructs everyone to bow their heads in prayer. I play along with the head-bowing thing but don't bother with the prayer. Instead, I listen to the ringing in my ears and try to ignore the stench of last night's beer and bourbon seeping through my pores. I remember napping in my car and believe it was parked on that hill on Buck Gish Road, but I might well have been parked behind the dumpsters at Kroger. A blind drunk, a walking blackout, a semi-suicidal binge. There are no pretty words to describe it, but now instead of praying or echoing the minister's lisped amen, I promise the old man that it was my last one. The money locked in the glove compartment of my car is a chance to start over, and I vow to the old man that I'm going to do just that. Stay sober, live respectably, spend some time reading the want ads until I find the right job and a new life - wherever it may be. There's nothing tying me to Greenview, and there's a whole world of roads out there. I know that now.

After the last amen, Deanna sprinkles a handful of dirt on her daddy's coffin and the service ends. Anxious to be out of the cold, the mourners bum rush Deanna and Ronny Wayne Curtis, kissing cheeks, shaking hands and then scurrying up the sloping hill to the warmth of their cars and SUVs. I whisper a final thank you to the old man and trudge towards my Monte Carlo. I wait until I'm a respectable distance from the grave to light the cigarette I've been craving for half an hour. Halfway up the hill, I pause and look toward the rows of graves beneath a bare willow on the far side of the cemetery. Alicia's buried there, two plots over from my mom and dad. I haven't visited that grave in nineteen years, but suddenly, it seems important that I do it soon. Not today. I'm not ready for that, not yet, but soon. I make it a promise.

Before I get into my Monte Carlo to warm myself with the half pint of whiskey that I've been waiting to open all day, I turn back to the old man's grave. Most of the mourners are gone now, but Deanna Browning is bending on one knee to hug a whip-thin little girl with corn-colored hair. Flanked by a tight-lipped couple in their fifties - the foster parents I assume - an older girl watches them, glaring and trying to look a lot harder than she is or has any right to be.

"Deanna! We got somewhere to be right now!"

The shout makes me jump and drop ash across the front of my suit. - Ronny Wayne Curtis stands by his bumblebee colored pickup, glowering at Deanna and her daughters. She's throwing away her children for him, and he won't even let her say a proper goodbye. She squeezes the child tighter, kisses her forehead and then lets go and heads toward the pickup truck, struggling to not look back at her kids. When she gets there, Curtis says something and she shakes her head. Then he grabs her arm. Even from this distance, I know that his grip is a tight one that's likely to leave bruises.

I look back at the little girls and see they've watched all this. Their dresses billow in a gust of wind, and they might be the ghosts of any of the buried and forgotten children in this graveyard. Thinking that brings gooseflesh to the back of my arms, and the craving for a drink is so sudden and overpowering that it nearly buckles my knees. Inside the bumblebee truck, Curtis seems to be screaming at Deanna as they pull out of the cemetery. I know it's not going to end with shouting. I lean against my Monte Carlo and press my palms to my eyes.

I stay there until the last of the mourners

have left the cemetery. The gravediggers who'll finish the burial haven't yet arrived so it's just me and the dead - the old man, my parents, my daughter, the ghost of what she might have been.

"I don't owe anybody anything," I say aloud.

But the dead are the most silent and obstinate of creditors, and my excuses bounce back at me.

* * *

An hour after the last light goes out in the little weatherboard farmhouse, I load the .22 automatic and step out into a frigid, moonless night. It's the day after Thanksgiving, over a week since the old man's funeral, and I've waited as long as I can. I dig around in my trunk for a couple of screwdrivers, one Phillips and one straight-head, squint at my watch in the feeble glow of the light from the trunk lid. It seems impossible that the beating happened just seven hours ago.

Every night since the old man's funeral, I've kept my vigil, and for most of those days nothing much has happened. They bought groceries, argued, drank beer, ate a lot of takeout food, argued some more, watched TV.

Still, it felt important that I be here. It's the only place I've felt at peace since they stuck the old man in the ground. Then this afternoon Curtis's pickup roared into the drive with Deanna Browning behind the wheel. The passenger's door opened, and Curtis stumbled out into the yard, still chugging from a can of Pabst Blue Ribbon. He rushed around the pickup's grill, yanked open the driver's door, grabbed a handful of Deanna's hair and pulled her out into the gravel. She landed hard on her shoulder, rolled to her knees. Then he grabbed her hair again, pulling her to her feet and slapping her, a hard backhanded slap across the mouth that I could hear even though I was too far away for that to be possible. She broke free and staggered towards the house, but Curtis caught her by the neck of her sweatshirt, pulled her back. The punches and screams seemed to come from everywhere. When she went to the ground, Curtis was on her kicking her in the legs and back, cursing and shouting at her as he did it. This was ugly and shameful, nothing like the things you see on television or in movies. It froze me in my place, left me weak and trembling. I wanted to stop it, wanted to charge down the hill and shoot him right then and there, but I couldn't move, couldn't do anything but watch and curse myself as a coward.

Then it ended. Maybe he just got winded or maybe whatever fury that had possessed him passed, but it stopped as quickly as it started. He stumbled away from her, dropped on the edge of the front porch and drank his beer. A few minutes later, clothes torn, her face scraped and bloody, she pulled herself to her feet, hobbled up the porch steps, paused before she touched his shoulder and then took his hand and led him inside.

Now I slip, stumble and fall my way down the muddy hillside to their front yard. The porch looks risky, likely to creak and pop and make a lot of noise so I move around to the back of the house, trying to remember everything about lock picking and breaking and entering I've seen on TV.

After I wedge the straight-head screwdriver in the door jamb and succeed in doing nothing but making too much noise and digging out a couple of chunks of rotted wood, the knob turns in my hand, and I realize it had never been locked to begin with. Evidently, Ronny Wayne Curtis had been too busy swigging beers and Deanna too concerned with nursing her wounds to bother with locking the door.

Bare fluorescent bulbs over the sink throw a thin, bluish light through the kitchen. The room is small but cleaner than I expect from the mess in the yard. The dishes are washed and put away and, except for half a loaf of bread, the kitchen table is empty and covered with a spotless, white tablecloth. Looking at the scrubbed countertops, the ceramic salt and peppershakers and the Home-is-Where-the-Heart-Is plaque mounted over the electric stove, I'm sure I've made a mistake. This looks like a home where normal people live, people who hold hands at the movies, watch their favorite shows snuggled on the living room couch and put on their best clothes to eat dinner at a Red Lobster or Outback Steakhouse when they can afford it. I want to slip back outside, forget I've ever done something this crazy. But I can't forget the kicks and punches, the blood on her face, the pathetic way she led him back inside or the nagging question of what if she were my daughter out of my head.

There's a dim, blue light from a muted television at the end of the hall, so I pass by a bedroom door, saying a silent prayer that one of them will be sleeping on the living room sofa. The idea of shooting Curtis while Deanna Browning snores peacefully beside him breaks out sweat on my forehead and makes my hands tremble. If I have to do it, I will, but I know it isn't going to be easy.

Sports Center silently flickers on the television, and I stand at the edge of the living room watching college basketball scores scroll at the bottom of the screen. A single, ragged snore brings me back to myself, and I see that for once I've caught a break. Ronny Wayne Curtis is passed out on the couch. The blanket that Deanna Browning must have draped over him makes my head roar with anger, and I step towards a fireplace that doesn't look as if it's been used in years. There are a half dozen framed pictures on the mantel. I squint at the freckled little girls and think of Alicia and the child she might have been. She's lost, I know, but these two don't have to be, not with Curtis dead, not if their mother takes this chance to turn her life around.

Steeling my nerve, I lift the .22, stride across the room and bang my shin into a coffee table. A nearly empty fifth of Jim Beam falls to the floor and my heart stutters, but Curtis simply grunts once and goes back to snoring, and I stand over him and watch the jagged rise and fall of his chest. I'm close enough that I can smell onions and bourbon and tobacco on his breath. I try to focus on what I witnessed in the front yard, but the vulnerable, moon-faced man lying in front of me doesn't seem anything like the one who used his feet and his fists on a defenseless woman. I close my eyes and struggle to summon my anger and outrage, but I just feel tired and shaky and ashamed.

Suddenly I want to wake him and ask for an explanation. I need to know how we got from wherever we were to this place we are now. Surely no one sets out to be a wife beater or a drug dealer or an out-of-work sales manager with a loaded gun in his hand. Yet somehow people end up in these places all the time. It's a mystery I can't figure out on my own.

"You're a monster," I whisper.

The words are forced and empty and I'm not sure whom I mean anyway. What I know for certain is that I can't pull the trigger. Whether it is a moral virtue or a moral failing doesn't matter. I can't kill him and was a fool to have ever thought I could.

And so I promise myself that tomorrow I'll send Deanna Browning what's left of the old man's money along with an anonymous letter explaining what almost happened. I'll tell her that her father had nothing but the best intentions. I'll say that there are numbers she can call, places she can go to get help. I'll remind her of her daughters and how easily she could lose them forever. Maybe I'll tell her about my own life - the things I lost and those that I threw away.

I've just stepped into the kitchen when a light flares on in the bedroom at the end of the hall. I want to run but my legs feel like stone pillars and the rest of me is trembling so hard I nearly drop my pistol. Then Deanna Browning steps into the hall.

"Who are you? What are you doing here?" she asks.

Her face is swollen, scraped, already bruising, and for a heartbeat, I wish I'd had the guts to pull the trigger when I had the chance. Then she begins to bellow.

"Wake up, Ronny Wayne!" she shouts. "We got an intruder!"

"Listen," I say.

"Oh good God, Ronny Wayne! He's got a gun." A fat, pink tongue creeps to the corner of her damaged lips. "Who are you? Answer me, damn it. Are you looking for drugs? Are you some kind of psychopath or something?"

"No," I say, "I'm a salesman."

She isn't listening. "Ronny Wayne! Wake your drunk butt up! I tell you we got an intruder!"

"No listen," I say. "I don't want to ... I'm not here to hurt you."

I hear scrambling in the other room, the creak of a door. For a moment, I think Curtis has decided to bolt from the house and leave her on her own. Then he stumbles into the kitchen, still half drunk or half asleep or maybe a little of both. He's swaying on his feet, and there's a shotgun cradled in his hands. This is not a good combination. When he sees me, his eyes widen, and he lifts the barrel in my direction.

I lift the pistol and am a little surprised to see that it's still in my hand. A Mexican standoff. That's what they called it in the westerns and gangster movies my dad watched when I was a kid. I can almost hear John Wayne or Lee Marvin saying, "Looks like we got us a Mexican standoff, boys. The question is where do we go from here."

"What do you want from us?" Deanna Browning says now. "What are you doing here?"

I want to tell her everything I intended to put in tomorrow's letter. I want to say I understand how easy it is to set out for one place and end up somewhere completely different. For the first time in nineteen years, I need to speak of the loss and helplessness and the bitter sense of relief I'd felt when Laura and I lost the baby. I want to talk about love both husbandly and fatherly. And I want to say to them, "Everything we do we do for love." I need them to help me understand whether or not that's why things sour so easily, why lives and best intentions go so wrong. I am compelled to say, "My name is Kincaid. I'm a salesman with nothing left to sell."

But my voice seems to have left me. Still, it's not too late. I know it isn't. There are choices to be made. I understand that we could point the guns to the floor or put them down altogether and walk away into whatever life is left to us. Yet we're caught here, frozen, watching, waiting for someone to pull a trigger. From the corner of my eye, I catch the barest of glimpses of our reflection in the kitchen window. I know that it's still dark outside and likely to stay that way for a long time, but I also know that in some places the night is nearly over.

"Listen," I say to them and the strength of my voice surprises me.

"Somewhere out there, maybe not here ... but somewhere, it's almost morning."

Then I do the only thing I can. I squeeze the trigger.

Where Will You Be When the Waters Rise?

1935.

He stands in the side yard, staring through the mud-specked glass of her bedroom window, shoulders hunched against the falling drizzle and the needle-wind, which whips across the Green River. She doesn't know how long he's been watching or what it is he believes he's seeing. She flicks her hand, a gesture meant to shoo him, but he's only seven, and he wriggles his small fingers in a wave. She knows she should stop, roll off the bed, clutch the sheet around her, and either screech at him to get away or cower in shame, but she doesn't. Instead, she goes on riding Finis Young in the way he likes to be ridden, her back turned to his face, her body swaying gently like a reed in the wind.

She closes her eyes and keeps moving, faster now and then faster still. Finis reaches around to lift her heavy breasts and grunts "Uh, nuh oh," the way he always does. Then she feels him throb inside her, and it is over. She opens her eyes and sees her son has gone, bored, she supposes, with what's proven to be not much of a spectacle.

"Did you?" Finis asks. "You know, how women do?"

"No," she says.

"Oh." His sigh is sad and weary. "I'm sorry."

She says it's sweet of him to ask and then kisses his fingertips. His hand is smallish and soft, a storekeeper's hand. His fingernails fascinate her. They are trimmed short, kept clean, tinged pinkish from the blood beneath them. Her husband, Lester, has yellowish, nearly clubbed nails, hard and sharp and black underneath from grime and coal dust.

She widens her thighs and places his hand where she likes it, whispers, "Go ahead. With your fingers. The way you do."

A moment later, she arches her hips and clutches at the graying mattress and swallows a scream lest it should frighten him. When the shudders pass, she lifts his hand again and kisses his fingers once more for good luck.

After everything is over, he pulls on his pants and his white, round-collared shirt, hooks his suspenders over his narrow shoulders. She smokes one of his Chesterfields and studies the bald spot on the back of his head.

"I got to get back," he says. "They sent me a new clerk, but he don't know lard from lace."

"Okay," she says.

"I'd stay if I could."

She tells him that's all right, makes sure she sounds a little pouty, a little disappointed. The truth is she's anxious for him to go, the way she always is. She likes Finis pretty well, but the afternoons, the too-brief hours before her older children come home from school and Lester returns from the mines, are hers. She prefers to spend them alone or with Jimmy Ray when she's kept him home from the mine-camp school for no reason other than she doesn't want to part with him.

"We're supposed to get some horehound in on Monday," Finis says, lacing his shoes. "I'll bring you a nickel's worth if I can."

"I don't need no candy."

"For the boy then."

"Sure," she says. "For the boy."

She thinks of telling him that he doesn't have to bring anything, that these times when her husband is deep underground at Holt Mining Company's Paradise No. 3, isn't about what he gives her or the way he sometimes forgets to note purchases on her and Lester's monthly tab at the Holt store. But she's afraid saying such a thing will make him distrustful. He is fifty-one, a widower, a small, balding, owl-eyed clerk, not the kind of man who is used to being welcome in another fellow's bed. If she tells him the real reason, he might think her crazy, and even if he didn't, he'd ask questions, and she doesn't want to waste the time it would take to answer them. Besides, the gifts - the dime left on her dresser, the occasional free sack of flour or bucket of lard - come in handy.

"How about butterscotch?" he asks. "I could bring you butterscotch if you'd prefer."

"Yes," she says. "I like butterscotch just fine."

He grunts and bobs his balding head. He's satisfied. Their relationship is on solid ground.

The first time was on the cot at the back of the mining camp store. Twelve years ago. She was a few days past her twenty-first birthday, and the trip to the company store came at the end of the waiting time after the birth of her second daughter. She had heard that Finis Young's wife, Katie, had passed from the cancer not long before, but lying with him was far from her mind. Then she stepped up to the counter to ask the price of a bolt of fabric, and he was calculating in a ledger, and she happened to look down at his hands. They were white and soft and clean, little different than they are now except with a few less cords and wrinkles. She thought how she had never seen a man with such hands. Her daddy and her stepbrothers and her husband and every man she knew had hard, scabbed and callused hands with thick fingers and a lifetime of grit and grime beneath the nails. They were hands that were meant to smear and stain and hurt someone. She stood there at the front counter, her question drying up on her lips, and stared at Finis's fingers, noticed how pale his skin looked against the gold of his wedding band. She had left the baby with her momma, but she latched onto a lie that would excuse a too-long trip to the store. She would say that old Mrs. Taylor, who her mother dreaded like a bout of the trots, had tied up the shopkeeper with a dispute over her bill, and her mother would roll her eyes and snort, "As if that old bat will ever pay it anyway."

Trembling a little, she came around behind the counter and lifted his hand from his ledger and placed it on her breast. He sputtered for a while, but after a time, he led her to the backroom and laid her on the cot. With a few pauses thrown in for the birthing of her sons,

Jackie and Jimmy Ray, and during the time when the miners were on strike and Lester hung around the house to plague her, it had been steady ever since.

Now Finis bends to kiss her forehead. "I'm not sure when I can get back," he says. "I'll try, but I don't know."

"That's fine."

"Well," he says, awkward as a thirteen-year-old boy.

She smiles, thinks to ask a question that Lester himself would ask should he find himself in this position - and the idea of that nearly sets her off into a thirteen-year-old girl's giggles. "So is it true?" she asks once she has swallowed her laughter. "Is Holt going to walk out of them talks? They going to force another strike?"

He shakes his head. "I don't know," he says. "They don't tell me nothing about things like that. They just tell me to hire the boss man's halfwit nephew or to stop ordering so much cornmeal or to collect my delinquent accounts before they find somebody who will." He sighs and pats what's left of his sandy-gray hair. "I wouldn't doubt it though. Times are tough, Ada. I ain't got to tell you that."

"The Holts got plenty of money."

"That's right," he says. "And they want to

hold onto every penny of it if they can."

It's about what she's figured, what the wives know and the miners refuse to admit. She's heard people talking about the President's New Deal for the last two years, but it looks pretty much just like the old one as far as she can tell. Whatever you want to call it, new or old, the thing that never changes is that the coal companies are always dealt a winning hand.

"Send Jimmy Ray in," she says. "Tell him to warm himself in the kitchen and stay there until I come out."

He nods and promises he'll do his best to remember that butterscotch candy and then leaves her. She stubs her cigarette, reminds herself to pitch the butt into the weeds at the edge of their backyard. Lester smokes home-rolled Durham. He isn't the sharpest man she's ever met, but he ain't altogether stupid either.

Yawning, she stares out at the rain beating down in their dirt yard. By the calendar it's only a few days until spring, but the rains and the gray skies and the razor wind still carry the bite of winter. She hears the front door shut, and Jimmy Ray's footsteps heading for the kitchen. She knows she should get up. Knows that she's doing wrong - by Jimmy Ray and the rest of her children, by Lester and by herself -

but the bed is soft, and she likes being naked, likes being splayed wide. That very phrase makes her shiver.

She runs her hand down her throat and over her breasts and then down between her legs. Her fingers move, and she tries to remember Finis, the way his hands feel, the way it is when he puts his thing, whiter and smaller than any man she's known, inside her, the way the whiteness of his skin makes her feel clean. But it never works when she's without him. When he's here, she can hold onto those thoughts, but gone, he takes them with him.

She widens her legs and uses two and then three and then four fingers until it hurts so bad that she whimpers. When she closes her eyes, she does not think of Finis or Lester, but of her older stepbrother, Rex, who would take her into the bottoms at the edge of the river. He was twenty, already work-hard and filthy from the mines, she not quite fourteen, and when he would leave her with her dress bunched up beneath her, she would look at the mud and coal dust smeared on her pale thighs.

This time she does not strangle her cry, doesn't even try to hold back. She screams and screams and is still shivering, riding the wave of it, when the bedroom door opens. Luckily, she still has enough presence of mind to roll onto her side and spare him from the worst of what he's witnessing.

"Mr. Young gave me a quarter," he says. "He said you'd know what we ought to do with it."

In one quick movement, she rolls onto her back and snatches the sheet over her nakedness. She props herself on her elbow, forces a smile.

"Well wasn't that nice of him," she says. "We'll talk about it after I get dressed."

He nods but does not leave. He stands there pinning her with his clear, blue eyes. She holds onto her smile as long as she can and then glances down and notes that the sheet has slipped so that her breast is bared. He is staring at it - the heaviness, the faint, blue veins beneath the skin, the dark rise of her nipple - but he doesn't seem to be truly looking at her, not in any way that she understands, not with her husband's mixture of contempt and lust nor Finis Young's embarrassed desire. Not even with the innocent mingling of shame and curiosity she's seen on her older boys' faces when they've happened to glimpse her stepping from the bath. It is as if Jimmy Ray is simply registering what he is seeing and storing it away for later consideration.

"Go on now," she says.

He nods quickly and then turns his back. She takes a deep breath and wonders why there is something wrong with her, wonders why she can't shake the image of him standing at the bedroom window, watching through the mist of rain like a ghost that hasn't quite figured out that he is dead.

* * *

An hour later at Pop Gaddis's Cafe, Jimmy Ray finishes his hamburger, grins at her. She pushes aside her coffee and grins right back.

"Feeling full?"

"Yes, ma'am," he says. "Thank you."

"Thank Mr. Young. He's the one who gave you the quarter."

He nods and looks down the neck of his bottle of Coca-Cola. "But you didn't have to bring me here."

"No," she says.

"You didn't have to."

"I know."

"I wouldn't tell Daddy."

His eyes are blue, and he sees everything. She's known that all along he's been watching and judging her in his own, quiet way. Letting her son stay home on days when Finis is set to visit is like playing Russian roulette. Perhaps, she wonders, she wants him to tell, wants to blow up her world and her marriage, but no, she knows that isn't true because, faced with that possibility, she's trembling, terrified. It has to be something else. It has to be that she wants a witness, wants Jimmy Ray to see that his momma can be touched by something other than filth and grime and callousness.

Now she swallows hard, forces herself to be calm. "Tell Daddy? About what?"

He shrugs, swirls the soda around at the bottom of the bottle. "Anything."

She nods solemnly and then winks at him. She's itchy and so warm that her skin seems to be burning, and she doesn't know why exactly, just that neither Finis nor her own hand has put an end to it. Sighing, she lights a cigarette, a home-rolled Durham this time instead of a Chesterfield - and shifts on the booth's seat. Old Pop Gaddis has a radio on a shelf behind the counter, and she tries to focus on the commercials for perfumed soap and patent leather shoes and motorized washing machines and a half dozen other things that she's never seen outside a catalog and will never be able to afford. But today the voices seem far away and cruel, as if they're mocking the hayseeds and miners for their dirty, underfed children and their wash worn clothes.

Pop Gaddis catches her eye and nods. He's a short, fat man with stubby hands and burn scars up and down his forearms. When he smiles, he shows a few teeth and a lot of gum. The retarded fellow who lives in a tarpaper shack just off the trail she and Jimmy Ray walked to get here is sitting at the far end of the counter, slurping coffee and mumbling to himself. He is large and thick-shouldered with corn yellow hair and a sweet, almost angelic smile, harmless as a baby. Lester and half the miners in the Paradise Camp are always yapping about how something needs to be done about him, how he ought to be locked in a facility or kept in a cage or something. "Feeble minded are dangerous," Lester says. "They're unpredictable and can go off at any moment like a loaded gun."

She always wants to say to Lester, "Well if ignorance is a crime, why are you still walking free," but doesn't quite dare.

Now, looking at the man's broad back, her mind begins to wander, and she finds herself wondering if it's true what they say about the feeble minded having a big sex lust to go along with their big peckers. When she catches herself moving her legs beneath the booth, she takes a deep breath, glances at Jimmy Ray, sees that he's watching her, his gaze intent, as if he knows exactly what she's been thinking.

"Let's go," she says. "Drink up and let's get out of here."

She's prepared for his whining and complaining. He loves being here in the diner with the smell of coffee and freshly fried hamburgers and the radio playing in the background. But today he just nods and swigs what's left in the Coca Cola bottle.

"Sure," he says, smiling at her. "It's time."

* * *

Their path home is narrow and curving and follows close beside the rain-swollen and still rising river. Its roar rages in her head, and glancing at it makes her queasy with something that almost feels like desire. Dark brown water swirls and eddies, bites at the banks, carries away trees and scraps of lumber and some poor man's work boots.

Jimmy Ray leads the way, picking his steps carefully and truly. He does not stop, does not glance to his right to see how close he is to falling in. It's just one foot in front of the other until he gets where he's going.

She mimics him. One foot in front of the other, but the ground sinks beneath her and mud seeps over her shoes. They pass the tarpaper shack where the retarded man and his older-than-Abraham daddy live, and she sees the old man leaning against the front wall of the shack, a home-rolled cigarette dangling from his mouth. He does not wave or acknowledge that he's seen her, just stares dead-eyed at the roaring water. Further on, the path twists and turns. In the distance she can see smoke rising from the crumbling chimneys, the shabby homes of a handful of Negroes who were imported as scabs and who had the poor judgment to stay. Now they live huddled together in a ring of rotting cabins like old-timey settlers surrounded by hostile Indians.

The path narrows even more and begins to drop sharply. Her foot catches in the mud and her ankle gives. She falls hard, squealing in pain.

"Momma!" Jimmy Ray shouts.

He runs to her, arms open, his eyes wide and terrified. She tells him that she's all right and grabs his arm to pull herself up. When she makes it to her feet, he hugs her, his face pressed against her upper stomach, his fingers digging into her back. She pries them away, holds his hands in hers, smiles to reassure him. Then she happens to glance down and notices for the first time how small and white his hands are, how soft the skin is, how clean the nails.

She hugs him again, pulling him tightly against her. The feeling comes without expectation, without warning, and her legs nearly buckle. Warmth floods upwards from between her thighs. Her breath quickens, and her face burns as if she's suffering from a high fever. Suddenly every inch of her is alive, hungry, and the extent of her appetite, the nearly overpowering urge for an unrestrained and inexcusable gluttony both appalls and tempts her.

She forces herself to let him go. When she looks at the boy, she is certain that he sees into some dark and horrible place in the center of her, a place that she has never known existed but one that he's been aware of for some time. Trembling, she reaches down and grabs a clump of mud and smears it across his pale cheek before she can he stop herself.

"Momma," he says.

It is more of a judgment than a naming. She shoves him, and he stumbles a little. Then she shoves again, harder, and he falls backwards into the river.

He comes up twice, and she knows that it isn't too late, knows that she could reach him. But she's unsure exactly which of them she would be saving. Then there's no wondering at all because the river claims him, and it is as if he were never hers, never truly existed at all.

* * *

She moves through the rooms of their rented company house, broom in hand, sweeping and sweeping. It does no good. No matter how hard or how often she cleans, there are cobwebs she can't reach, coal dust she can't scrub off the walls or out of the curtains.

The sun has set, and she hears the far off sound of baying hounds. They'll be back soon, but that's okay. She has told her story, and she will tell it again and again if need be. Jimmy Ray held onto his birthday money. This morning he begged her to take him to Pop Gaddis's for a cheeseburger. She will say once again, "So I did. God help me, I couldn't think of a reason not to." There will be more questions or there won't. Either way it doesn't matter. In the end they will believe her. What other choice do they have? They are men, and their minds like to snatch onto comfortable explanations, reasons that they can easily understand. Someone will pay for this. She knows that. People, men particularly, like for ledgers to balance.

She is stubbing a home-rolled Durham when Lester comes in, tracking mud on her freshly cleaned floor. She speaks their son's name, and Lester's head droops like an ear of corn on a broken stalk.

"I'm tired," he says.

She studies him for a moment. He's saggy-shouldered, branch-whipped, covered with mud and leaves and scratches.

"He just walked off to take a leak?" Lester says. "And he never came back?"

"That's right," she says.

He shrugs and says something about old wells and mineshafts in those thickets, but then slaps his cap against his thigh. "I don't believe it though. Somebody got him." He considers this a moment, adds, "That retard lives awfully close to there."

"I know."

He sighs and says, "I reckon I should go to your mother's, fetch the other kids home."

"Not yet," she says. "Close the door."

"I'm tired." He steps deeper into the living room. "I'm so tired I can't stand it."

But it doesn't matter. She's already on the floor with her dress pushed up and her legs open wide, and soon he's on top of her, leaving his stains all over her cold, white skin.

Breaking Ground in Paradise

I was out in the barn sneaking a cigarette and trying not to think about the hole that the old man would soon have me digging when the girl came weaving her way past the puddles in our washed-out drive. I pegged her to be seventeen or eighteen. She was dragging a suitcase behind her and not having an easy time of it. Watching her made me think of a little girl trying to wrestle a reluctant dog towards bath water. Every few steps, she stopped to look around with a scowl on her face and her hands on her hips. They looked like pretty good hips from where I was standing. Maybe they were a little on the skinny side but good nonetheless. She shook free a cigarette and bent her head to light it. With her rolled dungarees and her powder-blue blouse tied beneath her breasts, she looked just like one of those wild girls who was always hanging on the arm of Marlon Brando or Vic Morrow in the movies, the kind of girl you dreamed about but hardly ever saw in real life, at least not here in Paradise, Kentucky, where a girl in dungarees would have been as horrifying as President Eisenhower making a speech in a cocktail dress or Nixon coming on live television to announce he was a Red.

She dragged her suitcase to our backdoor, knocked. It took a couple of minutes, but Carol Ann answered. She was the latest stray my old man had brought home from one honky-tonk or another. It was clear that she knew the girl but didn't seem particularly happy to see her. That wasn't much of a surprise. Carol Ann hadn't seemed particularly happy about anything in the four and a half weeks she'd been shacked up with my old man. As far as I could tell, bored and edgy, drunk and boisterous, hung over and sullen pretty much covered the extent of her emotional range.

"Now won't you look here," my old man said from the shadows deep in the barn.

The old man had a knack for sneaky. Sometimes it was as if you could conjure him from thin air by just thinking too hard.

He stepped up beside me and laid his heavy hand on my shoulder. "It's a fine old world, ain't it?" he asked, his blue eyes flickering to the cigarette in my hand.

I swallowed hard and said a silent prayer that whatever this girl's business, it would distract him from the pack of Lucky Strikes I'd filched from his dresser. I watched while Carol Ann shook her head no, listened a minute and then opened her palms in an I-guess-I-don't-have-a-choice gesture. She stepped aside so the younger girl could drag her suitcase through the door.

"Yes sir, a fine world when pretty women just drop out of the sky. Ain't that right, Jackie?"

I said I couldn't argue with that, and he winked and said he was going to take a walk down to the river. He had some thinking to do. I didn't ask him what about because I already knew the answer, just like I knew that despite what he said, he'd already made up his mind. I'd seen the flicker in his eye when Carol Ann burned yesterday's biscuits. Of course the burned biscuits weren't the real reason he intended to kill her and have me bury her on the back of the farm. Like I said, Carol Ann didn't have the sweetest disposition, and he'd already grown weary with her, and she'd seen too much of his business for him to just boot her out the door. When it came to killing, my old man could always find a reason.

He stopped and turned back to me. "Hey Jackie," he said as if something had just occurred to him. "You know what they do to thieves over there in them foreign countries? They chop off their right hands, so they won't forget what they done wrong and won't be tempted to do it again. I read about it in the *National Geographic*."

He was smiling, but that didn't mean a thing. My old man was always smiling.

"They got some peculiar ways in them foreign places, don't they?"

I said yes sir they did and then added, "I got a quarter in my pocket."

"Put it on the dresser where you found those cigarettes," he said. "Then thank the Good Lord you was born and raised right here in America instead of one of them heathen foreign lands."

* * *

They were about half drunk and dancing to Patsy Cline songs that they played over and over on our Hi-Fi. Carol Ann still wore the silky, cream-colored slip she'd had on at breakfast, and her hair was mussed and her lip stick smeared, but my old man kept pinching her ass and telling her she was as pretty as

Marilyn Monroe. She'd cackle and tell him to hush his nonsense and bat her eyelashes in hopes he'd say it again.

My old man was ignoring the bourbon and sticking to dripping cold bottles of Miller High Life. He was in a fine mood.

"Who would have thought it?" he said more than a couple of times. "Pair of rough old west Kentucky hicks like us passing a summer evening with two genuine beauties like these girls? I tell you, Jackie. We must be living right."

Carol Ann cackled some more. Her daughter, Ellie, rolled her eyes. I liked that she wasn't buying my old man's bullshit. There was a lot I liked about her - the tanned skin of her bared belly and the rise of her breasts and the natural, redness of her lips. She wasn't a beauty. Even at fifteen, I knew that. Her chin was a little too pointed, her teeth gapped and small, her eyes squinty and too close together. But the way she sipped her beer and smoked one Chesterfield after another made her seem glamorous and mature.

"You don't have anything but Patsy Cline?" she asked when my old man started "Walking after Midnight," for the fourth time.

"Ain't nothing wrong with Patsy Cline," he said.

"Don't pay her no attention," Carol Ann slurred, glowering at her daughter.

My old man flared a match with his thumbnail and lit a Lucky from the pack that he'd taken back from me even though I'd left my quarter on his dresser. "I bet you like that Negro music don't you? Chuck Berry or Little Richard or Elvis?"

"Elvis is white," I said.

His eyes flickered in my direction. "Not beneath his skin"

"I like all kinds of music," Ellie said. "I even like Patsy Cline only not when I hear the same song every ten minutes."

I opened myself another beer even though I was feeling queasy at the thought of what was coming. The old man had already said something about how we were going to party all night and then take a blanket, some beer and some sandwiches outside to watch the sunrise. Carol Ann had said it sounded romantic to her, and her eyes had pleaded with her daughter until Ellie said sure, it might be fun. I figured that's when he'd shoot them, while it was still pitch black but close enough to dawn so I'd have first light to help me see where I was digging.

I wasn't sure why the old man was the way he was. Maybe there was something missing in him or maybe he was sick or maybe he was just mean to the bone. I didn't know. I just knew that I'd worshipped him when I was a little kid and he'd swing me up on his shoulders and parade me around or slip me a lemon drop when my momma wasn't looking. Things changed after she got run over by a drunken railroad man. As I got older and realized some of the things my old man had done, I learned to fear him. Now it seemed that all that love and fear were so mixed up that I couldn't tell where one left off and the other began.

My old man made his living by running bootleg liquor into dry counties all over west Kentucky, by cheating in card and dice games and, on occasion, by pimping out the women he brought home, but what he really was, was a killer. I'd helped him bury a half dozen women, a couple of irate drunks who'd figured out they'd been cheated in five card stud, a Negro who'd come to the door with a razor when he'd heard my old man had bedded his daughter, and a rookie deputy who didn't believe he had to abide by the arrangement my old man made with Sheriff Keeling.

"I'd give you a penny for your thoughts but I'd feel like I was over charged," the old man said, winking over Carol Ann's shoulder.

"I need some fresh air."

"Sure you do," he said. "But you take it easy on them beers, Jackie. The night's young." His stare felt as cutting and jagged as broken glass. "I don't want you all pooped out before the fun really gets started."

* * *

I'd been down to the barn for ten or fifteen minutes, just sitting there smoking and watching the bugs swarm the gas lanterns, when she came out to find me. She had two beers, one in each hand.

"I figured it was the bullshit not the beer that was making you sick at your stomach." She passed me one and grinned. "I brought an opener. It's in my back pocket if you can manage to get it out."

She turned her hip towards me. My mouth went real dry and my hands shook, but I reached in there and promised myself I'd never forget the feel of her denim-covered cheek against my hand.

"Thanks," she said when I handed her the opener.

She sat down on a hay bale and took a drink and reached into her blouse pocket for her pack of cigarettes. I wanted to act natural and cool and charming, but I couldn't stop thinking about reaching into her pocket. Then I felt myself getting hard, so I tried to sit in such a way that she wouldn't notice.

"The turtle raises its sleepy head," she said and giggled, the first hint I'd had that she was tipsy.

My face burned hot. I stared down at the mud tracks and hay on the barn's floor. For that one moment, I couldn't wait to dig the hole.

"I'm sorry," she said, wiping her lips with the back of her hand. "I didn't mean to embarrass you." She gave me a slight, teasing smile. "I think it's sweet that you like me."

"I'm not a little kid." Only God knew why I said that.

"I didn't say you were."

"Good," I said. "Because I'm not."

But I felt like one. At supper I'd picked up a little about her past. She'd lived with Carol Ann until she was eleven, but when her momma had taken up with some man, Ellie had been sent to live with her maternal grandmother, a tight-fisted Pentecostal who'd somehow gotten confused about the difference between home and prison. After three years, Ellie had had enough and took off with a traveling salesman she'd met outside the IGA. He'd ditched her in Lima, Ohio, but she hadn't come home. She'd lived all over - Louisville and Cincinnati and Columbus and even Detroit, Michigan. Then on her eighteenth birthday, she'd made the trip back home. After ten days of banging on doors and hassling her momma's old friends and acquaintances she'd finally tracked her down to our farm three and half miles outside of Paradise, which meant three and a half miles on the far side of nowhere.

"Why'd you come back?" I asked, wanting to change the subject. "If I ever got away from here ... "

"You'd be surprised," she said. "When the money runs out, home don't seem like such a bad place to be."

"Did you miss your momma?"

"You're kidding, right?"

I shrugged. "You came looking for her."

"I didn't have any other place to go." She gave me an earnest look. "You think your daddy will let me stay here with you all?"

"Sure," I said.

"But probably not for long."

"Longer than you think," I said.

She smiled at that, and I felt guilty saying it. "He seems like a nice guy."

"He isn't."

She laughed and flipped back her hair. "I didn't think so. It just seemed like something I ought to say."

Crickets chirped from the weeds at the edge of the barn. They sounded like off-key fiddles as they blended with Patsy Cline's muted voice drifting from the house.

"What's it like living in a city?" I asked.

"I loved it. Detroit especially. Soon as I can get some money together, I'm going back. There are all kinds of things to do and places to see and foods to eat. There's buildings so tall it hurts your neck to look up at them, and bright lights and music that goes on right through to the morning." She took a long drag from her cigarette and exhaled in my direction. "I ain't going to stick around these pissant towns any longer than I have to."

I tried to imagine it, a big city with broad sidewalks and buses and taxis that could take you anywhere, a place where men wore suits to work and women had real diamonds sparkling in their ears. Most of all I thought about the lights, about how they'd burn all night and drive back the dark. City folks never know pitch black, not the kind you have in the country. I thought how in a place like that you'd never have to sleep if you didn't want to and how you'd always be able to see what was waiting to grab you.

"It sounds great," I said

There didn't seem to be much else to say, so we drank our beers and smoked our cigarettes. I listened to the crickets and tried not to think about what would come later. My eyes were restless, so I watched Ellie and studied the way her hair curled around her neck and the way her chest rose and fell with her breathing. I wished she hadn't come here, wished that she would have just stayed in the splash of all those lights far away from me and my old man. Then I thought about what my daddy would have said about such a hopeful way of thinking. Wish in one hand and shit in the other and see which one gets full faster.

"Sounds like Patsy's turned in for the evening," she said after a moment.

It took a second for me to understand what she meant. The crickets were singing solo now. The music that had been drifting from the house stopped, and all that silence scared me. My first thought was - he's done it, and any minute now he'll be down here to finish the job. Then Ellie suggested another possibility.

"I wonder if they made it to the bedroom, or if they're screwing on the living room floor," she said.

And the air came back to my lungs.

"Probably they are," I said, giggling with relief.

She rolled her eyes. "My momma's such a whore. She wonders why I ain't Miss Prim and Proper."

I let that alone and slowly my heart returned to its normal beating. That good feeling didn't last long though. Probably it hadn't happened yet. My old man didn't like to kill in the house because it left him with too much cleaning to do. But it would happen. I knew that as surely as I knew that once the dark really settles on the world, it's a long time until morning.

"So," Ellie said. "How old are you, Jackie? For real."

"Fifteen," I said. "Sixteen in a couple of weeks."

"Well hell," she said. "That's not *that* young." She tipped her beer bottle in my direction. "You ever been with a girl?"

"Sure," I said.

"For honest?"

I wasn't a hundred percent sure if it was technically true. On the last day of school, Peter Franklin and Merle Henry and I had bucked up our nerve enough to visit Roseanna Epley's house trailer out in Cleaton. Roseanna was about fifty and only charged two dollars a pop. She didn't let me put it in her though. She had me push it in between her thighs until I was finished. I still couldn't help but feel that I'd been cheated. Although to be fair, I hadn't done a lot of complaining at the time.

Now I figured it was close enough for horseshoes so I said, "Hell yeah, I have."

"Good. I wouldn't want to be robbing the cradle or nothing like that," Ellie said.

Then she stood up and untied her blouse and began to work on the buttons. When she let it fall away from her shoulders and wobbled over to me and took my hand, I couldn't stop thinking about the way the shovel sounded when it first struck in unbroken ground.

* * *

In the end, it was the thought of all those bright lights that did it. Even while Ellie and I were lying there in the hay, both of us sweaty and tired, I couldn't stop thinking about them, about how they'd blink through the night and keep away the dark. By the time I heard the backdoor slam and my old man and Carol Ann calling our names, I was grieving over those lights, as if they were part of a world where I'd once belonged but had been yanked out of - even though I'd never been to a town bigger than Owensboro in my whole life.

"I ain't going to ask what you two have

been doing," my old man said, winking at me.

He had a knapsack filled with beer bottles and sliced ham and a half dozen of Carol Ann's burned biscuits slung over one shoulder and a flashlight in his other hand. He had his big old .45 automatic tucked into the front of his belt, too, but he'd pulled out his shirttail to cover it.

Carol Ann was carrying a folded up blanket and saying something about what a beautiful night it was and how it had been ages since she'd watched the sun rise and wasn't this just the most romantic thing anyone had ever heard of. As drunk and groggy as Ellie was, she seemed willing to play along. Me? I just kept thinking about how the shovel would blister my hands and how all those winking bright lights of the city were fading further and further away.

"Run up to the house and get the twelve gauge," my old man said to me. "We might come across some varmints, and I'd hate for them to get away." Even in the dim light of the gas lantern I could see his blue eyes sparkling. "It's in the hall closet!" he called after me.

I knew where it was. Ever since I was nine, he'd had me carry that shotgun in case someone made a run for it or things went wrong somehow. So far I hadn't had to use it.

When I came back with the Browning short

barrel, all three of them had fresh beers. Even Ellie was laughing at some joke my old man was telling about the Pope, a nun and Senator Kennedy.

He led us along a path that wound in and out of a cypress thicket and sloped down to the river. He talked a lot about the view of the sunrise over the water, but I knew he was just doing me a favor. The ground was softer down here in the bottoms.

At one point Ellie took my hand and squeezed it. In the dim beam of the old man's flashlight, I could see that she was looking up at me, expectant and needy. It struck me then how odd it was that the thing we'd done had changed her. Earlier, she'd seemed so much older and smarter and worldlier than me, but now she was looking at me as if I needed to protect her, as if I was the one in charge. No one had ever looked at me like that before.

When we came out of a copse to level ground, the old man set down the knapsack and told Carol Ann to spread the blanket. Then he pulled her close to him. She'd changed into slacks and a loose sweater, and he worked his hand up under there and kissed her. Ellie looked away, but I couldn't. It made me a little sick to my stomach to see the way he pawed at her, knowing he was going to kill her at any moment. I promised myself that I would never be like him. I wouldn't be a pimp and a user. I'd never tell a woman that I loved her and then have her spread her legs for every hayseed willing to hand over five dollars. I'd never have that twinkle in my eye. I'd never kill for the sake of killing.

"Here you go!" my old man said to the women. "You all step right up there and look down where the bank drops off."

"What?" Ellie said, holding onto my hand.

The old man broke our grip. "Those beech trees block the view. Jackie's already seen it. You and your momma just step right up there. You won't regret it."

She gave me a questioning look and I nodded. Then she and Carol Ann moved forward, both on wobbling legs.

"Don't let no varmints get away," my old man whispered in my ear.

He took a deep breath and held it, wanting the moment to last, I guess. Then he flipped his shirttail and pulled the .45 automatic from his waistband. He thumbed off the safety and leveled the gun at the back of Carol Ann's head. I heard crickets. I thought about what was going to happen. Two shots. That's all it would take. Then he'd turn to me and tell me to get the shovel and be quick about it. I'd finish before noon and he'd hand me a cold beer when I walked through our front door. A few days from now, he'd bathe and shave and put on his most expensive aftershave and go out to the Yellow Rose or some other bar. It would all just be one more thing I'd seen and done, one more thing to bind me to him.

I thought about killing him then. I had my finger on the trigger. But a thought flickered through my head. If I saved them, I'd be responsible for them. With Ellie that didn't seem like such a bad thing, but Carol Ann was old and a drunk and she might not understand why I'd had to do it.

"Look for it," my old man said to them. "Just wait for it to come."

He pulled the trigger. Carol Ann jerked and then crumpled, and Ellie started screaming and my old man let out his breath with a shudder and turned the gun on her. It was the bright lights that did it. I could see them winking out one by one, and I didn't want to let them go. I pointed the twelve gauge right at the old man's kidneys and fired both barrels.

He stumbled forward, tried to turn around but couldn't quite make it. He went face first into the dirt. I didn't look down at him. I just dropped the shotgun to the ground and held onto Ellie until she stopped screaming.

"He was crazy," I said. "He was going to kill you. Do you understand?"

She nodded against my chest. "What are we going to do?"

"We're going to bury them," I said. "Then we're going to take the nine hundred or so dollars my old man's got hidden in the root cellar and we're going to catch the first bus out of here, wherever you want to go just as long as they got bright lights and music."

"I'm scared," she said.

"I know," I said. "But we got to do ... "

She glanced down at her mother. "He killed her."

"Yeah," I said. "He was going to kill you, too."

She nodded and then kissed my cheek. "Just tell me what to do."

And of course I told her to go back to the barn and get the shovel. I handed her my old man's flashlight to help her on her way.

It seemed to take her forever. While I waited there in the dark, I swatted mosquitoes and bent down on one knee and took the pack of Lucky Strikes from my old man's shirt pocket and my quarter from his pants. I smoked three cigarettes and listened to the crickets. Then Ellie was there, dragging the shovel along behind her.

I took the shovel and kissed her forehead and when I turned around, the sun was rising. It streaked the sky purple and red and gold. I stood there a second and watched it. It seemed as if I was being born again, and I made that new dawn a lot of promises. I swore that I'd never be like my father. I glanced back at Ellie and vowed that I wouldn't use her or hurt her. I promised myself that I'd never kill anyone ever again.

But there was a lot I didn't know then. I didn't know how those bright lights could melt and shift until they weren't an illumination but just a part of the dark. I didn't know how quickly nine hundred dollars could go away or how hard your stomach could ache when it was empty or how easy it was to convince a woman to use her mouth or open her thighs to pay for a good night's sleep or a warm dinner. I had no idea how a woman's needy, I-love-you look could dig barbs under a man's skin. I didn't know how a finger can itch to pull a trigger.

All I knew was that for the moment I had Ellie beside me and a new day was beginning. For that one moment, I believed my promises mattered. And I was foolish enough to believe that as I broke the ground, I was digging my last hole.

Happily

Clayton finds the Beauty Queen in the backseat of a new '87 Monte Carlo on a cold, cold January night, and his life boards a Greyhound for a destination unknown. It's a Monday night, just a week from his twenty-first birthday, and he's been rambling through the old Sugar Creek strip mine, mindlessly driving deserted haul roads since well before dark. Then he tops a small rise that opens to a coal pit and finds the Monte Carlo parked at the edge of dark water. He high beams the car, races his old International pickup's engine and waits for the car's taillights to flare. Nothing. He reaches under the seat for the Smith and Wesson .357 that his granddaddy willed to him and then lays on the horn. He waits. Five minutes later, still nothing, so he sets the emergency brake and steps out on frozen ground.

"Well, what have we here?" he says, peering through the Monte Carlo's window.

Of course there's no one to answer. Most of the mines in this part of south-central Kentucky have been abandoned for close to a decade, and there's nothing out here now but hundreds of acres of weeds, rusting machinery and overgrown trails that curl back upon each other like sleeping snakes.

Clayton pushes his glasses back up to the bridge of his nose, smiling the slow, loopy smile of his that had made his teachers nervous and his classmates swear he was retarded. He goes to the International, digs out a big, Black and Decker flashlight that he'd stolen from his old man's Peterbuilt and hurries back to the Monte Carlo. He opens the rear door. No dome light so the battery's shot. He spotlights the Beauty Queen and Lover Boy and stares as hard as he can, wanting to scorch the scene into his memory. The Beauty Queen is sprawled in the backseat, a thick, white sweater patterned with Christmas trees balled up and pitched into the front, a lacy, cream-colored bra unsnapped and hanging loose from her shoulders, her stonewashed Levis unzipped to grant access to searching fingers. Lover Boy is slumped forward, his head touching the front seat, his pants and BVDs down at his ankles. There's a fifth of vodka on the seat between them, a half case of Falls City Beer on the floorboard beneath the Beauty Queen's feet. Clayton reaches in for the vodka, unscrews the cap and takes a swallow.

Wiping his mouth on his wrist, he listens to a stray dog's howl from the far side of the pit. Clayton holds his breath, waits for the sound of a motor. Nothing. During the summer the strip mines are party central for high school kids looking to drink beer or score pot or fuck without worrying about prying parents. But now patches of snow still linger on the hillsides and the place is the way he likes it - quiet and empty, a ghost world that belongs only to him.

Satisfied that no one is coming, he sets the vodka bottle on the ground and swings the flashlight's glare into the front seat. A plastic baggie of grass on the dashboard, a half-smoked number in the ashtray, a prescription bottle open on the passenger's seat. He opens the front door, drops the pot and the prescription bottle, Valium, into his parka's big front pocket and then turns his attention to the backseat again. It doesn't take Sherlock Holmes to figure it out. The Beauty Queen and Lover Boy came out here to fuck and get fucked up. It's been brutally cold for the better part of a week, so they would have been running the heater. They'd passed out or maybe she'd blown him and they were stoned and sleepy and it sneaked up on them. He doesn't know and it doesn't really matter. What does is that carbon monoxide got the best of them. Clayton checks his watch. It's early yet, just a little past eight, so he figures they must have come out here last night or maybe even the night before. He runs the flashlight over Lover Boy's face, doesn't recognize him and doesn't give a damn. It's the Beauty Queen that matters. Traci Greenwood, the daughter of the School Superintendent. She'd been a year behind him at Harps County High, a cheerleader, without a doubt the most popular girl in school. He licks his lips. A year and a half ago, right after her senior year, the town made it official and crowned her Miss Harp at the county fair. Clayton stood in the sweaty, sour-smelling crowd at the Ag Center and watched her ass twitch as she paraded across the makeshift stage in her powder blue swimsuit. Lately, he's been hearing that the Beauty Queen has fallen on hard times. She dropped out of Murray State after her first semester, came back to town to party, got kicked out of her parents' house after they caught her screwing a married man right on their living room sofa. He's heard she moved in with Cindy Seegers, a thirty-year-old pill-head divorcee with a half dozen arrests for dealing and solicitation. Clayton didn't believe the rumors, but now he thinks maybe they're true since times don't get any harder than dead.

He flashes the light on the Beauty Queen's face, thinking absently how peaceful she looks even with the bluish tinge around her lips. This is the way he always imagined Sleeping Beauty looked when she was discovered by Prince Charming. He leans into the car and kisses her dry, cold lips, but there's no resurrection. He wonders what would happen if there were. Would she scream or call him a weirdo or would she be so grateful that she would let him touch her breasts, maybe even put his hand in her pants? Thinking about it gets him hard, and he shivers like a horse waiting for the saddle.

"There's no harm in it," he whispers.

And surely there isn't. No one's here to see, and the Beauty Queen's past caring, so he hunkers beside the car, pulls down the straps on her bra and cups her heavy, chilled breast in his hand. Moaning a little, he leans forward and takes her nipple in his mouth and suckles. His heart hammers in his chest, and he feels feverish and dizzy. He thinks of the way he'll stroke himself when he's home in bed, what he'll have to remember and that makes him even harder. As smitten as he's been with the Beauty Queen, he's never jerked off to her before, the same way he's never jacked off to his posters of Samantha Fox and Christi

Brinkley even though they grin down at him from his bedroom wall. Even in his fantasies, Clayton's humble. Middle-aged waitresses with varicose veins and saggy breasts, the pimpled fat girl at the drive thru window at Druthers and his cross-eyed cousin Lorraine are the best looking women he can imagine being with, a fat, four-eyed weirdo like him. The Beauty Queen? To him she's every bit as majestic and unattainable as celebrities or the girls on the pages of Playboy Magazine. But now she's here within easy reach.

He slips his hand inside her panties and yanks it out when the dog howls again. This is crazy, he tells himself. He needs to leave it alone. No one's likely to come out here tonight, but if they do and they see him, he might get in trouble. The thing to do is get back in his truck, head on home, eat some dinner, forget about it. When someone finds them out here, Sheriff Simmons won't look twice. He'll just shake his head, call for an ambulance to take them to the morgue and have something to talk about at his next Stay Straight and Stay Alive lecture at Harps County High. But if someone sees Clayton fooling around with the body, there's no telling what they might think.

Still, he doesn't want to leave the Beauty Queen behind. How can he give her up? If he lives a thousand lifetimes he'll never have such a beautiful and pliable female in his grasp again.

He stands up, shivering in a gust of wind. His hands are aching, half numb. He glances back at his pickup, an idea taking hazy form and then suddenly becoming clear and possible as he seizes upon the image of the old smokehouse near the back of his parents' fourteen acres. He reaches into the car for one of the frozen cans of beer, heaves it towards the dark water, giggles when he hears the splash. It hasn't been above thirty for nearly a month, and in the last week, it's gotten as cold as seven below. If the water's not frozen this close to the bank, the pit must get real deep real quick. Why not, he thinks. What harm would there be in it? Who would ever know?

* * *

Two and a half hours later, Clayton sits at his parents' kitchen table, crumbling crackers into a bowl of tomato soup and reliving the last couple of hours in his mind. He's had the Beauty Queen twice since he unloaded her in the smokehouse, and he's cold and spent. He slurps his soup and thinks about her, nude and covered with an old blanket, lying on a stack of milk crates, waiting. The idea of rats troubles him. It would be wrong to let them get at her. The Beauty Queen deserves better.

"You didn't come in to say hello," his momma says on her way to the fridge for yet another light beer.

Clayton winces at the sound of her voice and hopes she doesn't see it and wills her to get her beer and head right back to the living room. "I thought interrupting Carson's monologue was forbidden at all costs," he says.

She opens the can, sips, and then, of course, sits down with him at the kitchen table. "Your daddy called tonight," she says. "He's in Fort Myers, Florida. Says its warm enough down there to ride with the truck window open."

"Huh," Clayton says. "He coming home soon?" he says, thinking please God no.

"A couple of days," she says. "He's picking up another load in Panama City and running it over to Shreveport. Then he's heading this way."

It's too soon, but Clayton figures a couple of days without his old man's constant nagging and his greasy farts stinking up the living room is better than no days at all. *Get a job, go to work, get a job.* The old man has been as persistent and repetitive as a trained parrot since Clayton quit high school.

"You should have come in and said hello," his momma says, her beer-addled mind chasing itself in circles. "I get nervous with your daddy gone. I might have shot you as a burglar."

Clayton shrugs and then grins at her over his bowl. "What kind of burglar breaks in and makes a can of soup?"

"A hungry one."

Clayton smiles a genuine smile despite himself. He hates it when she catches him off guard with her goofy humor or with displays of almost-true affection. It makes the rest of the time, when she is distant, judging, disappointed, even worse. He doesn't blame her for feeling that way. She's thirty-nine, an attractive woman just edging toward a plumpness that would fall away if she'd give up her nightly six pack. She has strawberry blonde hair and a playful smile that can be flirtatious when she's dressed in one of her "business suits," and showing a reluctant client around a three-bedroom ranch or a four-bedroom split-level at Cherry Wood Estates. She was never a cheerleader or a Beauty Queen, but he's seen her high school yearbooks. She was a pretty girl who got better looking with time. The same isn't exactly true of his dad. Too much time sitting behind the wheel and too many truck stop meals have thickened him and worn away his muscles, but he still looks all right with a fresh shave and a haircut. How such "normal" looking parents ended up with a close-to-three-hundred-pound, myopic, greasy-haired and acne-scarred kid is probably the great mystery of their lives, the one question they've been asking themselves since he was five years old.

"So what have you been up to tonight?' she asks, her tone light but the question not casual.

The lie comes easily. It should. He's been telling the same one for the last four years.

"I was down at the pool hall."

"Beasley's?"

He tries to keep the impatience out of his voice. "It's the only one in town, mom."

She runs her thumbnail along the rim of her beer can. "I'm not sure I like you hanging around there. Mabel Clemmons says they sell drugs out of that place."

"She doesn't know everything."

"She knows more than you think."

"A lot of people know more than you think."

Her head ticks to the side and her jaw sets. "What's that supposed to mean?"

For a second he holds her eyes. He wants to say to her, you know exactly what it means.

Things have been tense between her and the old man recently with fights roaring up from nowhere and without warning the way thunderstorms churn up in the summer when the air is too hot and too heavy to do anything else. But those fights - over a joke that his mother deemed inappropriate or the money needed to pay an unexpected bill - never give rest to anything, just the way those quick summer storms never seem to break the heat and humidity. Lately, his mother has become restless, complaining about the time she spends alone, suddenly dissatisfied with the old farmhouse they'd bought when Clayton was four. Now she wants a place closer to town without the overgrown fields, the crumbling barn used to store junk his daddy hasn't gotten around to hauling away, the ivy-covered old smokehouse with its low roof just visible over the weeds and pawpaw bushes. Clayton suspects that the real tension around here has come from how often his mother mentions Ray Massey, her boss at Massey Real Estate. A couple of weeks ago, Clayton spotted the two of them, his momma and Ray Massey, leaving the Royal Palm Restaurant. When he mentioned it she said it was a "working" lunch. He didn't comment, but he was pretty sure you didn't come out of a working lunch and linger by the side of the building for a quick kiss. Now, he holds her eyes, wanting to let her know that below her makeup and quick smile, she isn't so pretty after all. But then, as usual, he loses his nerve.

"It doesn't mean nothing, mom," he says. "I was just saying ... "

Then he falls silent, thinking about the Beauty Queen, how she's out there right now, waiting, thinking how she's his and no one can take her away from him. She'll never cheat, never slip off for a quick kiss with another man. Most of all she won't look at him the way his mom's looking at him right now - her expression distrustful and full of angry questions: *Why are you always smirking? How did you get so ugly? Why don't you do something - lose weight, cut back on the chocolate and sodas to clear your skin, wash your greasy hair? Are you ever going to get a real job, a girlfriend, a life? Will you always be the cross I have to bear?* And the thought of the Beauty Queen makes it all better, nearly tolerable for the first time in as long as he can remember. He has something, someone, and the rest of it is just petty shit that doesn't matter. Suddenly, he's on the verge of laughing out loud.

"What's got you grinning like the Cheshire

cat?" his momma asks.

He shrugs, takes his bowl to the kitchen sink and runs water in it. When he turns from the sink, she's still watching him.

"I met someone tonight," he says.

"A girl?"

His resentment flares at the surprise in her voice. "Yeah," he says. "Believe it or not, she seems to *like* me. Or at least she hasn't told me any different."

"Well," his momma says. "Good, good for you."

"It's early yet, but who knows? Maybe I'll end up with happy ever after, after all."

Then he does something that he hasn't done since he was nine years old. He bends and kisses her forehead on his way to bed.

* * *

Three days later Clayton has come to understand: this is Romeo and Juliet, John and Yoko, Luke and Laura, baby. This is love with a capital L. For the first time in his life he knows why they play all those syrupy songs on the radio. Before the Beauty Queen, he'd been an Iron Maiden, Megadeath, Guns 'n Roses kind of guy. Now, he can't get enough of pop ballads on FM radio. It makes him feel foolish, but in a nice kind of way, and even his dad's presence can't spoil his good mood.

He goes to her at sundown, kisses her cool, dry lips and is warmed by her presence. The Beauty Queen is more beautiful than ever. He likes the whiteness of her skin, the exotic blue tinge to her lips, the grace and peacefulness in her eyes.

The morning after he found her, he dug through the barn for an old chest freezer his dad had moved out there three years before. He'd washed it and let it air out for a while and then about busted his spine loading it into his International and lugging it into the smokehouse. But the Beauty Queen is worth the effort. Now she sleeps her days away safe from rats and field mice and raccoons, waiting for his return.

They lie on a lumpy, mildewed mattress that he rescued from the town dump - not exactly the bed of roses the Beauty Queen deserves, but it will do for now, he supposes. He tells her about his trip into town with his father, skimming over the way the old man harangued him about applying for a real job before finally asking, "What the fuck, Clayton? You think you can cut yards and rake leaves and pick up odd jobs for the rest of your life? You think your momma and I are always going to support you?" There's no point in getting too deep into that. The important news is that no one really thinks she's missing. Everyone in town seems to believe that the Beauty Queen and her Lover Boy, who owed some not nice fellows a lot of drug money, took off for warmer weather - Florida or maybe even California.

"It's just the way I told you it would be," he says even though he hasn't told her that at all, just hoped it would be true.

And in his head the Beauty Queen says how she never doubted it. He was always smarter than people gave him credit for. Then she confesses that unlike the rest of their schoolmates, she never really believed he was weird. In fact, she says, she always secretly thought he was kind of cute. She was just afraid to say it to her friends. He tells her not to worry about that, not to worry at all. He forgives her completely. He kisses her again and then opens her thighs and rolls on top of her.

Afterward, he lies with her beneath the blanket, speaking of the things that trouble him in his life. He tells her that he never meant to be weird, didn't know he was until the first day of kindergarten when Jeremy Mayes spotted him digging at a chigger bite on the back of his thigh and shouted, "Look at that! The weird kid's an ass picker!" For a long time he hated

Jeremy Mayes, he tells her, but he gave that up when he finally realized that if it hadn't been Jeremy who branded him a freak, it would have been someone else. Everyone could tell by just looking at him. He forgave Jeremy Mayes. But he couldn't forgive his parents.

"They knew," he says. "Once I saw the way people at school looked at me I could see it on their faces, too. My whole life they knew I was a weirdo, but they didn't tell me. I wasn't prepared. They just sent me off to school like it was a big fucking joke."

He cries then, can't help himself, but the Beauty Queen doesn't mind, doesn't think of him as less of a man. He can feel sympathy and love rising from her cold skin.

"It doesn't matter," he says. "I've got you now. And we're going to have each other forever."

But he hears the Beauty Queen in the back of his mind, and her words make him shudder. It's been warmer today, she tells him. Spring will be coming soon. And then I'll rot, the Beauty Queen says. There's no electricity in here, no way to keep me fresh. I'll rot and be gone and you'll be alone again. It breaks my heart to leave you, she says. But it's bound to happen.

He promises her that he won't let it. He'll

do something. Stop the rotation of the earth, banish both spring and summer, whatever it takes for them to be together. But he knows even as he's saying it that those are foolish, hollow words, boastful nonsense from a terrified and inexperienced lover. This isn't the way happily ever after is supposed to end. But it will. And he realizes that there's nothing he can do about it.

"Yes," she says. "There is."

And Clayton is sure that the Beauty Queen has spoken aloud. And yes he knows that it's impossible, but he can still hear her voice, feel its vibration in his ears and the boards of the building.

"Tell me," he says.

She does and of course he's known all along. And of course he resists at first. And of course he gives in because, after all, true love has its sacrifices and in the end its demands are inevitable.

* * *

His parents are sitting down for dinner - his mother's pork chop casserole with Minute Rice and cream of mushroom soup - when Clayton kills them. In the moment before he lifts the .357, so heavy and reassuring in his hand, he leans against the kitchen door, watching them. His mother is pushing her food around with her fork, a glass of ice water by her hand. She never drinks beer when the old man is home. That's okay though. He drinks enough for both of them. There are three empty Pabst cans on his side of the table. His head is close to the plate as he shovels the food in, pausing only long enough to wash a mouthful down with a swallow of beer and then complain that the rice is dry and the pork chops fatty.

Clayton's mind is racing, and he flashes on a memory from when he was five or six. His mother in a loose white dress sitting in a lawn chair and shouting out "warm" or "cold," while he runs through the back yard, an Easter basket banging against his chubby thighs as he searches for the colored eggs his old man hid. His eyes water, not because of what he's about to do, but because there are so few of these good memories and the ones he has are getting harder to recall every day.

"Your supper's on the stove," his mother says, barely glancing at him. "Wash your hands before you sit down."

His old man doesn't bother to look back at him at all. "The least you can do is show up to eat on time. If I had my way I'd have dumped your plate in the garbage."

"Dad," Clayton says.

"What?"

"I love you."

That stops the old man. His shoulders tense, and he drops his fork on his plate, turns in his chair, his eyebrow raised in a question.

"Is something wrong?" he asks.

Clayton squeezes the trigger. The .357 bucks in his hand, its roar setting his ears to ringing. The shot hits the old man just below the breastbone, punches him back against his chair, one arm flailing out wildly, knocking empty beer cans from the table. He grabs at the wound, his mouth working the way a fish's mouth works when it's dropped on the bank, the hook still biting deep into its gullet. Clayton fires again. This shot catches the old man in the throat, comes out the side of his neck in a spray of blood and skin and bone, ricochets off the sink.

Wide-eyed, his momma holds up her hands like a cornered suspect in a television show. She's trembling, Clayton sees, and her skin is nearly the same bleached white as the Beauty Queen's. She doesn't try to run or fight back or even scream. She just sits there with her hands up, her lip quivering. Finally, when he turns the .357's barrel to her, she finds her words.

"Oh Clayton," she says, more sad than

surprised or frightened. "Oh Clayton."

* * *

The afternoon of his twenty-first birthday Clayton stands at the living room window and watches a Sheriff's Department cruiser bounce along the ruts in the drive. His legs tremble when he thinks of how lucky it is that he decided to put his family away before he ran to town to shop for his birthday dinner. In the last couple of days he's taken to leaving them out more and more, his parents on the living room sofa, sitting with their legs touching, their hands interlaced, happy and in love, the Beauty Queen either at the kitchen table to share a romantic meal or, more often, waiting for him in his parents' marriage bed, her smile knowing, her legs parted in an invitation. But this morning the Beauty Queen spoke up. "Better safe than sorry," she said, so he dragged them all into the bedroom, drew the curtains and shut the door.

Now he pulls on his parka, thinks of the .357 magnum lying on the nightstand in his bedroom. He wants to go get it, but the knock on the door comes before he's three steps down the hall, and he stops, panicking, unsure what to do. He wants the gun, but maybe Sheriff

Simmons will get suspicious if he makes him wait.

He has kept the thermometer on fifty since he carried the Beauty Queen into the house, but now sweat breaks out on his forehead and runs down the small of his back. His heart wallops in his chest. There's another knock at the back door, and he gives up on the idea of the gun. On the way through the kitchen he thinks of his father's skinning knife in the catchall drawer beside the sink. He takes the time to get it and slip it into his pocket, knocking be damned.

"I thought I heard you in there," Sheriff Simmons says, grinning a little.

Clayton closes the door behind him. "That was me all right."

Sheriff Simmons is a tall man, six two or three, raw boned and wiry in his youth but potbellied and slump-shouldered now as he creeps towards retirement. He's balding on top, wears a thick black and gray mustache, has kind eyes.

"How you been getting along?" Simmons says. "I'm asking cause I ain't seen you in town very much lately."

"I was there this morning."

"Huh," Simmons says.

"I been busy lately."

Simmons glances over his shoulder, but

there's nothing for him to see on the other side of the small pane of glass in the door. "Say you have? You working?"

"Well, I ... " He thinks of lying but something like that would be easy to check. "No," he admits. "Just watching a lot of television."

"That keeps you busy?"

"I've pretty much made it a full time job," Clayton says.

Simmons smiles at the attempt at humor, but it's not a genuine smile. Clayton can tell that. It doesn't even come close to reaching his eyes, which are sharp now and distrustful and not at all friendly.

"You got any idea why I'm out here?"

"I figure ... "

"It's got something to do with your momma and daddy," Simmons says. "Ray Massey called me this morning, said your momma hasn't been to work all this week and no one out here's answering the phone."

"Huh," Clayton says because he can't think of anything else.

"He's worried."

"I bet he is," Clayton says quickly, picturing Ray Massey's suntanned face and white-toothed grin and wanting to take a chopping axe and split his head wide open.

"What's that supposed to mean?"

"Nothing."

Now it's the Sheriff's turn to say huh and then, "I called out to Peterson Trucking. They say your daddy's had a load waiting for two days. They been calling too. Nobody's been answering." He reaches into his coat pocket for a pack of Pall Malls, thumbs one out. "I figured I ought to swing by here and see if everything's okay." He lights his cigarette with a Zippo engraved with crossed pistols and exhales smoke at the sky. "Is it?"

"Is what?"

"Everything okay."

"Sure it is," Clayton says, trying to force himself to smile but not quite succeeding. "Why wouldn't it be?"

"I don't know. That's why I'm here." He exhales another little cloud of smoke. "Your daddy home?"

"No."

"Even though his rig's parked down there by the barn and his Ford Ranger's sitting right there in the drive?"

"Even though," Clayton says.

"What about your momma?"

"No."

Simmons smiles around his cigarette. "Even though that's her Plymouth I parked beside?"

"Right."

"Say, you wouldn't happen to have some coffee in the pot would you? Cold gets to me these days, and I need all the warming fuel I can get."

"We don't have none."

"No coffee?"

Clayton feels his face burn and his tongue wanting to tie up into a stammer. "Instant," he says quickly. "We don't have one of those Mr. Coffee's. Instant's all we got."

Simmons smile is broad and friendly. "Well, hell, son that's fine with me. Beggars can't be choosers. That's what they say isn't it?" He steps closer and Clayton can smell his aftershave, English Leather like his old man wears. "How about we go in, have a cup of coffee where it's warm and see if we can't make sense out of all this?"

"No," Clayton says. "I mean I don't have time. I got to ... "

And now Sheriff Simmons isn't smiling at all. His eyes - how could Clayton have ever thought they were friendly - are as hard and narrow as a hawk's that has just caught sight of a rabbit breaking cover.

"You're telling me I can't come in?"

"Yes," Clayton says, his voice barely above

a whisper, his eyes turned away. "That's what I'm saying."

Simmons shakes his head and sighs. "So I've got to go to all the trouble of driving back to town, waiting around until Judge Watkins' cuts me a warrant and then coming back out here? Because that's exactly what I'm going to do. Come back with a warrant."

"It's just that ... " he lets the words trail away and tries again. "The place is dirty," he says. "And I haven't been feeling all that well lately, not like myself. I didn't mean to be rude."

"I don't need a warrant?"

"No," Clayton says. "My momma's probably going to kill me when she finds out I let you in with things looking this way, but I don't want you to go to all that trouble for nothing."

Clayton opens the door and stands aside, ushering him in. Simmons claps his shoulder and crosses the threshold.

"Cold in here," he says, stepping into the kitchen.

Clayton closes the door behind them. "Furnace hasn't been working all that well lately."

Simmons glances down at the birthday cake, the slowly thawing steak, the melting ice cream Clayton's left on the table. Then his eyes move to the hallway.

"Smells funny in here," he says.

And when he says it, he seems to recognize the scent for what it is. His hand drops to his gun belt, his thumb unsnapping the trigger guard on his holster. But it doesn't matter. The old Sheriff has made the rookie mistake of allowing someone to get behind him, and Clayton already has the knife in his hand.

* * *

Clayton has finished his porterhouse and baked potato and is waiting to light the candles on his birthday cake when he hears the cars approaching. He gives into temptation and rushes to the living room to see how many are coming. Five of them, three locals and a couple of state troopers, are rushing into the drive, lights dim, sirens off. He lets the curtain fall closed and hurries back to the kitchen where his family is waiting.

Before joining them at the table, he takes a second to admire the scene. On the night of the murders he'd carefully washed and then bandaged his parents' wounds, and now, his father is dressed in the charcoal gray suit he only ever wore to weddings and funerals, his mother in her favorite skirt and sweater, the one that always made her seem like a college girl. The Beauty Queen, stunning in her nakedness, sits at the head of the table next to Clayton's chair. He smiles at her and sits down as he hears the thud of slamming car doors.

He uses his left hand to hold hers, grips the Sheriff's lighter in his right. He hears them out there, taking up positions, hears someone say, "That's the Sheriff's cruiser sitting right there in the open."

That surprises them but Clayton isn't sure why. What would have been the point of moving it? When Simmons didn't come back to the office or answer his radio, they would have come looking anyway. He had better things to do with his time - like make love to his woman and cook his birthday dinner and then, when he was finished, unhook the gas line from the stove. They're moving around out there. Sooner or later one of them will knock on the door. He shakes his head. They're too close to the house, too close to the big old propane tank that's likely to blow once things get started. For a second, he thinks about stepping to the door and warning them but decides against it. Why bother? It wasn't like anyone had ever done him any favors.

He takes a deep breath. It's almost over

now, but he has no regrets. The last few days have been the best of his life. And isn't that what true love really is? A few snatched moments of solace on the way from one darkness to another?

"Happy birthday to me," he says like Frosty in that old cartoon.

Then, still holding the Beauty Queen's hand, he fires the lighter. And in the stuttering heartbeat before the explosion, he has time to wish for happily ever after - whatever that might mean in the blackness that is to come.

We Will Find Each Other

Cheryl Ann Caskey had been missing for five days when I found her torn and bloody sweatshirt hidden beneath a tangle of blackberry bushes on a hillside at the border of the old Sugar Creek Mines. I was only fifteen, but I knew that finding that sweatshirt meant all the things we'd been saying were lies. Cheryl Ann hadn't skipped town with a Fort Campbell soldier or sneaked away to Nashville to have an abortion. They were foolish, hopeful delusions, but for five days all of us had believed them. This was 1983, and back then three-quarters of the houses in Harps County still had antennas bolted to their roofs, and no one had even heard of the Internet. The world felt farther away somehow. Of course we were aware that kids and teenagers were sometimes kidnapped and raped and murdered. Every so often their faces turned up on our milk cartons, but those kind of things never seemed to happen in our nowhere corner of south central Kentucky. I'm not sure we believed they could.

That day I sat on a jutting lip of sandstone and stared at the jagged hills and pine thickets of the abandoned strip mines. I ran my finger over the rubbery Molly Hatchet logo on the sweatshirt and then brought the damp fabric to my face and sniffed. I smelled Ivory Soap and cigarettes and cinnamon perfume, but that might just have been my imagination. Cheryl Ann was a scrawny, fragile girl. She was a couple of years ahead of me but was one of the older girls who had struggled her way from Basic Math to Algebra, so we shared one class. I remembered her sitting in the back row, staring out the window, dreaming, I guess, of a better life somewhere else.

There was no question about what I should do, but I didn't do it. Finding that sweatshirt was the biggest thing that had happened to me, not to my mom or my dad or our family, but to *me*, and I wanted to hold onto it. I took the pack of Winstons that I'd stolen from my dad's dresser and lit one and thought about it for a while.

A cold rain was spitting, and I hunched my shoulders against the chill. A cool damp summer had given way to the coldest and wettest fall in more than a decade. Off in the distance, the Green River raged against its banks. Then I heard the rustle and snap of branches followed by a dog's bark in the beech thicket behind me. If someone found me with the sweatshirt, they'd think I did it. I imagined my face on television and in the paper and thought how, even when they let me go, people would still believe me guilty. I looked at the rusting coal shovels and slag heaps rising on the far side of the mines and wanted to make a run for them, but my legs were stiff and stupid, and all I could do was gasp for air like a fish yanked from deep water. Finally, I caught hold of my fear and stuffed the sweatshirt inside my coat just before a short, broad man in a yellow rain slicker burst into the clearing. A sable-colored German shepherd trailed behind him, teeth-bared, waiting for the attack command. For a moment, I believed the old man might give it even though he'd known me for most of my life.

"Mr. Eason?" I said. "It's me, Chance. Charles Russell's boy."

"I know who you are." He tongued at a fever blister, dropped his hand to lightly touch his dog's head. "Easy now, Igor," he said. "Easy, boy."

Lowell Eason was our nearest neighbor, a widower who lived a quarter of a mile closer to the main highway in an unpainted farmhouse with a crumbling soffit and rusted gutters. His fourteen acres of scrubland were fenced and patrolled by the pack of shepherds that he bred and trained and then sold for what my father said was "an ungodly price for a mangy animal."

Now he moved down the muddy hillside with amazing speed and sureness of foot for a man in his late sixties. "Your daddy know what you're up to?"

I thought about the sweatshirt and what he might have seen. "I'm not doing nothing," I said. "I don't know what you mean."

"Them cigarettes you got in your hand." He touched a damp gray patch that was all that was left of his hair. "I don't reckon you brought them out here to admire the pretty colors on the package." He grinned at me. "You come out here a lot, boy?"

"Some. Not a lot."

He nodded as if it were about what he'd expected. "You don't ever get to messing around my place, do you?" He tugged at the crotch of his filthy khakis and smiled. "I wouldn't want my dogs to get a hold of you. He cleared his throat and spat near my boot. "What about the old Zachary place? You ever fart around up there?"

The Zachary place was a crumbling three-story Colonial near the dead end of our road. A decade before I was born, Cecil Zachary blew off the back of his wife's head with a .12 gauge shotgun, then worked the barrel into his own mouth and pulled the trigger with his toe. He had no children, and the house had stood empty since they loaded him and his wife into the back of a hearse. A lot of kids swore it was haunted, and when I was little, the fact the Zachary farm bordered my dad's land gave me nightmares, but my father said all of that was nonsense. Cecil Zachary had been nothing more than a crazy bastard who'd been overly jealous of his young wife. There weren't any ghosts or evil spirits haunting the Zachary place. The real trouble, he said, came from vine-hidden wells and rusted nails, wasps and copperhead snakes.

"No," I said to Eason. "I don't mess around there."

"Afraid of old Cecil's ghost, huh?" His grin widened. "It's the living you got to watch out for." He tongued at his fever blister some more and squinted hard at the ground. "You got pretty big feet for a boy," he said. "But not that big, I don't reckon. You ought to be heading on home, boy. There's no telling what might come scurrying out of those old mines when the sun goes down."

He turned to his dog and clucked his tongue, and the shepherd came to the old man's side. I started to say something about him being a beautiful dog, but I could tell that I wasn't wanted here, so I nodded a goodbye and climbed the hill towards the thicket.

"Mr. Eason?" I said when I reached the top. "What are you doing out here in the rain?"

He snorted as if I'd said something so stupid it was funny. "Your daddy's land, hell all the land on this road, is pie shaped. Broad in the front and narrow in the back. I know it for a fact, for it was my own daddy who parceled off this here property. You understand what that means?"

"No."

"It means these weeds and the thickets and that hill you're standing on belong to me. It means that whatever I'm doing, it ain't none of your business."

I did what I should have done a long time ago. I headed for home.

* * *

That night after stories about the deployment of American Cruise missiles in Europe, about a joint study from the EPA and the Kentucky Department of Fish and Wildlife that identified sixty-three, potentially toxic chemicals found in the Green River, and about an eighty-three-year-old widow over in Crofton who'd had President Reagan's face tattooed on her shoulder, the local news ran a segment on Cheryl Ann Caskey. But there was nothing new to tell. The Sheriff's Department was pursuing leads; her parents were utterly distraught; anyone with information was urged to contact the Kentucky State Police.

"Those poor people," my mother said. "My heart breaks for them."

For a second I wanted to confess about the sweatshirt, but I told myself I didn't know for sure it belonged to Cheryl Ann and that it didn't matter anyway. Those old strip mines went on forever, winding back on themselves and curling around Harps County like a sprung Slinky. Even with an army of searchers it was unlikely that Cheryl Ann's body would be found. There were too many slews and gullies and ravines out there, too many packs of scavenging dogs and coyotes. Maybe it would be better if the Caskeys never knew what happened to their daughter. They could choose to believe whatever they wanted, that she had run off to Florida with a boyfriend or hitchhiked to California to become a movie star. Surely it would be better to live your life hoping that at any moment you might get a phone call or turn on the television and spot your long-lost daughter than it would be to know she was buried six feet underground.

My mom looked at me, frowned. "What are they saying about it at school?"

"Nothing," I said, but I knew she wouldn't leave it at that. "Some people say she ran off with Mr. Whitaker, who used to be a substitute teacher. Or a serial killer like Michael Myers got her. One kid even told me he thought aliens abducted her."

"Aliens my ass," my dad said. "She'll turn up when whatever soldier or college boy she's been shacked up with drops her ass at the end of the road."

My mother said, "Your children are awake and listening."

This was only partly true. My little sister, Amy, had conked out in the living room floor halfway through *Knots Landing.*

"You know how girls are at that age," my dad said. "Or have you forgot you were wilder than an unbroken pony."

"I'm warning you, Charles," she said. "You're about to earn yourself a lifetime of pain."

She punched his bicep, and he tickled her. They goofed around like that for a few minutes, acting silly, giggling. A year ago it would have embarrassed me to see it, but now I was thankful. It had been an eternity since either one of them had anything to laugh about.

I don't know how long my mom knew about the lump in her breast, but by the time she came home from a doctor's visit at the end of last winter, the cancer had spread to both breasts. A week and a half later, she'd checked into the Owensboro hospital for a radical mastectomy that was to be followed by weeks of radiation treatments. A few days later, she came home and spent the next few months shuffling around our house like a ghost that was unsure of exactly what it was supposed to haunt. At first my dad had tried to hold onto an illusion of cheerfulness. But as the days went by, he grew quiet and brooding. He couldn't do anything - work on a car or watch television or face the morning - without a drink in his hand. He always sat alone, sullen and glaring, his silence broken by sudden explosions of temper that ended with holes punched in walls, kitchen chairs stomped to kindling, threats to take after me or Amy with a belt. He spent most of his time in the barn he'd converted into an auto-body shop, swilling beer and blaring Waylon or Willie on his tape deck, hammering fenders and quarter panels as if metal were responsible for all the trouble in our lives.

One night in June I had watched my mother through our cracked, bathroom door as she stood naked in front of the mirror, weeping, an open bottle of pills in her hand. The next morning I'd overhead them talking. He told her she needed counseling, needed someone to help her move past this thing. She told him he was drinking too much, that the smell of whiskey on his breath made her want to vomit. They spoke of divorce but agreed that neither wanted that. In the end, they came to an arrangement. She would visit a counselor at Harps County Community Health, and he would put aside the bourbon, never touch it again, never bring anything stronger than beer into the house. I spent the next few weeks certain it was just a matter of time until my mother went back to her haunted, lifeless shuffle and my dad came home staggering and reeking of whiskey, but I'd been wrong.

Now my mother sat up straighter, flushed and smiling. "Put your sister to bed, Chance, and then head that way yourself."

When I roused Amy, she blinked a couple of times, grinned and let me guide her to her bedroom, walking as stiff-legged as a zombie. "I'm not sleepy," she said.

But she was snoring when I turned out the

light. My mother shouted for me to brush my teeth before I got into bed. Things were quiet for a minute, and then I heard her laugh, low and throaty.

"Let's turn in, Charles," she said.

There was a pause that seemed to drag on forever before he said, "You heard the weather. Clear in the morning, rain in the afternoon. If I'm ever going to finish Ed Cisney's pickup, I need to shoot it first thing and hope like hell it dries before the rain sets in."

"So?"

"If I'm going to shoot it in the morning, I need to prep it tonight."

There was another heavy silence. "It's been forever," she said. "If you don't' want to ... with me, I mean ... "

"It's just about the rain, Donna," he said "Nothing else, but the goddamn weather. I have to get the truck finished so I can get paid. Times are hard around here. I don't have to tell you that."

I shut off the water in the bathroom sink and waited for what would come next. But nothing did, so I slipped down the hall to my bedroom. When our back door slammed, I winced. I took a toy horse from my dresser and ran my thumb over the mane. It was posed in full gallop, intricately carved, lacquered, hand-painted. There were a half dozen others of varying colors and sizes, all made by my dad when I was five or six years old. Back then he would tuck me in at night and tell me how one day we would get us a couple of mounts and ride off into a wild west that only ever existed in his imagination.

I set the horse back down and crossed to my window and moved aside the curtains. The yard and the fields and the garage were lit from the streetlights my dad took as partial payment for fixing the county judge's truck. Now I saw my father sitting on our back porch steps, shoulders hunched, a beer in his hand, a cigarette dangling from his lip. After a moment, he took a long swallow of beer and reached into his coat pocket. I knew what I was about to witness, and I wanted to turn away, but I couldn't do it. He uncapped a pint bottle and brought it to his lips. When I shut my eyes, it was as if I could see the wetness on his lips and smell the smoky-sweet bourbon on his breath. I thought about those carved horses, how he'd spent hours notching the wood. I imagined myself slamming them off the wall and grinding them beneath my heel, leaving them on the table for him to find. But I knew I wouldn't do that. Instead, I opened my eyes and watched him cross the field towards his garage, staggering in that old, familiar way.

* * *

The next morning I walked Amy to her bus stop. My mother had insisted on it every morning since Cheryl Ann Caskey disappeared. A couple of minutes after we reached Cedar Hill Road, Amy boarded the bus, took a seat and then waved at me through a fogging window. I stood there a minute, thinking about Lowell Eason and dreading the walk alone to my own bus stop over on the main highway. Then my dad's battered, old International pickup rounded the curve. He stopped and leaned across the seat to open the screeching passenger's door.

Despite the chill of the morning, he wore a short-sleeved work shirt that gripped his biceps. He was scrawny but strong with a body that seemed made solely of bone and gristle. Unlike my mousy brown hair, which I'd gotten from my mother, his was nearly black. His eyes were ice blue, his skin always darkly tanned even in the middle of winter. I understood why my mother was jealous of him and why whenever he entered a room women turned to stare.

"You got something on your mind,

Chance?" he asked as we waited at the Highway 70 crossroads.

"I saw you last night."

"And?"

I dropped my eyes and focused on the mud smears and empty cigarette packs on the floorboard. "I don't know."

"Answer my question. What exactly did you see?"

"I saw you drinking whiskey."

He flicked his cigarette butt out of the window. "That's better," he said. "If you're going to accuse a man of something, you ought to have the courage to speak it to his face."

"You promised you wouldn't."

"That's right," he said. "But don't go getting wound up. You and your mother, I swear to God," he said. "Listen, there's nothing wrong with a nip every now and then to keep out the cold." He sighed and flicked his hair from his eyes. "You and your mother don't like me drinking whiskey, but you all aren't the one out there trying to make enough money to put food on the table, are you?" He said, "I drank too much last spring. I know that. I let it sneak up on me, but that's not going to happen again."

"Okay."

He turned onto Eagle Lane, and we merged into the crawl of traffic heading towards the drop-off zone at the front of the school. "There's no reason to worry your mother," he said. "She overreacts to things. You've seen how she's let that girl's disappearance get to her."

"It is kind of weird. Knowing someone like that, I mean."

"Yeah, I guess so. But she'll turn up eventually. Girls like that ... " He shrugged and lit another cigarette. "But here's the thing, Chance, and you need to listen. I hope that girl's all right, I truly do, but whatever did or didn't happen to her has nothing to do with you. Life's hard enough without taking other people's troubles as your own."

Usually, I liked it when he spoke to me seriously, man to man, but today I wanted to ask him if he was so smart, why couldn't he stay sober. Instead, I shrugged and let him take it how he wanted.

He squinted at me through his cigarette smoke. "You can tell your mother whatever you want. But sometimes being a man is about knowing when to keep your mouth closed. The way I've kept mine shut about that half pack of cigarettes you took from my dresser." He met my eyes. "Watch what you say. I gave you the respect of telling you the truth about my whiskey. I expect the same in return."

"Yes sir," I said. "I just wanted to try them is all."

"That's why I haven't mentioned it to your momma. There's no sense in worrying her about something that doesn't amount to a hill of beans."

When he stopped in front of the school, I opened the door, winced at the hinge's screech and felt my face burn when a few guys and a couple of senior girls turned to stare at us. My dad said something, but I wasn't sure what it was, so I skulked towards the school, head down, wishing I was anywhere else in the world. I heard the International's rumble and felt him watching me, but I didn't turn around.

* * *

Late that afternoon while a cold drizzle fell and the day's light slipped away, I crouched in the cover of saplings and honeysuckle and watched Lowell Eason burst through a thicket at the far side of the Zachary farm. He stood still, taking deep breaths of cold air, and then glanced around as if he was concerned about someone watching him. Satisfied that he was alone, he walked to the front of the house and tested the rotted boards of the porch steps.

Despite the cold and damp, I was sweating.

Earlier, I'd been sitting on the sandstone lip with Cheryl Ann Caskey's sweatshirt in my hand when I heard him thrashing through the thickets. Once I was sure he was heading toward the Zachary place, I cut through deeper woods and briar-choked gullies that ran parallel to the clearing. Now he stepped back from the porch steps and walked to the side of the house where I lost sight of him.

I had a decision to make. Give up on following him or risk a dash across the open yard to the elbow of the thicket. Before I even realized that I'd decided, I broke cover and ran, fighting the perverse, maybe suicidal urge to let out a whoop that would have announced my presence. Those two-dozen yards seemed to stretch for an eternity before I finally reached the cover of stunted apple and peach trees.

Eason paused at the rear corner of the house, bent on one knee with his weight supported by his walking stick. A moment later, he struggled to his feet and moved to the backyard. He pulled a small flashlight from his pocket and thumbed it on and aimed it at the ground. He stood there looking down, digging at his earwax with his pinkie. Then he kicked aside a pile of wet leaves and broken twigs and lowered himself to his knee again. He grabbed something, tugged, stopped, tugged again.

This time when he stood, he swept the flashlight across the yard as if he were looking for something or someone, and I had to hold my breath to stop myself from crying out or making a break for home. He flashed his light back at the dirt and took out a plug of tobacco and cut himself a chew. Then he turned back towards the far side of the thicket.

I counted to three hundred and fifty just to make sure he was gone before I emerged from hiding. I walked around the front yard and tried the porch steps. They were sturdy enough for me, so I climbed them and peered through the busted front windows, but there was nothing to see, just buckled floors and crumbling walls and rotting furniture.

The wind picked up and I shivered as I retraced Lowell Eason's footsteps. A low, sprawling mound of dead leaves and twigs rose in the middle of the backyard. A grave, but the mound seemed too low and too regular, and the ground wasn't sunken. Then I spotted a door set nearly level with the dirt like a trap in an old movie. I hunkered, touched it. It was made of thick metal, nearly orange with rust but still sturdy. A heavy chain ran through the latch and around a fist-sized metal pole buried deep in the ground and was secured by a Master Lock that was gleaming and new, probably fresh off a shelf from Ace Hardware.

There was nothing I either needed or wanted to find here, but I'd come too far and the compulsion to know was too strong to just leave, so I stomped the door. There was only a dull thud. I stomped again, harder this time, and then harder still. I shouted even though I knew that shouting was crazy, maybe even suicidal. I called her name until my throat was raw and aching. Cheryl Ann, I screamed, Cheryl Ann, until my gasping breaths felt as jagged as glass in my lungs.

I was still there when I heard footsteps behind me. They were heavy and certain and so close I knew there was no point in running. For one heartbeat, I clung to the hope that I'd find Lowell Eason sneering at me, his walking stick raised behind his head, but I knew I wouldn't.

"Daddy," I said before I even bothered to turn around.

"You've made yourself hoarse for nothing," he said. "She's too deep underground."

* * *

In the end, it was my decision to see what he'd tried to keep hidden for so long. He lifted the metal door and in the pale, yellowish light that drifted up from underground, I saw a metal rung ladder bolted into the side of a concrete wall. He nodded for me to go ahead of him, but I hesitated. I was afraid that he might simply close the door and leave me down there to die.

He handed me the lock as if he knew exactly what I was thinking. I climbed down into an open room with concrete walls and a concrete floor. A couple of naked, low-watt bulbs rigged to a car battery splashed the room with feeble light. Rusted can goods lined metal shelves fastened to the wall. There were a couple of chairs and an unpainted wooden table sagging beneath the weight of a beer cooler and a fifth of Early Times.

I didn't want to look at the heavy, iron bed, but I couldn't help myself. Cheryl Ann Caskey stared back at me, her eyes wide and frightened. She was bound spread-eagled to the head and footboard, nude except for a dirty sheet bunched around her stomach, gagged with a dirty rag held by duct tape.

"Christ," I said. "Dad, what have you done?"

"You wanted to see. Now sit down and let's talk about this thing, try to work out what all this means for us. You owe me that." He said. "You're upset. I understand that, Chance. A thing like this?" He ran his hand through his hair. "It's pretty hard to take. I know that. I just wish you'd left well enough alone."

"What is this place?"

He frowned as if it were a trick question "A fallout shelter. Old Cecil Zachary was certain the Russians were going to drop the big one at any moment. This was back in the mid-fifties when a lot of people thought the same," He uncapped the bourbon bottle and took a pull. "He must have spent a fortune on this thing. It's eight feet down and lined with concrete."

"I don't understand."

"I'm not sure I do either," he said. "I don't know why the notion took hold of me, just that it did and I couldn't sleep, couldn't think about anything else."

"Was it mom? What they did to her?"

"No. Don't think that." He coughed and cleared his throat. "Or maybe that was part of it. Not because of her, you understand, but because of me. It started me thinking about how time was jack rabbiting away from me, how I was getting older, how before I knew it, I'd be buried six feet underground. I realized I'd never be young again and that I'd never have the chance to feel a young, healthy woman's body next to mine. That ate at me. You don't know how that feels." He sighed and gave me his serious I'm-speaking-the-truth-

and-you-better-listen nod. "But you will. God help you, boy, you will." He passed the bottle, and I took a drink before I even really thought about what I was doing. "Now listen, Chance," he said. "I'm not saying that was the only reason. I've always had things like this running around in my head, daydreams and fantasies, I guess. Your mother knows some of it. She tried to play along, but with her, it wasn't ... "

"I don't want to know," I said. "I don't want to hear anymore."

"All right," he said. "But there's a part of you that knew, isn't there?"

I remembered Saturday morning trips to Greenview to pick up parts for one car or another, the way we'd stop at Druthers for a ham and egg sandwich and how he'd always run into the post office and come out carrying brown-wrapped boxes with stamps from Denmark and Sweden. I thought back on the way he stared at the cheerleaders when he took me to a basketball game. I remembered waking in the middle of the night more than once to the sound of a leather belt slapping flesh and my mother's cries, cries that I sometimes thought came from pain and sometimes thought came from joy.

"You've got a good heart, son. You care about people. I know that. But listen, son. This girl? She's just a little slut. I know what I'm talking about. When I was toying with the idea, not sure if I was serious about it, I started watching her, and I saw what she was. You know what it took to get her in my truck? A cigarette and a six pack of beer."

"I don't want to hear about that either."

He ground out his cigarette "You're right. That doesn't matter. What does is what happens next."

He reached into the oversized pocket of his coat, fumbled for a second and then pulled out the small, snub-nosed revolver I last saw in a shoebox at the top of our hall closet. "You're going to kill me," I said.

He recoiled as if I'd slapped him. "You think that about me? That I would hurt you? I'm a lot of things, Chance, but I'm not a monster. Maybe you think I am, but I'm not."

He grabbed my wrist, and I tried to yank away from him but couldn't. He squeezed until I opened my hand, and then he slapped the butt of the gun into my palm and closed my fingers around it.

"What happens next is your decision, but the way I see it, you have three choices. You can put the gun in your pocket, climb that ladder, go on home to tell your momma what I've done. Or if you truly believe I'm a monster, you can aim it at my head and squeeze the trigger." He sighed and brushed a lock of hair from his eyes. "Who knows? Maybe that would be the best thing for all of us."

"Christ, Daddy," I said. "Why did you have to do this?"

"Or maybe you can just see this thing for what it is. A small part of me, nothing more than that. A tiny little part that doesn't have to change anything between us."

"And if I do see it that way? What happens then?"

He shrugged. "You give me the gun, get on out of here and let me do what needs to be done."

I couldn't kill him. I knew that even as I told myself I would. No matter what else he was, he was my father, the man who had once dragged me to shore when our johnboat capsized down at Lake Malone and who had spent long nights in his garage hammering and welding until he made me the go-kart I'd been begging for when I was ten. He was the one who'd carved all those goddamn horses for me when I was a little kid.

"I hate you," I said. But I wasn't sure if I were speaking to him or to myself.

I looked back at Cheryl Ann. She was watching us, terrified, waiting. I decided to climb the ladder and run home to tell my mother what I'd found, but then I thought of the police cars and the flashing lights and the television cameras. Whispers and taunts would follow all of us for the rest of our lives. A thing like this might make my mother sick again. Amy would be tormented and then shunned, avoided as if she carried some horrible and contagious disease. They would hate me. Maybe they wouldn't say it, maybe they wouldn't even admit it to themselves, but they would hate me for doing what was right instead of what was right for them. And, of course, I thought about myself, about what my life might be like after all of this.

"Chance," he said.

"Lowell Eason was out here," I said. "He knows something ain't right. He'll tell."

My dad shrugged. "I don't think so. I know for a fact that he fell down a ravine on his way home, bashed his brains out on a rock."

He thought he had it figured out, but there was a fourth option that he hadn't named. I could jam the barrel against my temple and squeeze the trigger, leave him to deal with the mess. But I knew I wouldn't do that either. There would be questions. The answers would end with my father in handcuffs and my mother and sister shattered beyond repair.

I crossed the room and stood beside the iron bed. I looked down at Cheryl Ann Caskey. The bruises, the scrapes, the dark, cherry-wood smears of dried blood on the dingy mattress. Her eyes were open, watching me. I thought about her in Algebra class, staring out that window and dreaming of a life that she was never going to live.

Then I gave the gun to my dad.

"Go home, Chance," he said.

"I don't think I can," I said. "I don't know .... I can't face momma."

"Go home," he said.

I shrugged and then crossed the room and climbed the ladder. The rain had stopped and the sky had cleared, but it was colder. Shivering, I headed towards the thicket. I was halfway across the yard when I flinched, certain that I'd heard a gunshot although I knew that was impossible.

I shut my eyes and imagined a future. I saw myself cutting through the thickets and woods until I reached the main highway where I'd hitchhike until I found someone who would carry me somewhere, anywhere else, but I figured somehow, some way, everyone would know what I'd done, no matter how far I ran. Then I imagined myself bolting for the Sugar Creek Mines, where I'd sleep in caves and roam with packs of coyotes and unwanted dogs until I was old and gray.

I opened my eyes and looked up at moonlight shining through thinning clouds. When I was little, my dad would take my hand and point to the sky and tell me to look for the man in the moon. He always asked didn't I see him smiling down on us, watching out, and I always said yes, yes I did. My dad always made the same, lame joke. "What I want to know," he would say, "is how that poor son of a bitch is going to get down."

But there was no man up there. The moon was just a cold dark rock caught in its mindless orbit, lost and hopeless, carried here by chance without even a light of its own to shine.

"The moon doesn't care," I said.

I winced when the metal door slammed shut, and then I turned and saw my father on level ground. He nodded as if he had expected me to wait for him, and I realized that in his mind, there had never been any doubt. It was why he put the gun in my hand in the first place. He'd always known where I was going even before I took my first step. I thought about those carved horses on my bedroom dresser, remembered my favorite story he told to go with them, one I never got tired of hearing.

He would say you ride west to flank those Apaches, and we'll meet up once we've taken care of business. My heart always thrummed inside my chest, and I would ask him what would happen if I didn't get there, what then. He'd always tell me that I would ride like the wind, that he had faith in me. I'd ask him, but what if I can't find you, Daddy, what then? And he'd say, don't worry, we'll always find each other, and we'll ride for home where your mother will have biscuits and gravy waiting. But I could never leave it at that. I'd always say, but what if we've gone too far and we can't get back home? He'd ruffle my hair and tell me, well that was okay, too, that everything would be fine as long as we were together.

And that night with Cheryl Ann Caskey lying dead in the fallout shelter, together was the way we walked home.

Something about Teddy

Halfway between Indianapolis and Louisville, snow spitting and slush gathering on I-65, Tom Lennox regretted telling Teddy his secret. Teddy, nineteen or twenty with greasy blond hair smashed to his forehead by a sock cap and the tattoos and piercings that even nice kids his age had these days, wanted to make it a game.

"What about her?" He asked when they passed a woman in a Honda Civic. "How would you kill her?" Teddy propped his feet on the dash, licked his bottom lip. "You'd play with her first though, wouldn't you? Do her before you did her."

Lennox checked his rearview mirror and measured a car length distance before he glided the Buick back into the right lane. Twenty-seven years on the road as a sales rep for Lindite Bowling Balls had made him a lot of things - twenty pounds overweight, enough money to support his wife's addiction to Home

Shopping, a few friends, and a cautious driver. Once the Buick had settled into its lane, he glanced at Teddy's filthy Reeboks on the dash and fought the urge to slap him.

The boy was crude. That was his wife's term for boys like Teddy. Muriel taught Geometry in their hometown of Fort Wayne, Indiana, and she said these days most of her students were crude. She was thankful that they had never had children. Lennox wasn't sure. Maybe children would have changed things, would have given him a reason to come home from the road. Muriel's womb had been the source of their problems. It still was. This afternoon she had an appointment with an oncologist who would confirm what both Muriel and Tom knew. She was beyond treatment. The fact that Muriel had insisted that he continue his sales route instead of coming home to accompany her to the doctor both angered and frightened him.

"Get your shoes off my dash," Lennox said.

Teddy dropped his feet to the floor, sucked air between his teeth and grinned. "Hey, you'd pop her before you popped her. Right?"

"I wouldn't rape her."

"Sure you wouldn't," Teddy said. "In a pig's eye."

"I've never raped anyone."

Teddy leaned forward and took a last look through the rearview mirror. "I'd do her," he said. "A lot of women like that. I read it in a book once."

Lennox quickened his wipers against the snow and shifted his weight behind the wheel to give his hemorrhoids relief. He reached for a pack of Camel Lights, told himself he could wait ten more miles before he smoked another, then lit it anyway. He'd been trying to quit for months but nothing worked. Not the patches or the gum or even the fear he felt when he climbed a flight of stairs and felt fluttering in his chest. He was forty-nine, a big, balding man carrying too much weight in his upper stomach, with high blood pressure and an even higher cholesterol count thanks to a lifetime of eating in diners and truck stops from South Bend, Indiana to Jackson, Mississippi - the endless ribbon of interstate that he'd traversed for decades. Sooner or later, a half-clogged artery would clog completely or a platelet would burst free and hit his heart and Tom Lennox, excellent salesman, competent Canasta player, mediocre husband, would be a lump of dead weight for a maid to discover. And more recently there were nights when he lay in bed at a Motel Six in Indiana or a Comfort Inn in Kentucky or a Ramada in

Tennessee and prayed for sooner rather than later. He couldn't imagine life at home without Muriel. The three-bedroom ranch house would be quiet and empty and there would be nothing but the sound of the television for company while he ate and drank alone. It would be exactly like being on the road.

Lennox took a hard drag from his cigarette and thought of the .22 stuffed beneath the front seat. He imagined pressing the barrel to Teddy's left ear and squeezing the trigger and knew that doing it would push away the worry, the same way saying his prayers before bedtime had kept nightmares at bay when he was a boy.

"What about Fred and Wilma?" Teddy asked as they pulled even with a minivan and a fat, dark-haired man and his redheaded wife. "Gut shoot them, right? Make them suffer a little bit."

"It's not about making people suffer," Lennox said. "I'm not disturbed."

Teddy cocked his eyebrow and slouched back against the seat. Lennox stubbed his cigarette. He didn't know how to make the kid understand or see the order and self-control of his murders. Lennox wasn't a sadist, and he wasn't excessive. One a year. Twenty-four murders so far, the first a vagrant who slept behind a liquor store in Paducah, Kentucky, the last a seventeen-year-old runaway who solicited travelers at a Waffle House in Batesville, Mississippi. Lennox had been so discreet in choosing his victims and so cautious in his methods that the police had never had a clue all of the murders were connected.

"You make them beg?" Teddy asked.

The boy would never understand. Lennox wasn't sure *he* understood it. Occasionally, he tried to figure out why he'd started killing, but he'd never come up with a satisfactory answer. Sometimes, he thought it was just the road. Years of driving the same, unchanging highway and staring at the same billboards and the same cityscapes, and the patches of pine trees and pastures that were always the same, whether the signs told you that you were in northern Indiana or southern Tennessee. And eating in the same restaurants and diners and listening to the same songs on a dozen different radio stations and vomiting the same sales spiel a dozen times a day to bored Bowl-A-Rama managers made life as meaningless as the fragments of graffiti he read on overpasses and bathroom walls - Jesus Saves or Sandra's a Slut, perhaps. One murder a year gave him a reason for his life on the road. The boy would never understand. With his endless chatter and his crudeness, Teddy was making even murder seem meaningless.

"Sure you do," Teddy said. "You make them beg. I bet you get off on it."

"Shut up," Lennox said, surprising even himself with his anger.

Teddy blinked his bright blue eyes. "You don't have to get pissy," he said. "I was just talking."

"That's the problem."

Teddy pretended to be fascinated by the billboards advertising Louisville FM stations and Budweiser. Lennox shouldn't have told the boy about the murders and wasn't sure why he did other than there was something about Teddy that drew Lennox to him. He'd felt it when he spotted the boy hanging around a payphone at a rest area just south of Gas City, Indiana. The feeling had been so strong, Lennox had broken his own rule and offered the boy a ride. He told himself it was because, in his baggy jeans, thin windbreaker and sock cap, Teddy was likely to freeze on a snowy January day, but knowing that in truth he didn't want to be alone today, not when the world was as gray and cold as Muriel would be under the hospital's florescent lights.

He'd regretted his decision five minutes after Teddy got in the car when the boy leered at him, scooted across the seat, and offered to give him a blowjob. Lennox had recoiled, threatened to put him out on the side of the road. He told Teddy that one thing Tom Lennox was not was a faggot. Didn't he see the wedding ring on his finger? Teddy had shrugged and said there was no reason to get angry. A lot of straight guys wouldn't turn down a blowjob, and he'd just wanted to say thanks for the ride.

Ten miles later, Teddy launched into a long discourse on why he always wore a sock cap. He said if you took your cap off your body heat leaked out, which was bad, but sometimes your soul went with it and then where the hell were you, walking around without a soul? That was crazy talk, and it scared Lennox. But Teddy had just smiled as if the whole thing were a joke, and Lennox couldn't decide if the boy was putting him on or if he really was crazy. Twenty minutes later, Teddy told Lennox he'd served five years in a juvenile home for armed robbery and while he was there he'd knifed two boys but no one had been able to prove it so he walked away free as a bird. Something about Teddy was like a key turning inside Lennox's mind, and when the boy finished his story, Lennox told his own. Now, Lennox looked at Teddy slumped against the door and felt guilty for the way he'd spoken to him. He wasn't sure why, just that indefinable something.

"I'm sorry," Lennox said. "Never mind what I said."

Teddy's head popped up, and he reached for a cigarette without asking. "You're probably just tense," he said. "You sure you don't want me to blow you?"

Lennox squinted through the snow at the high rises and bridges that marked the beginnings of Louisville. "I told you I'm not a homosexual."

Teddy blew a smoke ring. "Me neither. I mean not really. But I don't mind doing a guy a favor."

Then Teddy said he had a great idea. Why didn't they kill someone? Make it a special occasion. If they killed somebody together, Lennox would know his secret was safe. The only other way to guarantee it was if Lennox killed him.

"And I don't meant to be offensive or anything," Teddy said. "But I'm pretty sure I could take you."

Lennox told him to stop talking. Traffic was picking up, the road was icy, and he needed to concentrate. They headed south through Louisville. With its snow tires and steady wipers, the Buick glided through traffic as anonymous as the first wayward cells of cancer.

* * *

They stopped at a Ramada just south of Greenview, Kentucky, and Lennox had Teddy lie across the front seat while he registered. Except for his diet and his smoking, Lennox was cautious in all things. If anything went wrong tonight, he wanted no one to be able to connect him with Teddy.

The sky was stained a molded gray, and snow swirled in a whipping wind that whistled from the hills outside of town. Three quarters of the parking lot was already full and yellow lights glowed from dozens of steamed motel windows.

"Nice room," Teddy said when Lennox unlocked the door.

It was just a motel room - worn carpet, heavy green drapes, a paisley bedspread on a hard, queen-size bed, a couple of vinyl chairs, a burn-scarred writing table, and a television bolted to a stand on the dresser. Lennox unpacked, thinking of a man he'd worked with who lived around here. Massey something or other. Or was it something or other Massey? He couldn't remember and that worried him. A salesman who starts forgetting names was as useful as a fastball pitcher with a blown arm. Lennox fretted while Teddy paced the room, turning the faucet on and off, bouncing on the bed, flipping through channels on the television.

Lennox pulled off his sweater, uncomfortably aware of the way his gut sagged over his Dockers. It was five thirty, which meant Muriel should be home from the doctor. Lennox pulled a fifth of Jack Daniel's from the side pocket of his suitcase, broke the seal, and poured a double shot into a plastic cup and then offered Teddy the bottle.

"I never drink the stuff," he said. "A beer now and then, but that's it. That junk will kill you. You don't believe me? Ask my old man."

Lennox downed his whiskey. He poured another two fingers into his cup.

"Don't get soused," Teddy said.

"I can handle my whiskey."

Teddy fiddled with his sock cap. "I'm not preaching or anything."

Lennox drank, refilled his cup and told Teddy to keep quiet while he called home. He sat on the bed and dialed the number and was surprised that his hands weren't shaking. The phone rang four times before the answering machine kicked on.

"Pick up," Lennox said. "It's me, babe. Pick

up, okay?"

The phone beeped to let him know his time was over. He hung up, wondering if Muriel was there, alone in the living room with the lights off, terrified by the certainty of her dying. He dialed home again.

"It's okay, babe," he told the machine. "Things will be all right. Just pick up."

Maybe she'd sent him on the road because she knew what the doctor would say and knew what she was going to do about it. He could see her lying across their king size bed, her eyes closed, an empty pill bottle on the nightstand.

"Goddamn it," he said.

Lennox slammed the receiver on the hook and then dialed again.

"Muriel, please answer," he said. "Let me help you."

Still no answer. Lennox had another idea that was as horrible as the first. Maybe she'd sent him on the road because there was someone else she wanted to comfort her.

"Okay," he said. "I'll be home tomorrow night. We'll talk then." He held the phone, and then, just before his time ended, he remembered to say, "I love you."

He was as tired as he'd ever been in his life. He unlaced his shoes and pulled his shirt from his trousers and lay back on the bed and closed his eyes.

"Trouble at home?" Teddy asked, his voice soft and concerned.

Lennox sat up on the edge of the bed. He told Teddy about Muriel. When he finished, it was as if his body was a balloon that had lost its air. His shoulders sagged, his muscles quivered, and he flopped back on the bed, his eyes burning as if the effort of staying open was too much for them. He didn't think he was crying, but maybe he was.

"Just take it easy," Teddy said. "Rest a while."

Teddy helped him beneath the covers. Then Teddy stood and stretched, took off his windbreaker and tennis shoes. Lennox wasn't surprised when Teddy slipped in beside him. But then Teddy moved closer and laid an arm over his shoulders, and Lennox stiffened.

"Don't touch me," he said.

Teddy put his mouth close to Lennox's ear. "Don't push me away," he said. "Just let me stay here with you."

Lennox shut his eyes. The whiskey still buzzed through his head, and he felt as if the world were disappearing down a long, narrow tunnel. A few minutes later, he rolled onto his back and told himself it was because his shoulder was aching. When Teddy's hand moved under the covers, Lennox didn't stop him.

"I'm not gay," Lennox whispered.

"Relax," Teddy said. "You don't always got to put labels on everything."

Then Teddy pulled the covers away. Lennox lay still and let the boy do what he wanted and told himself that the moaning in the room was coming from the wind rushing at the windows.

* * *

Afterwards, Lennox dozed and woke later when he heard the door closing. He sat up, blinking stupidly and then rushed to the window in time to see the Buick's taillights easing from the parking lot. His mouth was dry with panic. The boy had stolen his car and probably his wallet and how in God's name would he explain why he'd picked up a hitchhiker and what they were doing in a motel room with one bed.

"Little queer," Lennox said. "Goddamn hustler."

He went for a drink and found the note that Teddy had placed beneath the whiskey. Teddy had "borrowed" a hundred bucks from his wallet and gone after supplies. Lennox took a shot of the whiskey and lit a cigarette and swore to himself that his relief came from not having to offer an explanation about what happened and not from his fear that he'd never see Teddy again.

Lennox finished his drink and went to the bathroom, stood staring in the mirror at his fat face with bloodshot eyes and broken capillaries in his cheeks. The self-loathing started slowly like water heating on an electric stove. It began with the sight of the bags under his eyes and moved to his hairy gut and then to the shriveled old prick that had stiffened at the touch of another man.

"Faggot," he said to the mirror.

His disgust passed. He hadn't touched Teddy. Not once. That proved that he wasn't gay. A gay guy would have touched back wouldn't he? By the time Lennox sat back on the bed with another cup of whiskey, he was sure that almost anyone would have done the same thing under the circumstances. Tonight they would find a victim, kill him or her together, and say goodbye in the morning. It would be as if none of this had ever happened, and the pain he felt in his chest at the thought of parting with Teddy was just heartburn brought on by too many cigarettes and too much whiskey.

* * *

Lennox followed Teddy's directions. After a lifetime of Fort Wayne winters, he drove expertly in the snow, guiding the Buick around snowdrifts and ice patches, as the glowing lights of the fast food joints and strip malls faded and gave way to rolling hills and stretches of fields broken only by the occasional farmhouse. Teddy was hyperactive, his hands moving constantly to light a cigarette or pick at the insulated hunting vest he'd bought with Lennox's money or adjust the sock cap on his head.

"A good time," he said every few minutes. "This is just too cool."

Lennox grunted his response and scanned the side of the road for deer. Teddy had been saying the same thing since he came back to the motel with a Walmart bag loaded with a hunting knife, his new vest, duct tape, and a flashlight. He'd spread the supplies on the bed like a kid showing off his toys on Christmas morning and told Lennox that he'd taken a drive and spotted a target, a house far enough outside of town to give them privacy and yet not too far from the main road to make getting out quickly a problem. Then he stood with his hands in his pocket and waited for Lennox to offer his approval.

"Next right," Teddy said now.

Lennox took the turn. The snowdrifts were higher here, the road curving and narrow.

"That's it," Teddy said.

A small farmhouse sat back from the highway, the last home before a crossroads. Lennox guessed the nearest neighbor was at least a quarter of a mile away. Teddy had chosen well. Lennox cut his headlights, eased into the drive and killed the engine. His throat was dry and his temples pounded. Teddy was grinning, rubbing his hands together, his eyes wide and manic. Lennox had the urge to let Teddy step out of the car and then lock the door and drive away. He was no stranger to the nerves that came before a killing, but this was different. Teddy was a wild card. Lennox had made him promise that they would play by Lennox's rules - they would not be brutal; they would terrorize the people as little as possible; when they finished they would slip away, taking nothing with them. Teddy had promised, but now his eyes gleamed and his muscles quivered with anticipation.

"Just do what I tell you," Lennox said as they started up the drive.

"You're the expert."

Teddy slid into the shadows, moving quickly and easily in the dark to the side of the front door just outside the glow of the porch lights. Lennox trudged straight to the door, out of breath, the snow swirling in his eyes. He kept one hand in his pocket on the butt of the .22 pistol. The ruse was simple. He was a stranger lost in the storm, having car trouble. Just his luck that his cell phone had gone out the first time he really needed it and would they be kind enough to allow him to call Triple A? When they invited him in, Teddy would follow.

He knocked once, waited five seconds and then knocked again. A thin, thirtyish man with horn rimmed glasses and a UK sweatshirt opened the door.

"Sorry to bother you," Lennox said. "But I guess I'm lost and my car's quit running."

The man frowned at the intrusion. A woman in the background asked who it was. Before the man could answer, Teddy jumped from the shadows, pushed Lennox aside and rammed his shoulder hard into the door, knocking the thin man off balance.

"Wait!" Lennox shouted.

The thin man brought up his arm, but it was too late. Teddy jabbed the knife hard into the guy's leg and then hit him in the chin with a right cross that sent him to the knees. A vaguely pretty blond in a bathrobe dropped a bag of microwave popcorn and started screaming. Teddy smiled at her and kicked her husband in the face.

"Please," the woman said.

She seemed to realize what was happening and broke for a cordless phone on the coffee table. Lennox had no choice. He pulled his gun and told her if she took another step he'd shoot her. Then Teddy hit her.

"Way too cool," Teddy said when the woman brought her hand to her bloody mouth and stopped screaming.

* * *

Half an hour later, Lennox sat on the sofa, smoking a cigarette, while Teddy paced the room, brandishing his knife and talking incessantly about zombies and vampires and bogeymen. This was ugly and disorderly, but Lennox was too tired to stop it.

The couple looked at him with pleading eyes, but Lennox shook his head and smoked his cigarette. They were gagged and duct taped to straight back kitchen chairs. Both of them were bleeding - the husband more profusely than the wife. Lennox figured before long the man would go into shock, since it looked as if Teddy's knife had nicked an artery - and Lennox just kept thinking, "Thank God they don't have children."

Teddy went into the kitchen, came back with a bottle of Budweiser and a salami sausage. "This is a good fucking time, man."

He downed the beer and pitched the bottle through a mirror over the mantel. Then he tilted his head and let out a grating yell. Lennox gave the woman the embarrassed, uneasy smile of an indulgent parent trying to explain the behavior of a toddler. Then he touched the .22 in his lap. He could put an end to it now. All he had to do was lift the gun, aim at the man's head and then the woman's. Their suffering would be over. But he couldn't find the energy to do it.

"It wasn't supposed to happen like this," Lennox said.

Teddy took a bite of the salami. "Relax. You're too uptight man." He chewed with his mouth open. "It's all rock n roll, baby."

Lennox stared at the television. They'd interrupted the couple's Netflix night. On screen a frightened little boy told Bruce Willis that he saw dead people. Teddy picked up the remote and clicked off the movie.

"I saw that when I was little," he said. "It's

spooky shit. Gave me nightmares."

Teddy plopped down on the sofa beside Lennox and pointed the knife at the husband. "How long until he bleeds to death?"

Lennox didn't answer. Teddy said maybe the next one would be in the gut to speed the process along. Then he cocked his head to the side and smiled at the woman and licked his lips.

"What do you think about her?" he asked.

What Lennox thought but wouldn't admit was that there was something about her hair and the line of her jaw that reminded him of Muriel. He told Teddy to leave her alone.

Teddy smirked. "Don't get jealous, Pop. We can share her." His smirk spread into a leer. "I mean both at the same time. That's a real big fantasy for a lot of girls." He leaned forward and pointed his knife at the woman. "You ever thought about it, hon? Two guys doing you together?"

The woman's eyes widened and she began to cry and shake her head. Lennox felt sick to his stomach.

Then Teddy crossed the room. He whispered something in the man's ear that made him thrash his head and strain against the tape. Lennox didn't want to watch, so he stared at his fingernails and thought about how they needed cutting. When he looked up again, the woman's robe gaped open, and Teddy stood smiling and whistling his admiration for her body.

"How'd a geek like you get a babe like this?" he said to the man. Then he slapped the guy's shoulder. "This is some fucking party." He came back to Lennox and flopped on the couch. "Let's do her man," he said. "That would be too much."

Lennox shut his eyes and shook his head. His world swirled. Then Teddy's laughter broke in, a deep, knowing laugh that Lennox found repulsive.

"Suit yourself," Teddy said. "Tell you what. I'll do her and you can watch." His hand found Lennox's lap and squeezed. "Then I'll take care of you the way you really like it."

Lennox willed himself not to respond to Teddy's touch, but he couldn't help it. When Teddy massaged his erection right in front of the man and woman, Lennox felt ashamed and filthy. Teddy let him go and went for the woman. He cut the tape from her arms and legs and dragged her from the chair by her hair. She struggled and thrashed, but Teddy hit her once and put the knife to her throat, and she stopped fighting. The husband stomped his feet on the floor and thrashed his head and came close to tipping over.

"Come on, honey," Teddy told the woman. "You know you'll like it."

Instead of leading her to the bedroom, he pushed her to the floor and ripped her robe away and told her get on all fours. The woman kept shaking her head but she did as he told her.

"Doggy style!" Teddy said. "That's the way uh huh uh huh I like it."

He ripped her panties and pushed his jeans down and wrapped his arm around her neck to hold her head in place. The woman didn't move. She just held still and waited for the inevitable.

Teddy craned his neck and grinned at Lennox. "You change your mind you can have sloppy seconds."

When Teddy turned to mount the woman, Lennox raised the pistol, aimed slowly, and then squeezed the trigger. Blood splattered the husband, who stopped struggling and stared at Lennox in disbelief. Teddy fell forward and his weight drove the woman to the floor. Teddy struggled to get back his knees. He'd almost made it when Lennox shot him again. Teddy fell on top of the wife, and she bucked her hips until he rolled off onto the floor.

"It wasn't right," Lennox said.

He nodded his head as if agreeing with himself. He'd repeat that as long as he needed to make himself believe it. If that didn't work, he'd swear he shot Teddy because the woman reminded him of Muriel. Under no circumstance would he ever believe that a second before he pulled the trigger, he'd thought, the son of a bitch is cheating on me.

"It just wasn't right," he said again.

Lennox helped the woman to her feet and set her in the chair and grabbed the duct tape to secure her. Then he went to the front window and squinted outside. It was still snowing.

"I'm sorry," he told them when he turned around.

He pulled the bottle of Jack Daniel's from his overcoat pocket and sat on the couch and took a long pull. He lit a cigarette and leaned forward with his elbows on his knees, searching for the words to tell his story. He wasn't sure where to begin, but he knew he wanted them to hear all of it - the years on the road with nothing but miles in front and behind him; the times he'd awakened alone and frightened and certain that he was dying; how he'd first met Muriel at a skating rink in Ohio; the absurd rituals they'd followed in their efforts to conceive a baby; the way she'd turned away from him now that she was dying and didn't want him with her and wouldn't answer the phone.

Afterward, he'd have to decide what to do with them. Would he kill them and move on down the road or was this the night to put an end to his useless traveling? He took a deep breath and glanced back at the window. He made a bet with himself, a traveling game that he'd played a hundred times to make meaningless decisions - if he'd eat at McDonalds or Denny's, stay on the interstate or break up the drive by taking a state road, stop for a drink or wait until he checked into his motel. If it was still snowing when he finished his story, he'd cut them loose, take one last swallow of bourbon, and put the barrel of the gun in his mouth. If it was clear, he'd make their deaths as quick and as painless as possible and get back on the road.

Lennox smiled at them and then glanced at the dead boy lying on the floor. He knew where his story would begin.

When he finished, Lennox went to the window to discover the future.

The Last Day of Your Life

On the last day of your life, you eat Corn Flakes with sliced bananas, your favorite breakfast, but this morning the phone rings just as you finish pouring skim milk over the cereal. A nasal-voiced telemarketer offers you a chance to win an all expenses-paid vacation to the Bahamas if you take a few minutes to apply for a Visa Gold Card, and although you do not need a Visa Gold Card and don't believe you'll win a trip to the Bahamas, you wait for the man to stop talking before you tell him you aren't interested. By the time you get back to your breakfast, the flakes are soggy and the milk is warm. It is not a good breakfast.

* * *

You sit on the worn vinyl sofa in your living room and make a shopping list: bread, margarine, tea bags, paper towels, toilet paper, panty liners, cigarettes.

At the last minute, almost as an afterthought, you scribble Chocolate Cake at the bottom of the list in large, bold letters. But, for one reason or another, you never go to the grocery store, and later, the police will find a crumpled grocery list on the coffee table.

"People change their minds," Detective Harold Washburn will say to his partner on the drive back to the Atlantic Avenue precinct of the Daytona Beach Police Department.

* * *

Maybe it is irony or fate or maybe just a coincidence that on the last day of your life you see the man who will investigate your murder. It happens a few minutes past noon at a red light just west of the Sea Breeze Bridge. Your cars are side by side. Detective Washburn has spent most of the morning at Raintree's garage trying to get his wife's Toyota fixed, and he is in a hurry to get back to the peninsula so he can stop at PJ's Bar and hustle down a couple of cold ones before going back to work. He glances at you, and you glance back at a forty-something man with gray in his sideburns and beads of sweat on his forehead. Neither of you thinks much of the other. Later, when he stares down at your corpse wedged in the sand beneath the pier less than two miles from the traffic light, he'll have no recollection of having seen you before.

* * *

You do not go to work at Pablo's. Today is Thursday, your day off. You hate your job, hate the constant noise of the arcade and the thick stench of hamburger grease and fried onions and draft beer. You hate serving drinks and mopping floors and telling sullen twelve-year-olds that no you will not give them change for a dollar because there are a half dozen change machines in the arcade. Of course, if you did go to work today, you might have gone home at the end of your shift and might not have met the man who took you under the pier, hit you with a right cross that cracked your jaw, ripped your denim shorts from your thighs, raped you, and stabbed you thirty-seven times.

No one can say for sure.

* * *

Just across the Sea Breeze Bridge, you stop at a 7-Eleven, buy a couple of packs of Marlboro Lights, a twenty-ounce Pepsi, and a lottery ticket. You choose the same numbers you always play, the date of your high school prom - your lucky numbers even if your luck has never come in.

The clerk, a twenty-year-old kid from Ormond Beach, working this crap job on his summer break from UCF, will remember you because he catches a look down the front of your bikini when you bend over to circle your numbers. He thinks you have very nice breasts and guesses that you are twenty-three or twenty-four, which would have made you happy since you've been worried about getting old for the last three months.

You are thirty-one years old, and your full name is Christine Diane Reynolds but most people call you Chrissy. You were born in Greenview, Kentucky, and grew up there, but now you live on Fawn Way in Daytona Beach and Kentucky seems like a strange place you might have visited once or twice as a child.

When you finish filling in your lottery numbers, you glance up and catch the clerk peering down your top, but you don't make a big deal of it because what's there to make a big deal about? You've worked enough waitressing jobs in your life to know what men are like, so you just smile at him and hand him your ticket, walk out of the store and forget about it.

He doesn't forget. He spends five or ten

minutes thinking of things he should have said to you, lines like "I don't know if I'm falling in love with you or not but I think I'm beginning to stumble," or "Hey, are your eyes bothering you, because they sure as hell are killing me," lines he's heard a frat brother use, words he is sure are charming and irresistible. Later, he will see your picture in the paper and tell everyone he knows that he met that woman who was murdered under the pier. One night, he'll get drunk and tell his pal, Jeff, that you came on to him but he'd had to work and nothing had come of it. Then the story will play out, disappear from the papers, and he'll quit talking about it.

* * *

You had a half-Siamese cat named Snoogie that was dying of feline leukemia and that you just couldn't consider putting to sleep even though you ran up a fortune in vet bills. You owned every record Bob Dylan made and played them over and over again when you were drunk or stoned. You liked gin and tonic without the lime. You loved chocolate. *Friends* was your favorite television show. For the last seven months you had been sleeping, on and off, with a forty-four-year old married man who owned an electronics store a few blocks from your apartment. You knew he would never leave his wife for you, and you knew you weren't in love with him anyway. Two or three nights a week you would lie in bed and think about your ex-husband, Derek, whom you still loved even though he was a loser, a part-time drug dealer and a full-time car salesman who had moved you down to Florida and then left you for a girl who danced at a strip club called The Bottom's Up in Coco Beach. One Thursday every other month, you drove forty-five miles north on A1A to Marineland to watch the dolphin show because you loved to see the expressions on their faces when they exploded out of the water and hung suspended in the air and although you knew it was silly, you always believed that the sound they made when they came crashing down was laughter. Every Christmas Eve, you watched *It's a Wonderful Life* and cried when Jimmy Stewart and the cast sang "Auld Lang Syne." You had plans to take a course in Real Estate Management at Daytona State College the next fall.

* * *

On the last day of your life, you spend most of the afternoon at the beach. You listen to a

Bob Dylan album on the iPod your ex left behind. You do not read the paperback Stephen King novel you brought with you. You aren't much of a reader, and anyway you only bought the novel in the first place because you thought if you were going to start college classes in the fall you should read something. You lie on a beach towel and listen to the sound of the water and the sounds of teenagers shouting over a game of beach volleyball. You think, absently, about how good the sun feels on your skin and how you love the taste of salt in the air and how you will never go back North, not even if you have to work at Pablo's until you are old, gray, and arthritic.

* * *

A sixty-seven-year old retiree from Bloomington, Indiana, walks past you on his way to a concession stand and notices your dark tan and the way your nipples poke through the thin white material of your bikini and thinks of his own wife when she was your age and wonders if you bite your bottom lip when you come the way she did. Later in the afternoon, while you are lying on your stomach, listening to yet another Bob Dylan album and half dozing, a seventeen-year-old boy from

Deland spends fifteen minutes staring at you. Then a thirty-seven-year old insurance salesman from Valdosta, Georgia, notices you lying on your back and that your cutoff shorts are unbuttoned to tan your lower stomach. You haven't been careful. Your shorts are unzipped slightly, and he catches a glimpse of pubic hair curling around your zipper. Later that night, he will make love to his wife and close his eyes and pretend she is you. He will have no idea that his fantasy girl is already dead, wedged beneath the pier less than a mile away.

* * *

You grow tired of the beach, gather your things, stop at the public shower, wash away the sand from your calves and ankles and feet. You put on a pair of sandals and climb the stairs that lead to the concrete walkway that the locals call the Boardwalk - a half-mile of bars, cafes, arcades, gift shops - and you go to your car parked in the public lot behind Burger King. You have decided not to go home, so you pull a Disney World T-shirt over your bikini top, sit in the driver's seat and brush your hair in the rearview mirror.

You walk to The Neptune, a cafe and bar with the coldest draft beer on the beach. You order a dozen steamed oysters and a small pitcher of beer and talk to Craig the bartender. He tells you about the tragic events of his latest romance, this one with a hotel manager with a wife and three kids. You listen and nod in the right places. When the oysters come, you eat them with lemon and melted butter instead of Worcestershire or Tabasco like everyone else, and you ignore Craig when he rolls his eyes. You drink the pitcher of draft and then realize that you are thirsty and order another and know that you're going to get drunk again even though you've promised yourself a dozen times you're going to cut down before it becomes a problem. A couple of women you know from the Boardwalk come in and sit beside you at the bar, and the three of you spend a couple of hours drinking, complaining about your jobs, your boyfriends, your ex-husbands. Not long before the two women leave, you switch from beer to gin and tonic because you have a good buzz going now and don't want to lose it and the beer's making you full and sleepy.

When your friends leave, you think about going home, but you don't. Maybe you think how it's only a quarter till eight and how you'll spend the evening stretched out on the sofa watching reruns and waiting for Mr. Electronics Store to call but knowing he won't because it's Thursday night and on Thursday nights Alex and his wife go to the dog races. Maybe you think it's dangerous to go home because tonight you're drunk and depressed, tired from your day in the sun, and you'll do something stupid like call your ex-husband and beg him to come back to you or maybe, God help you, open another bottle of gin and use it to wash down half a bottle of Percodan. Or maybe you're just drunk and you want to stay that way for awhile, want to keep drinking and listening to music and walking from bar to bar on the Boardwalk with a sweet breeze coming in from the water.

* * *

You know quite a few people on the Boardwalk and quite a few people know you. Later, they will tell Detective Washburn that they saw you at McGoo's on the north end at nine-thirty, sitting at the bar, talking to a couple of regulars, drinking gin and tonic. They will say that at eleven they saw you at the Gator Grille, talking to a gray-haired man who was wearing golf pants and an Izod shirt. The last person who will remember seeing you is the bouncer at Razzles. He'll say that you were drunk, and that he didn't charge you the cover because he knew you, and that you blew him a kiss as a thank you and then disappeared into the club crowd.

No one else notices you until the next morning when a man and his wife and three-year-old son are walking on the beach. The little boy runs away from his parents and darts under the pier. The little boy refuses to come out, so his father goes after him and spots the child hunkered on his knees in the sand. Then he sees you - a woman with long brown hair hanging in her eyes, her body twisted slightly, blood caking her chest and stomach and bare hips. He grabs his son by the hand, pulls him away. The three of them will have their pictures in the paper, their faces on the local news, and a story to tell their friends back in Ohio.

* * *

It's after midnight and you're tired from the sun and the booze and the music, and you're thinking how you've really wasted your day off and how hung over you're going to be in the morning. The music keeps playing, but you don't know the song, and the heavy drumbeat gets in your head and pounds along with the ache in your temples. The place is crowded, and you shove your way to the bar and order a glass of ice water because you need to sober up before you drive home, and you gag at the smell of sweat and aftershave and cheap perfume. While you're waiting on your ice water, you think about your mother and father and remind yourself to call them before you go to work tomorrow. It's been too long since you talked to them, and you think you should make plans to go home for a week or so near the end of the summer because they're not getting any younger. You think about their cabin on the Green river and how you and your dad could make a lunch and spend the day on the water like you did when you were a little girl. The bartender brings your water and grabs your money from the bar, and you stand there, wishing the goddamn music would stop.

You notice the guy a couple of seats down the bar. He's not bad looking, mid-thirties, sandy hair, green eyes, nice smile. He tips his beer in your direction. You notice his wedding ring and think oh brother that's just what I need, and then you realize you're too tired to be horny anyway, so you shake your head and finish your water in a gulp.

Outside, the breeze is warm and soft coming off the water, and it clears your head a little. It's low tide, and the waves lap gently at the shore, and you think you might as well walk part of the way on the beach because you love the feel of sand and water on your toes. You haven't gone far, and you can still hear the pounding of the music in your ears. Maybe you're thinking about starting classes in the fall, wondering what it will be like to be back in school after so many years. You don't notice the heavy-set man who moves up fast behind you, and you're thinking this isn't happening to me, this isn't happening at all.

* * *

Or you're tired from the sun and booze and music, and you're thinking you don't want to go home, not now, not back to that apartment that's so goddamn empty. You squeeze into the bar and order another drink, feeling the push of bodies against you, smelling sweat and aftershave and expensive perfume. The music is pounding, but you're not sure what the song is, just something with a heavy beat, something with drums, which seem to get into your chest and pound with your heart, and let's face it, you're horny. You're thirty-one-years old, and you haven't had sex in two weeks because the asshole married guy you're dating hasn't been able to get away from his family, and there's nothing wrong with a healthy, thirty-one year old woman being horny, wanting to be touched and held and just fucked.

Then you see him, a nice looking guy sitting at the bar. He has a deep tan and blue eyes and a nice smile, although you notice a few wrinkles around his eyes and his face is a bit round, bloated maybe. You think, not bad, maybe not Johnny Depp but not bad. It's obvious from the way he's looking at you that he's interested and what the hell would the harm be in it anyway? He gets up and walks toward you, and you think he looks like a nice guy, a nice guy probably from Michigan or Maine or Minnesota because you like the sound of all those M words in your head. He smiles. He shouts something over the music. You shout back and let him buy you a drink even though you know you have had too many, and he squeezes in beside you at the bar. The two of you talk or at least try to talk over the roaring music, and he buys you another drink and touches your leg high up on your thigh, and that touch feels good, and you notice he isn't wearing a wedding ring, which you know doesn't mean anything but the two of you are following a don't ask, don't tell policy tonight. He asks you to come back to his room, just a short walk up the beach, and you go because he really seems like a nice guy and you're drunk and lonely.

Outside, the wind is warm and salty coming off the water, and he takes your hand and says, "Let's walk the beach, get our feet wet," and that seems like a good idea because you love the beach, love the sand and water on your toes. He stops under the pier, and it's just the two of you, and maybe you step toward him, lean on your tip toes because you're expecting to be kissed, wanting to be kissed, and when he hits you, you're not thinking anything other than this isn't what's supposed to happen, this isn't what's supposed to happen at all.

* * *

Or you order another gin and tonic even though you don't want another drink. You wait and smoke a cigarette and feel men push against you, and you think about the bottle of gin at home and about the bottle of Percodan in the medicine cabinet. You think about your parents and how they would feel and how that would serve your father right, the groping, grabbing, feel-copping son of a bitch, and then you think about your ex-husband and how he'd realize, finally realize, how much he'd lost when he left you. Then, when the bartender shoves your drink to you and grabs your money from the bar, you realize you won't do it. You'll go home. You'll think about it, maybe even take the pills out of the bottle when you get there.

Then you see him. He's sitting down the bar, and his eyes are locked on you, a tall, thin man with dark hair and a complexion the color of eggshells. You know him now, and he knows you, knows where you're going, where you have been, and when he comes to you, he doesn't even offer to buy you a drink because neither of you needs to pretend. This is him, the one you've been looking for all your life even though you haven't known you've been looking. When he takes your hand, you know you've found your Prince, your love, your one and only.

Outside, the wind is salty and warm on your skin, and you take him by the hand without speaking because there's nothing to say, not now. He's come to save you in the only way you can be saved, and you think of the diary you kept as a little girl and how you always imagined him with his dark hair and his pale skin, and you pull him to the beach because you want to feel the sand and water on your toes one last time.

Under the pier, you whisper that you love him. He doesn't answer but you can tell. When he hits you, you're not thinking anything except this is the way it's supposed to be.

Little Bell, the Beasley Boys, and a Long Road Home

Little Bell wasn't from Kentucky, and Little Bell wasn't even her real name, but Kentucky is where she ended up, and Little Bell is what people called her. The way it happened? Her momma sold her to Big Poppa, a hunchbacked old man who had body odor and a boil and who drove a pickup truck with more rust than either paint or primer. Little Bell didn't know the make or model.

There was a lot she wasn't sure of. For one thing, she was never certain of the circumstances of her birth, neither the when nor the where of it. She just knew that somehow she found herself alive and wandering the byways and highways with her momma. Year after year they wandered as Little Bell's legs grew longer and her breasts filled out and time moved on. Little Bell didn't know why. She wasn't sure what was wrong with her either, just that something was, and this something led her momma to shake her head and say with a mixture of affection and vexation, "Big as you are and as old as you'll get, you'll always have the mind of a child."

Uncertainty was as much of a part of her life as the endless highways, so it was no surprise that the only thing she knew about the particulars of the deal between her momma and Big Poppa was that he handed her momma a wad of money and a bus ticket to parts unknown. This transaction took place outside a Dairy Maid somewhere west of the tall hills she and her momma had crossed when they came into Kentucky. It was summer and shimmers of heat rose from the blacktop whenever a car passed by. Her momma bought her a super-big chocolate milkshake, kissed her cheek, reminded her to say her prayers every night, told her they'd meet on the other side of the rainbow if the Lord was willing and the creeks didn't rise.

Little Bell wasn't but about halfway finished with her milkshake when Big Poppa turned off the highway onto a narrow dirt road that cut through an endless cornfield and then, after they'd bounced through a half dozen ruts and washouts, pulled into the cornfield itself.

He didn't put his thing in her, but he made her lie back against the door. The seat was itchy, and her legs were so long she had to hang them over his shoulders. He used his hands on her. He had large, work-hardened fingers with untrimmed nails. It hurt pretty bad, and it seemed like it went on twice as long as forever. She was bleeding, and that scared her. He pulled his hand away and looked at it, and she thought surely he'll stop now, but he just smiled and smacked his lips and went right back at it. Desperate for it to end, she mimicked the howls and gyrations she'd witnessed her mother make in the backseats of cars and on cheap motel beds, bucking her hips and slinging her head and screaming, "Oh God, oh God. Goddamn." That seemed to satisfy him. His hand slowed, then stopped, and he pulled it away, wiped it on the leg of his already nasty workpants.

"You a sweet one," he said, putting the truck in gear. "It takes you a little while to warm up, but when you go off, you ring just like a bell."

The name stuck. Little Bell. She figured it was as good as any other.

As the truck bounced back onto the dirt road and over the ruts and then onto the blacktop, she realized blood was running down her thigh, and she wondered if she would bleed to death but decided she probably wouldn't. If having men put things inside you was fatal, her momma would have been dead and buried a long time ago.

"I'm bleeding on your seat," she said.

He glanced at her, raised a bushy eyebrow, finally got it. "Oh," he said. "Yeah, I suspect you are."

He reached into a greasy hamburger sack and pulled out a handful of balled napkins, pitched them on her lap. She stuffed a couple inside her underwear the way she'd seen her momma do, lifted her hips and spread out the rest on the seat the best she could.

They headed east back toward the tall hills, and she leaned against the seat and sipped her milkshake. It was melted now, but she didn't know when or if she'd get another, so she drank it anyway. The warm milk and sickly sweet syrup was too much for her though, and Big Poppa had to pull off to the side of road to let her vomit. She swore she'd never drink a melted milkshake again, not even if she was starving. Call it a hard lessoned learned in a life that was destined to be full of them.

* * *

Home became a rusted Airstream trailer at the edge of a gully on what people called Beasley Hill. The trailer was tiny, cluttered with broken furniture and rotting cardboard boxes. They gave her a kerosene heater for the winter, but there was no air conditioning or even a box fan to make the summer bearable, and on glaring July and August afternoons, Little Bell felt as if she lived inside a tin can that had been booted into a fire. The bathroom floor had rotted and collapsed. She relieved herself in a mop bucket that she dumped out of the back door every morning. The trailer reeked of mildew and raw sewage and the odor of the men who visited her at odd hours of the day and night.

She wasn't sure if those visits were a curse or a reprieve. She hated the feel of their hands and the things they did to her, cringed at their smell and the whimpering-dog sound the rollaway bed made when they climbed on top of her. But at least those visits broke up the monotony, the slow crawl of days. She began pretending that she was her mother, even saying aloud some of the hurtful things her mother was prone to say to make it seem more real. Some days she sat by a window that looked out over a trash-strewn gully and imagined that her mother was living in a pretty place near the ocean and that her mother had finally found "the good man" that she'd been looking for her entire life and that this good man had a "normal" little girl who never sassed or got whiny when she was tired or any of the other things that had angered her momma. When she imagined that little girl, the jealousy was like a fist in the pit of her stomach, but she made herself do it anyway. Other days when she felt particularly blue, she'd imagine her mother lying in a ditch beside a ribbon of asphalt, hidden from passing cars by waist-high weeds, the flies and beetles crawling over her staring eyes.

Twice a day someone came from a large, unpainted farmhouse farther up the ridge to bring her food and water - dry cereal or cold biscuits for breakfast, bologna sandwiches or two-day-old leftovers for dinner. Miss Ethel usually came in the mornings. She looked to be as old as the mine-scared mountains that Little Bell could see from the back window. She had iron gray hair and a saggy chin and milky blue eyes. Little Bell thought she looked just like that sweet old lady with the yellow bird that Little Bell had seen in a cartoon when she and her momma were staying with a man up in Pennsylvania. Her natural inclination was to run to the old lady and hug her tight and blubber against her shoulder, but this little old lady didn't have a bird, and she wasn't nice at all.

"Keep your filthy hands off me, split tail," the old lady said. "You do that again I'll loosen your teeth for you."

Little Bell came to hate Miss Ethel - her rounded shoulders, her puckered mouth, the way she leaned against the door and smoked a Kool while she waited for Little Bell to finish eating. Sometimes she imagined using a spoon to scoop out the old bitch's cataracted eyes.

"You're a scrawny thing, but that won't keep them away," Miss Ethel said that first day. "Men catch word there's a woman around, they swarm like flies."

When Miss Ethel was "feeling poorly," a raven-haired girl who wasn't much past five years old brought Little Bell her breakfast. She never spoke, never even met Little Bell's eye.

In the evenings, it was usually a man who brought her dinner, not always the same one and not one of her customers but one of the "Beasley Boys" as she heard the men who came to lay with her called them. Little Bell gathered that the Beasley Boys were "outlaws" and that everyone in this part of Kentucky was bad scared of them. God knew there were enough of them to fight a war. There was an older one with threads of gray in his jet-black hair and a cross-eyed one a few years younger and another who had a jagged scar across his forehead, as if someone had tried to scalp him but changed their mind. The one who frightened her the most when she first saw him was a younger man with snow-colored hair and tattoos scrawled from his neck down both arms. He called himself Cottonmouth and smoked home-rolled cigarettes and reeked of whiskey. That first day she was sure he'd come to kill her, but he'd just set her sandwich on the table, nodded and walked out the door. The next time he hung around, smoking a home rolled and humming some song that sounded vaguely familiar. The third time he actually talked to her.

"You like Kool-Aid?" he asked.

She said yes around a mouthful of cold, greasy hamburger. He told her he'd bring her a packet, said he sure wouldn't want to have to drink plain old water all the time. She thanked him, and he blushed a little and shrugged and said it wouldn't be no trouble, but she shouldn't tell anyone about it, especially not his grandma, Miss Ethel.

"Meanest old bitch God ever suffered to live," he said not with a hint of admiration.

After he'd visited a few more times, she

worked up the courage to ask after Big Poppa. When he'd dropped her off, he said he'd be back to collect her soon but a considerable amount of time had passed and she was wondering.

"Big Poppa?" Cottonmouth said. "Shit. Don't be worrying about him."

"I ain't," she said. "I was just wondering."

He nodded and flicked his ash out the cracked door. "What it was, see, was the old man needed to borrow some money from Young Sam, that's my brother. Old Sam he was my daddy but he passed on. Anyway, you was what they call collateral on the loan, but he couldn't never come up with the jack to pay what was owed."

"So he run off and left me?"

"Maybe." Cottonmouth shrugged and tipped a bottle of whiskey. "More likely the buzzards carried him away."

* * *

Her mind didn't register the men who came to visit. They were just a blur of leering faces and sour breath. She knew that she'd seen some of them before and that she was seeing others for the first time, but none of that mattered. Their coming and going simply marked the passing of days.

The first time the man in the uniform came was different. There was a quick, impatient knock and then the door opened, and he stepped inside - a balding, broad-shouldered man with a thick mustache, a badge on his shirt and a gun belt that hung loose on his narrow hips. Seeing him brought a surge of hope. Her momma had taught her to shrink away from men who wore uniforms, but Little Bell knew that those men could sometimes help you. When he first stepped into the trailer and looked her over from the top of her head to the tip of her toes, she was certain he'd come to save her. But he didn't say, "Everything's all right now," or "Lord have mercy, what have we got here?" or "I've come to rescue you," or any of the things she thought he might.

"You ain't as pretty as Young Sam said you was," he said instead. "But I reckon you ain't too bad."

Little Bell knew then and there that she wasn't ever going to be saved, that her momma and Big Poppa and all the Beasleys and the law and maybe the world itself had conspired to bring her here. She figured maybe this where she was meant to be, so she decided right then and there that she'd just give up thinking about any place else. This was her life.

She reckoned the best she could do was live it.

* * *

A few weeks later Cottonmouth brought her a gift - a pretty, yellow sundress with white flowers printed all over it.

"This used to be my sister's," he said. "Audrey Anne."

"She outgrow it?" Little Bell asked, twirling to model it.

"Nah," he said. "Son of a bitch she married choked the life out of her because she close danced with a lease man come down from Indiana."

"Oh."

He shrugged again. "I figured you got tired of wearing the same clothes all the time."

"Thank you." She stood on her tiptoes and kissed his cheek. "You're the only one who's nice to me."

A few weeks later as the grass was browning and the leaves falling, he brought her what was destined to be her best friend. A Raggedy Ann doll with yellow stains beneath its eyes and hardened gum in its mop-string hair. She thought it was beautiful, but Cottonmouth shoved it at her as if it were an unclean thing that he didn't want to touch anymore.

"Here you go," he said. "I thought of you when I found it. Because of the red hair."

Little Bell touched her temple. She'd forgotten that she was redheaded. There were no mirrors in the trailer, and the only glimpses she'd caught of herself had been distorted reflections in the trailer's dirty windows.

"I love her," Little Bell said. "She's just perfect."

He blushed but gave her a pleased smile. "You all grown up but you still simple," he said. "You know what that makes you?"

"Uh huh," Little Bell said. "Mildly retarded is the words my momma used."

"Well fuck her," Cottonmouth said. "It makes you special, makes you as pure as an angel."

She decided then and there to call the doll Angel Bell. She slept with it every night, hugging up to it the way she'd once hugged up to her mother when they were rough sleeping. In the long, gray days after the rain set in and the hillside turned to a slippery mire of reddish mud, Angel Bell became her very best friend. They shared imaginary birthday cakes and had tea parties. They complained about Miss Ethel's nastiness. They talked about how nice Cottonmouth could be and how gross it was that the short, dark-haired man, Young Sam, was always picking his nose. Later, when some smelly, overweight old guy drifted in to rut with Little Bell, they'd laugh about his belly or the way he shivered like a wet dog when he lay with her or how his face turned purple.

"Most of them ain't no different than hogs," Angel Bell would say, her flat blue eyes gleaming. "Snorting and rooting and thinking they're kings of the world."

Angel Bell could always make Little Bell smile. No matter how mean Miss Ethel had been or how many days went by without Cottonmouth coming to visit or how many men passed in and out of the trailer, Angel Bell made it bearable. Little Bell and Angel Bell. Two of a kind. Best friends forever.

* * *

Time passed the way it always does with days bleeding into weeks and weeks into months, months into years. During warm weather, Little Bell took to venturing outside to walk around the yard or pat the scroungy yellow dogs that hung around the gullies where the Beasleys dumped their trash or, more often, to sit on the trailer's rusted metal stairs with Angel Bell on her lap and watch the cars come and go at the huge metal garage next to the

Beasleys' farmhouse. At first the cars were long and rumbling. The men and boys who went into the garage came out carrying liquor bottles or cases of beer. Seasons passed. The automobiles got smaller and quieter and then large again but still quiet and strange looking as if they were hybrids of pickup trucks and cars. Now, the people, women as well as men, who came to the garage left with small, plastic bags instead of liquor bottles. Meth, crystal, crank, they called it. Little Bell didn't care. It was enough for her to watch the cars with the sun on her skin and her best friend on her lap.

Miss Ethel no longer brought her breakfast. A stroke, Cottonmouth said, looking all jittery and smelling like cat piss and garbage. They were going to bury her in Rose Hill cemetery.

"Oh," Little Bell said, trying to think of fitting words to say and grasping at what Cottonmouth himself had once said. "She was the meanest old bitch God ever suffered to live."

She didn't see the slap coming, so she took it full force right across the mouth. Her teeth shredded her lips and blood ran down her chin, stained her neck crimson.

"You ever talk about my granny like that again, I'll fucking kill you," he said.

Then he stormed away and slammed the

door so hard he nearly ripped it from the hinges. Little Bell sat on the floor and wept.

"He ain't no different from the rest of them," Angel Bell said, her sewn mouth twisting into a sneer. "They don't nobody care about you and me but you and me. Don't you ever forget it, Little Bell. Don't you dare."

* * *

The years went by. One day Cottonmouth stopped coming to the trailer. Little Bell asked after him.

"Dead," Young Sam - fat and bald now - said as he set a plate of moldy Hamburger Helper in front of her. "Fucking idiot slammed his truck into a pine tree up on Red Lick Road. They had to pick bits of him out of the weeds."

Time passed. The raven-haired girl who'd replaced Miss Ethel as the breakfast bringer and whose name was Millie had grown up now, and she had a stomach that looked as if it might explode.

"Pregnant," Angel Bell explained. "Stupid cunt's going to spew out another of those worthless Beasley Boys."

One day the raven-haired girl whose name was Millie didn't show up to bring her breakfast. No one came for three days, and

Little Bell couldn't stand the hunger pangs anymore.

There were dozens of balloons tied to the farmhouse's front porch rail and nearly as many cars parked in the drive. Little Bell and Angel Bell sneaked behind the house and looked through a window at a bunch of people sitting around a long, wooden table. They were laughing and the raven-haired girl had a wrinkled, red-faced baby in her lap.

"Wriggles like a worm," Angel Bell said. "And probably smells like shit and throw up."

Little Bell agreed that this was so. Then she and Angel Bell slipped down the hillside to where the Beasleys dumped their fresh garbage, and Little Bell ripped open plastic bags until she found half of a grilled cheese sandwich and a few chicken legs with meat still on the bones and a fist-sized ball of fried potatoes. She scurried back to the trailer, cleaned egg shells and coffee grounds from the sandwich, picked dog hair from the potatoes, then wolfed them down, holding her nose against the stench to keep from throwing it all back up again.

"Goddamn," Angel Bell said, showing a mouthful of teeth that Little Bell didn't know she had. "You eat like a stray dog while those fuckers sit up there with all the food in the world, living it up on money they made from pedaling your ass to every hillbilly in these godforsaken mountains."

Little Bell was shocked by both the language Angel Bell used and the hatred in her eyes, but she understood the sentiment. She understood it with every sour and moldy bite she took.

* * *

The world moved on. The men didn't come to visit her as often now. The ones who did seemed older or maybe just sadder. They all reeked of either whiskey or that cat-piss smell that she came to understand was "meth." None of these men wanted to look at her, and when they finished they slunk away.

More little red, wriggling babies came and grew older. Young Sam, fat and stoop-shouldered now, called them his grandbabies and put up a tire swing and a big trampoline. Little Bell stood at the window watching pint-sized Beasleys bounce up and down, up and down, their shrieks and giggles filling the world. The people who brought her food and water - only once a day now so that there was always a gnawing hunger in the pit of her stomach - were strangers. They looked at her as if she were no more than an unpleasant obligation, not much different from an old mule that had once been useful but now lacked the good sense and the common courtesy to lie down and die. They brought her food and sighed with the burden of it and went back to their lives. Angel Bell told her it didn't matter. They had each other. The rest of them could burn in hell with Miss Ethel and Big Poppa, Cottonmouth and her momma.

"Momma?" Little Bell asked. "You think she's dead?"

"Sure she is," Angel Bell said. "A whore like that? She wasn't worth nothing anyway. "

Little Bell cried at the thought of it, but Angel Bell rebuked her for her foolishness. Her momma hadn't loved her. If she had, Little Bell would have been somewhere else living some other life. No one had ever loved Little Bell but Angel Bell. That was just the way it was. In all of the world, they only had each other.

* * *

Late summer. God only knew what year. Little Bell sat on the trailer steps with Angel Bell on her knee. Some of the grownups were burning trash in a gully, and gray-black smoke seeped across the sky. A bunch of the little

Beasleys were playing in the yard. She wasn't sure who they were, just that they were all Beasleys, cousins and nephews and grandchildren. They weaved their bikes between new SUVs and sports cars with metallic paint gleaming in the sun and called each other sons of bitches and bastards and said "you fucker" whenever one of them did something the other didn't like.

"They all live up there like wasps in a nest or bees in a hive," Angel Bell whispered.

For once Little Bell ignored her. Her eyes were locked on a tall, lean boy of eleven who straddled a ten-speed bike at the edge of the fire. He was shirtless, his brown skin gleaming with sweat, his hair the color of freshly fallen snow. He was the spitting image of Cottonmouth. "You're the only one who's nice to me," she'd told him one time.

"He mashed your mouth for you when you spoke the truth about his damned old grandma. You ain't forgot that have you?" Angel Bell said.

Little Bell hadn't forgotten, but that seemed far away and unimportant. Now she descended the rusted steps and shuffled forward on trembling, uncertain legs.

"Hey little boy!" she shouted. "I knowed your daddy. Or maybe it was your granddaddy I knowed, but he looked just like you," she said.

The children turned to her, their faces red and sweaty in the sun. They were smiling, and she smiled back and held up a shaky arm.

"Hey little boy!" she shouted again, then couldn't think of anything else to say, so just kept shuffling forward, saying it over and over again. "Hey little boy!"

"Get out of here you old witch!" a girl with sunburned cheeks shouted.

Little Bell kept walking forward. The other children joined in with the little girl. Witch, witch, witch! Their voices were a singsong chant.

The boy with the snow-white hair didn't join them. He just stood there, straddling that big, shiny bicycle, a smile curling the corners of his mouth.

Little Bell held Angel Bell in front of her. "Look here at what he give me! Her name's Angel Bell and she's so pretty. Little boy, that fella who looked like you gave me my best friend."

He leaned forward and picked up a rock. She'd just called to him again when it hit her collarbone. Hard. She let out a surprised yelp, and tears watered her eyes.

Then he threw another rock and another and the rest of the kids joined in until she was caught in a thunderstorm of stones that bit the bones of her hands and arms and ankles. She tried to say please stop but the word wouldn't form on her lips. Then a sharp cornered rock caught her in the forehead and staggered her, and blood ran into her eye.

"Get on out of here, you nasty old bitch!" the boy shouted at her. "You ain't nothing but a goddamn haint!"

Another rock hit her and then another. Soon all of the children rushed her, kicking dust with their heels and throwing stones. Little Bell screamed in pain and ran, staggering to the left and right. Finally one of the adults stuck her head out of the door.

"Y'all leave that old witch alone now or I'm going to stripe all you asses."

One of the kids hollered a "fuck you" at the woman, and she ran out into the yard, fat jiggling in a pair of lime green shorts. The kids scattered, all but the snow-haired boy. He was looking right at Little Bell, waving something in her direction. At first she couldn't tell what it was. Then she looked down and realized that her own hand was empty. She'd dropped Angel Bell. In her selfish, stupid panic, she'd abandoned her only friend. Her legs wanted to buckle, her stomach heave from the weight of her sin.

"Hey!" she shouted, her voice a dry croak.

"Give her back to me."

The boy grinned. Then he turned and casually pitched Angel Bell into the trash fire. Little Bell pressed her hands to her ears to quiet the sound of her best friend's screaming.

* * *

On the third night of grieving, Angel Bell's voice called to her from the ashes. At first Little Bell was certain that she was dreaming, but even as she was rubbing her tear-swollen eyes and wiping the drool from the corner of her mouth, she clearly heard the voice again.

"Listen to me," Angel Bell whispered. "Put on your yellow dress and that pair of tennis shoes you found in the back of the closet. Then do just what I tell you."

* * *

It was long after midnight when Little Bell found her in the ashes of the trash heap. One leg was burned off; most of her hair was gone and what remained crumbled at the touch of Little Bell's hand; the left side of her face was crumpled and singed. But Angel Bell was alive and, when she spoke, her voice was stronger than ever.

The gas cans were in a lean-to shed beside the garage; the pliers were on a shelf just above the push mower and lawn trimmer and shovels. In a washtub of random tools, she found a big, deer skinning knife with specks of rust and blood on its blade. She grabbed a canvas bag laced with spider webs from a table near the door. Angel Bell told her to put the knife inside the bag. They'd both come in handy a little later.

It took longer to find the matches, but Angel Bell reasoned it out and guided her to the parked cars in front of the farmhouse. She found a matchbook in the cluttered glove box of a Ford F-150. Taking along empty McDonald's and Wendy's sacks for kindling was Little Bell's idea, and her heart thrilled with pride at having thought of it on her own.

Angel Bell told her how to loosen the valve on the propane tank and which way to turn it to flood gas into the house. Then Little Bell went to the back, sloshed gasoline on the door and along the windowsills, lugged another can around front and soaked the porch. Traumatized by her experience in the trash fire, Angel Bell insisted she be left on the hood of the F-150 before Little Bell lit the kindling.

It took her six tries to strike the first match her hand was trembling so hard, but finally she managed. She dropped the lit match into a McDonald's bag on top of balled up napkins. When it caught she used it to light the Wendy's bag, threw both of them at the backdoor and waited until the flames caught before she ran to the front and lit two more paper sacks and dropped them on the porch.

"Run, you crazy bitch!" Angel Bell shouted. "Run like the devil."

And so she did. She snatched her poor, scarred doll from the hood of the truck and ran for the trailer. She was almost there when the house exploded, showering the drive and the garage and the hillside with sparks and broken glass. Little Bell grabbed at the side of the trailer for support and then turned to look back. She saw the snow-haired boy standing at the attic window, his face pressed against the glass, his eyes wide with terror.

She waved at him. But he didn't wave back. He was too busy burning.

* * *

This is where she ended up - walking down the side of a narrow, winding asphalt road in the first, thin light of morning. Crickets chirped at her passing. Cars swerved to keep from hitting her, their drivers glaring through rearview mirrors. Finally, just as the road hit a level patch, a coal truck came rumbling along. It was barely past her when its brake lights flickered. The truck choked and shuddered as the driver geared her down and pulled onto the sawdust and sand shoulder of the road.

"Ma'am?" he said when he opened the passenger door. "Are you all right? Has something happened?"

She didn't know how to answer that, so she shrugged. Then she caught a glimpse of herself in the truck's side mirror. For the length of a heartbeat, she thought it must be someone else she was seeing - a stoop-shouldered old woman with more gray than red in her hair, deep lines in her face, a few jagged and brown teeth in her head, a bone-thin hag in a faded yellow dress that was ripped at the seams so that her thighs and her gray and bushy down-below hair was showing, her withered breasts sagging from the top, a charred and hideous Raggedy Ann doll dangling by her leg.

"What's happened?" the trucker asked. "Ma'am? Do you know who you are?"

She didn't. One thing was for sure, the reflection in the mirror told her that she wasn't Little Bell anymore.

"Get on in ma'am," the trucker said. "I'll find someone to help you."

She climbed into the cab, closed the door behind her as he shifted gears and pulled out onto the road. Settling into the seat, she laid the canvas bag on her lap to cover herself and set Angel Bell between them as protection against whatever it was the trucker might have in mind.

"It'll be all right," he said. "I'll get you someplace where they can help you."

His voice sounded kind, but when she glanced at his hands she noticed how the sandy-colored hairs curled around the too-tight band of his wristwatch and the way his knuckles whitened and swelled as he gripped the steering wheel. It occurred to her that she'd seen those hands before.

Then the truck began its climb up another steep hill. Little Bell felt its shudders and rumbles deep in her bones.

"You just hold on now," the trucker said. "I'll take care of you."

Little Bell nodded and listened to Angel Bell's whisper. "Tell him to pull off to the side of the road. Say you're feeling sick at the stomach. Men ain't nothing but hogs, no matter how nice they seem to be."

"He's just being helpful," Little Bell thought.

But Angel Bell wasn't having any of it. "You

done argued with me once and look what happened. Just do what I say and we'll both be better off for it. You believe me, Little Bell. Men are hogs. You know what you do to a hog, don't you? You butcher it. That's what it was put on earth for."

When the truck crested the hill, the world unraveled in front of them. There were trees and gullies and small white houses and a far off clump of buildings that was one town or another. That should have comforted her, but she knew there was plenty of dirt and gravel roads leading nowhere and surrounded by dark woods between here and there, and he might decide to take any of them.

Now the trucker geared down for the twisting descent into the valley. When she glanced at him, she saw he was paying more attention to her than to the road. His eyes lingered on her bare breasts, and his lips puckered the way her own did when she bit into something rotten hidden amongst the scraps the Beasleys threw her way. But there was a hungriness in his expression, too, and she thought of the times her belly had been so empty that she'd wolfed down that rotten, soured food and been thankful to have it.

"It's a shame," he said. "You got no idea who you are or where you came from, do you?"

he asked.

Now his voice didn't seem so kind. "Hogs ain't kind," Angel Bell said. "They're just hungry."

But surely not for the withered old woman who had appeared in the truck's mirror. And yet his eyes kept coming back to the sagging, ghost-white skin of her breasts and lingering on her puckered nipples. Then she thought of a funny book that one of her momma's "boyfriends" had shown her in the forever ago. This funny book hero had all kinds of powers, but what she remembered now was his special eyes that could see right through to the center of things.

"X-ray eyes," Angel Bell whispered. "That's what your whore of a momma told you they were."

Maybe that's what the trucker had, eyes that let him see right through the withered thing she was now to the Little Bell she'd once been. She slipped her hand inside her canvas bag and touched the knife for comfort.

"I wonder if anybody's looking for you." The trucker glanced at her and sadly shook his head. "I don't reckon they are."

Then he slowed down the truck even further, but she wasn't sure why. They were near the bottom of the hill and the town was getting closer, so that could have been it. But up ahead she saw a gravel road that sliced into the trees, and he might be preparing to take a turn.

She tightened her grip on the knife's handle. She closed her eyes and waited. Town or the dark woods? It didn't really matter. Either way, she was headed back to where she came from.

The Last Wrestling Bear in West Kentucky

This is where I am: sitting at a table in Redheaded Ray's Roadhouse five miles outside of Greenview, Kentucky, listening to my ex-convict son talk about the future while we wait for the wrestling bear. Danny is twenty-two, an optimist even though he's spent the last seventeen months at Roderer Correctional and has now landed back in Harps County with no girlfriend, no job and no real hope of landing either of them in the foreseeable future. Still, he believes finding the wrestling bear is an omen, a sign better times are coming. Me? I don't see the connection.

He strips the label from his bottle of Bud and grins at me. "Okay, listen," he says. "I've been talking about heading to Montana or Wyoming for years, and they've got bears out there, right? A week after I come home, we run across this one." He drops the stripped label in an ashtray, leans back in his chair and folds his hands behind his head. "You tell me."

There's no point in telling him that Redheaded Ray's is a place people come to drink, fight, maybe pick up a late-night companion, not to look for omens. Lynyrd Skynyrd plays over and over on an old jukebox; the shelf behind the bar is lined with jars of pickled pigs' feet, circa 1975; there are fliers that advertise a Wednesday night line dance and a Saturday night wet T-shirt contest; a banner on the far wall says, "Welcome to Redheaded Ray's, Home of Elmore the Wrestling Bear!"

It's six thirty on a Saturday, still hot and bright outside, but the bar is blissfully dark and mortuary cool. Beer-bellied farmers, out-of-work-miners, a few would-be outlaws, and hard-eyed women wearing too much makeup and short skirts that show the white, puckered skin of their thighs shoot pool in the back room or share pitchers at the tables or stand two-deep at the bar. A couple of women look our way, glance at the dance floor, smile at Danny. When he left for prison, he was a tall, gawky kid with chronic acne and a facial tic from years of snorting Crystal Meth. Now he is thick and healthy. With his crew cut, his clear, blue eyes, his broad shoulders and defined biceps, he looks more like a Marine home on furlough than a lawnmower thief out on parole.

I say, "You really want to wrestle a bear?"

He says he always had a thing for bears, used to collect stuffed ones, pestered his mom to take him to Yellowstone for summer vacation when he was a little kid. He lights a cigarette, grins at me through the smoke, his eyes crinkled, his lips spread tight - the same smirk his mother used to give when she beat me in a game of hearts.

"You probably wouldn't remember that, would you?"

By the late nineties most of the coalmines in this part of West Kentucky packed up their operations and lit out for shallower veins and union-free labor, leaving behind thousands of acres of ravaged land and a few rusting shovels to remind us of better times. I figured if it was good enough for Peabody Coal, it was good enough for me, so I loaded my life in the back of a pickup and left behind a soon-to-be-ex-wife and a five-year-old son. For the next fifteen years, I worked the oilfields in Texas and Oklahoma and Louisiana, but things went sour down there, too. After I lost my job and my girlfriend and got busted for a DUI in Shreveport, I decided it was time to see

Kentucky again. Now I work at an Ideal station, pumping gas, checking oil and wiping windshields for a nickel better than minimum wage.

When I first came back to town, Danny and I bumped up against each other at Wal-Mart and the Eight Ball Lounge. The first few weeks he'd just glare at me, the muscles in his jaw working and his lips twisted into what he probably believed was a tough-guy sneer. He seemed trying to work himself up to something, but I got tired of waiting. Finally, one night at the Eight Ball, I told him we had a choice. We could step outside or we could have a drink. He held my eyes for a minute as if he were debating it. Then flipped his greasy bangs from his eyes and said what the hell, yesterday was long gone anyway.

After that we shot pool a couple of times, shared a few pitchers. Then he went to prison, and I wrote him a few letters. Now this is what I know about my son: he got hooked on meth during his senior year in high school; he was desperate and foolish enough to believe that he could make a killing stealing lawnmowers from Rural King; he drinks Jack Daniels and Budweiser; he believes his good luck will start tomorrow, and tonight, he wants to wrestle a bear.

A waitress in cutoff shorts and a *Laid in America* T-shirt brings us another round and makes sure to brush her breasts against Danny when she reaches to empty our ashtray. I give her what used to be an irresistible smile, but she ignores me, rests her hand on Danny's shoulder.

"You need anything you just whistle, sweetie," she tells him. "Anything at all you want, I'll be right here."

He pats her hand, pitches a ten on her tray, tells her to keep the change. His mother, recently married for the fourth time and living in Lexington with her Geography-teacher husband, sent him five hundred dollars to help him get back on his feet. Danny calls it fresh start money, but he's already pissing it away on beer and whiskey.

Now I tell him that he's made a conquest and yeah, maybe the waitress is a little on the chubby side and her acne isn't exactly attractive, but I'd rather go three rounds with her than a bear. He grins and stares into the neck of his bottle and peels another label. His mother, Cheryl, used to have the same habit. I was always finding strips of paper on our coffee table or in the ashtray of our car.

"You look just like your mother," I say.

"She swears I look like you. I heard about it

every day of my life until I got away from her."

I try to make a joke of it. "Hey," I say. "I'm the one who ought to be ticked off. You aren't half as good looking as I was when I was your age."

These are things Danny and I do not talk about: our past, my marriage to his mother, what I did on the road, how he lived when he was strung out on meth, what happened to him in prison. This is what we can talk about: beer, basketball, women, the future and bears.

I say, "I'll tell you what, if it's a little bear I might go a couple of rounds with him myself."

Danny smiles but there's no kindness in it. "Old man," he says. "You better hope it's a cub."

* * *

There are three rules for wrestling the bear. No gouging in the eyes, no kicking in the nuts, no biting the bear. Redheaded Ray McAllen, owner of both bar and bear, stands at our table with a foot propped on an empty chair and explains all this between puffs on a Swisher Sweet cigar. Danny nods his agreement, and I remember him at three, sitting on his mother's lap, eyes wide, listening to my jumbled versions of fairytales.

"Fifty bucks up front. You last three full rounds with Elmore, you triple your money." He jabs his cigar in Danny's direction. "Three full rounds, no excuses, no explanations. You understand?"

Danny hands him the cash and then asks questions about the bear. Is it black or brown? Was it born in the wild? How did they train it to wrestle? When can he get a look at the bear? McAllen grunts and flicks ash from the toe of his boot with a long, yellowed fingernail.

"You ask a lot of questions. You think you're Jerry frigging Springer?"

"No," Danny says. "I don't think that."

McAllen snorts and squints through the cloud of smoke between them. "You sure about that? The way you've been flapping your gums, I thought maybe you had the delusion that I give a shit about what you've got to say."

Danny straightens in his chair, lifts his head, holds the older man's stare. His muscles are tensed, his eyes glimmering, and his grin is tight and cold, the kind of grin that a man with a gun to your head might give just before his finger tightens on the trigger. It hits me then that the man sitting across from me has nothing in common with the little boy I left when I went on the road, or the strung out, terrified kid they sent away to prison.

McAllen is a large man, infamous around Harps County for the shortness of his temper and his fondness for sending troublemaking drunks to the ER in the back of an ambulance, but something in Danny's expression spooks him. I can see it in the twitch of his finger, the nervous blinking of his gray eyes.

"I was just yanking your chain, buddy." He winks at me. "Kids these days. They take things too serious." He stubs his cigar and pulls out a couple of sheets of wrinkled paper from the back pocket of his Levis. "You'll be fifth on the list to wrestle, so I figure you'll be on at eight or eight thirty at the latest. And you'll need to sign this waiver here. It's the standard lawyer cover-your-butt document saying that you won't hold us responsible for any injuries sustained."

After the papers are signed McAllen wishes Danny good luck and saunters back towards the bar. Danny watches him, eyes hard, sneering a little.

"Yard bitch," he says. "I know his kind."

I nod and close my eyes. I can see the future coming at us like an eighteen-wheeler.

* * *

The jukebox repeats itself: Lynyrd Skynyrd, Hank Junior, Waylon and Willie, Lynyrd

Skynyrd again. McAllen is perched on a bar stool, talking with his cronies but every so often his eyes move in our direction, but Danny isn't paying him any attention. He orders a new pitcher of beer and a couple of shots of whiskey, chain smokes, drums his hands on the table. It's well past seven, but there's no sign of the bear and Danny's restless, talking too fast and endlessly about his plans for the future. He figures he'll end up heading west, maybe go to work on a ranch in Montana or maybe hook up with a buddy of his who has a fly-fishing business out in Wyoming. He makes it sound as if his only problem is deciding whether he wants to be Roy Rogers on the open range or the Bill Gates of trout lures. I nod and say "uh huh," or "okay" when it looks as if he expects a reaction, but he doesn't notice. That's okay though. The more he babbles about things that are never going to happen, the easier it is for me to forget about the full grown dangerous man who looked as if he might snap Ray McAllen in half with his bare hands and hold onto the freckled, sad-eyed little boy I want to remember.

Then a girl walks through the door. She's thin but not frail, nineteen or twenty maybe, striking with her baggy jeans and black halter and sneakers in a room filled with miniskirts, frilled blouses and high-heeled boots. She stands in the doorway, hands on her hips, scowling like a kindergarten teacher observing a group of unruly five-year-olds. Then she tucks a strand of her long, dishwater blond hair behind her ear, hitches her jeans and moves to the bar.

"She doesn't belong in here," Danny says.

I want to say that we don't either, but that would be a lie, so I just shrug, and watch as the girl steps close to a thin man in cowboy boots and a John Deere cap and taps him on the shoulder. He swivels on his stool, nudges the guy sitting next to him. Both of them look her over, but then the skinny guy says something to his buddy. They laugh and then turn back to the bar. The girl taps him on the shoulder again, holds her thumb and index finger an inch apart, and says something that makes the guy pop off his stool. Danny pushes back his chair, makes as if to stand.

"Leave it alone," I say. "She's just hustling drinks."

He gives me a look, partly pity and partly disapproval. By the time he pushes his way through the crowd, Ray McAllen has the girl by the elbow and is yanking her towards the door. Danny steps in front of them, says something that makes McAllen shake his head. Danny takes a step closer, and the skinny guy swivels on his barstool as if he means to get involved, but a quick flicker of Danny's eyes changes his mind. Danny reaches for the girl's hand, and McAllen lets her go like a reluctant father surrendering a daughter to the groom.

When they reach our table, she grins at me and sits in Danny's chair, elbows propped in front of her, stringy hair falling into her eyes. Her jeans are filthy with mud and grass strains, her halter so threadbare that it looks as if she's wrapped her breasts in black gauze. I look longer than I should, and Danny frowns, scoots a chair closer to her as if she might need protection.

"Hey," she says. "Is Galahad here really going to wrestle a bear?"

I say, so I've been told, and she says, that's really weird. She fills Danny's mug and licks foam from the rim before she takes a drink. Her name is Tennessee, well not really, but that's what she's going by now because it has personality unlike her real name, Lottie. Lottie, she says, is the kind of name you'd give to an unwanted dog. Besides, she says, she met some really nice people in Tennessee, which is nothing like Texas where the people are supposed to be friendly but aren't and where she'd been robbed outside of Dallas by a guy who was old enough to be her grandfather.

"Weird," she says again, refilling her mug. "I mean he had to be like sixty or something." She shrugs and wipes her mouth on the back of her hand. "Hey?" she asks. "Has anyone ever said you guys look alike?"

Danny says he always thought he was better looking than his old man, and Tennessee touches my hand and smiles. She says its real sweet that we're drinking together.

"I can't imagine drinking with my dad. He's a Baptist preacher back in Missouri, which is where I'm originally from in case I haven't mentioned it. I mean, my dad's all right," she says. "But he doesn't have much of a sense of humor."

She says in the end that's why she dropped out of East Missouri Community College and hit the road, well that and this bad break up with a guy who turned out to be a stalker. Since then, she's been to eleven states. Kansas was the weirdest, but Kentucky's pretty close.

Danny lifts a strand of her greasy hair from her shoulder and runs it between his thumb and finger as if it's precious silk, and she beams a smile up at him. Young love, I think, and thinking that makes me feel sour. Maybe because I'm not in love, and it's been a long, long time since anyone called me young. When the opening chords of "Desperado" start on the jukebox, Tennessee drains the last of the beer and says,

"So what do you do in Kentucky besides drink and rescue damsels in distress and wrestle bears?"

I give Danny a look and say, "We dance."

Her hand feels small and sweaty in mine. Danny's watching us, not smiling, not glaring, just watching. I guess he's thinking I shouldn't be dancing with this girl before he even had a chance to ask. Maybe I should feel guilty about that, but I don't. Instead, I pull her close and breathe in the smell of cigarettes and sweat in her hair and enjoy the feel of her breasts pushing against me. When I push back, she whispers in my ear that she ran out of money in Springfield, Tennessee.

"You like me, don't you?"

I say sure I do. Then she nips my earlobe and says she can take care of me for forty bucks, sixty if I've got a condom and want to go all the way. I touch her hair the way Danny did, but it doesn't feel like silk to me, doesn't feel like anything other than hair that needs a shampoo.

I say, "You're beautiful."

She steps back and looks at me, chin tucked, her expression so solemn that I nearly laugh. "Are you making fun of me?" she asks.

"No."

She nods and then smiles. "Cool," she says. "You can think it over."

Back at the table, she sits close to Danny and says she's danced up a thirst. He fills a clean mug from a fresh pitcher and reaches for his cigarettes.

"You were impressive out there, Pop," he says, making the word 'Pop' sound like a profanity. "You got the moves of a three-legged dog."

I say, "Why don't you give it a try, Fred Astaire?"

"Careful," he says. "You're showing your age." He squeezes Tennessee's shoulder but doesn't take his eyes from mine. "He doesn't know any dancers from this century."

She says, "I turned twenty-one yesterday." She lifts her mug. "Happy birthday to me."

When Danny asks if anyone gave her a birthday kiss, she says no one that matters and leans in. When they pull away from each other, she stares into his face, traces his eyebrows with her fingertips.

"You have gentle eyes," she says.

Then Danny starts talking. He tells the story about his scheme to get rich stealing self-propelled lawnmowers from Rural King and how he was loading one into the back of a truck when an Owensboro cop flashed a light on him, spit a wad of Copenhagen at his shoes, and told him the bad news that he was under arrest, the good news that he wasn't likely to give himself a hernia in the Davies County jail. Then he talks about Roderer Correctional, how it doesn't look so bad from the outside, but how looks don't matter.

Tennessee says, "Weren't you scared?"

I wait for the inevitable, tough-guy line, "Not me, baby," or "You just have to know how to look out for yourself," something he's heard in a movie and thinks sounds impressive. But Danny runs his hands over the bristles of his crew cut and then looks down at the water rings on the table and says that he was terrified, that it was two months before he could sleep through the night.

"After awhile you get so tired of being scared that you're like a frayed wire, ready to spark at any moment." He sighs and says, "I did a lot up there that I ain't proud of." He cuts his eyes at me. "And not what you think or what they always show about a young guy locked up for the first time." He lights his cigarette, and I notice his hands are shaking. "The scary thing is you get to like it, get so you believe that being mean proves you aren't scared. I seen long-term cons, guys who'd been in fifteen or twenty years, and they were all like that. You look at them and they seem calm, easy going, tranquil even, but they're like copperheads in autumn, you know? The way you see one lying in a pile of leaves and think it's just a stick. You get too close and you find out different, but by then you're already snake bit. That's the way people get in places like that. I guess I did, too."

"Hey," she says. "You're sweet," she says. "I can feel goodness seeping off you."

"No," Danny says. "I'm not a good guy, not really. But all that's over, you know? Tonight begins a new day."

He tells her about the bear being an omen, a sign that he should get out of Kentucky, head west where the air is clean and cold and a man can make his fortune if he's got brains and guts. I point out that he doesn't know anything about anywhere but Kentucky, that the west he's talking about never existed anywhere other than in old, black and white movies, and that one place is pretty much the same as any other, but I know neither of them believes what I am saying. Then Danny takes my shot of whiskey, downs it, slams the glass down on the table and says,

"Bring on the bear."

"He's a little strange when it comes to bears," I say.

Danny says even if old Elmore pitches him across the room, it will be worth it because it will be something he's done that not many have and he believes it's important to do things that other people don't do. That, he says, is what separates you from the herd, makes you an individual. Then it's as if he's suddenly realized that he's speaking aloud and gives an embarrassed shrug.

"You probably think wrestling a bear is stupid, huh?" he asks.

"Weird," she says. "But not stupid."

Danny stands and kisses the top of her head, tells us he'll be right back and then shoves and slides and sidesteps his way towards the men's room. Tennessee watches him, smiling a little to herself.

"He's nice. You did a good job raising him."

"I didn't raise him. I left him when he was five years old."

She tucks her bottom lip between her teeth as if considering that and shrugs, "No offense," she says. "But maybe you did a good thing by leaving."

I turn my mug upside down on the table. I say, "You still want to make forty dollars?"

* * *

In the cab of my truck, I lean against the window and watch cars pull into the parking lot and remember high school dates at the Oak Lake Drive-In, nights when Cheryl, six months and a missed period away from becoming my wife, would place her head in my lap and make me promise that I would never tell anyone about this, ever. Now I stroke Tennessee's hair, but it just feels greasy beneath my hand, so I close my eyes and catalog all the women I've known who have done this for love or lust or any reason other than a couple of wrinkled twenty-dollar bills.

Then it's over, and Tennessee wipes her mouth, pockets my money, and steps out of the truck. A couple of young guys sitting on the hood of a Monte Carlo have been watching, and she raises her hand in a wave. When I zip up and climb out of the pickup, one of them gives me a thumbs-up sign and cackles.

Danny isn't laughing. When we get back to the table, he has a fresh pitcher of beer and a couple of shot glasses, one empty, the other filled to the brim. There's still no sign of Elmore, but Danny looks as if he's already gone ten rounds with a grizzly. His head is hung, his eyes narrowed, his shoulders slumped and tense at the same time. Tennessee grabs the shot, knocks it down and then scrubs at her lips with the back of her hand. Danny barely glances in her direction.

"Did you two slip outside to do some more dancing?"

Then his hand explodes up, connects with my cheek, his elbow sending the ashtray shattering off the floor. It's a slap, not a punch, but it's hard enough to ring my ears and water my eyes. While I'm still trying to blink them clear, he lunges across the table and grips me by the throat. I flail and kick my heels on the floor, but his hand tightens, and there's nothing I can do to break free. He's stronger than I am, stronger than I ever was. He squeezes a little harder, cutting off my wind, but then opens his fingers, leaving me gasping, and I know this was just a warning, a way of letting me know that he could kill me if he wanted and all I could do was sputter my way to Jesus.

"Oh, wow, hey," Tennessee says. She smiles at Danny, brushes his cheek with her fingertips. "I'm sorry."

Danny's hands are shaking. He blinks tears from his eyes, but then takes a quick breath and stiffens his jaw. He looks as if he's about to say something, but then he just shakes his head.

"That's all right," I say although I'm not sure why I say that. "It's okay."

Tennessee takes his hand and makes him look her in the eye. "I'm going to go now. I mean I've got to keep traveling. Okay?"

He lifts her fingers to his lips and kisses them. It's odd, like something you'd see in an old movie, and I'm proud of him. Then she calls him Galahad again.

"Take care of each other," she says. "Good luck with the bear."

She pushes her way through the crowd and out the door. I tell myself that she'll be okay, that girls like Tennessee always turn out all right, but I doubt if that's true. Anything could happen to her. She might get killed and tossed into a drainage ditch or find herself in a place like this ten years from now when she's too tired to keep running or she might go home, marry a car salesman or a banker, have babies, and forget that places like Redheaded Ray's ever existed. How can you read someone else's future when you can't or don't want to decipher your own?

Danny pours us fresh beer. Then "Sweet Home Alabama" begins on the jukebox yet another time, and while the couples are still dancing Ray McAllen rushes them off the floor to make room for a makeshift wrestling ring.

Danny pulls a ten from his wallet and throws it on the table. "To hell with the bear," he says. "I want to go home."

* * *

The sun is a small, thin sliver of fading orange when Danny walks past my truck and stands at the edge of the road, frowning. He looks one way and then the other, and when he turns around he seems as disappointed as a kid who woke on Christmas morning to find Santa Claus didn't come. I know he was expecting Tennessee to be waiting.

"Listen," I say. "I offered her forty bucks. She needed the money is all."

He studies my face a moment and then smiles. "I want to see the bear."

He walks to the back of the roadhouse, shoulders squared, boots crunching off the gravel. I glance at the road one last time and then hurry to catch up with him.

The bear is not in a cage or pen. It is chained to a withered oak tree in a patch of weeds that have been worn down from its constant pacing. For a second, I'm not sure that it's really a bear. It looks more like a large, mangy black dog that has been trained to stand on its hind legs and give a performance.

"Jesus Christ," Danny says.

I don't know a lot about bears, but I do know that Elmore is miles away from the fierce ones I've seen on television and in movies. It's a small, black bear about the size of a Saint Bernard. When we approach, it growls and then whimpers and tries to shrink behind the oak tree. Feces and mud cake its graying haunches, and there are bald spots and open sores on its back and legs. Once it realizes there's no place to hide from us, it lies in the weeds and whimpers.

Danny kicks away an empty food bowl and steps up to the bear, his hand out, palm down to show he's friendly. He calls the bear by its name. Elmore, he says, you're all right, Elmore, you're a handsome bear. Elmore rears, flashes his teeth, but then drops back down when Danny comes closer. I tell him to be careful. Even a little bear can be dangerous, but Danny ignores me. He lets the bear sniff his hand, and then reaches the top of its head.

"This ain't right," he says. "That bastard. I ought to chain him out here all day, see how he likes it."

It seems like something you'd say when you're angry, the kind of thing that no one is meant to take seriously, but I can tell from the set of Danny's jaw and the flare of his nostrils that he means it. I say, "It's a hell of a way to treat a bear, all right."

"No," he says. "It's more than that."

An idea occurs to me, and I hope it's good enough to get us out of here and into my truck. "We'll call the Humane Society. They'll have that bear out of here and into a sanctuary in no time."

Danny looks at me as if I've lost my mind. "Screw that," he says. "Bears ought to be free in the wild, not locked up in a damn petting zoo."

"Danny," I say.

"No," he says. "You keep a tool box in your truck don't you? We're taking Elmore with us when we go."

For a moment, I clutch at the idea that he's joking, but I can't hold onto that for long, not when Danny's already tugging at the rusted lock to test its sturdiness. "You're serious?"

He looks up at me, and I know exactly what he's thinking. He's thinking okay, Pop, are you going to come through this one time or are you going to let me down again? And, of course, I'm going to disappoint him. Taking the bear is crazy. People don't do things like that, and even if they do I'm not one of them. Besides, I'm not sure what the penalty is for stealing a bear, but I'm sure there must be one.

"Look, son," I say and realize that it's the first time in a long time I've called him that.

"Help or don't," he says. "Either way I'm taking this damn bear."

I say, "I'll see if I can find some wire cutters."

But I never get the chance. I've just unlocked my truck when I hear voices coming from behind the bar. There are two of them, and neither one sounds happy. Dropping my keys back in my pocket, I hurry that way, my feet crunching on pea gravel, but it feels as if I'm struggling through quicksand. I've just reached the side of the building when I hear McAllen say that he's giving Danny a choice. Get the hell away from the bear or get carried out of here in the back of an ambulance.

I hear Danny say, "Try it, asshole. I'm a lot tougher than that poor, little bear."

My pulse pounds and stutters in my throat, and I can't seem to breathe in the thick, summer air. This is bad, I think over and over. This is bad. For once in my life, I'm right. When I reach them, McAllen is reaching for something in his back pocket. A gun, maybe, and my legs nearly buckle with that thought. He's got a gun, and he's going to kill Danny. There's nothing I can do but watch my son die.

"McAllen!" I shout although I'm not sure

what I can accomplish other than to end up on a slab next to Danny at the Harps County Morgue.

McAllen glances in my direction. It's really just a flicker of his eyes, but that's all Danny needs. He crosses the gravel like a linebacker cutting off a running back, his shoulder lowered, the muscles in his legs pumping. McAllen's hand is still trapped in the pocket of his blue jeans when Danny slams into him, driving him against the bar's block wall hard enough to snap back his head. While McAllen is gasping for breath, Danny moves back a couple of inches, brings up his knee into the man's groin three times, then moves back to let the man fall.

That's the end of it, I think. That's the end of it, and it didn't turn out so bad, but Danny drives his forearm into McAllen's throat and then delivers a quick right to his solar plexus. He steps back to give McAllen room to fall.

"Let's get out of here," I say.

But my voice is small and croaking, and Danny isn't listening anyway. Once he has McAllen on the ground, he kicks him four, maybe five times, in the ribs and stomach, and McAllen is gagging and gasping, whimpering a little.

"You're a big man, aren't you?" Danny is

shouting. "What about it, tough guy? You think it's funny to treat a helpless animal like that? You think because it's small and loves you, you can do whatever you want? You think it's a joke? Who's laughing now, asshole? Tell me."

But McAllen can't tell him anything because Danny ends every question by kicking him in the ribs, and foamy blood is bubbling at McAllen's lips. Somehow he's managed to free his hand from his pocket, but there's no gun or knife, just a thick, white hand that flops helplessly on the gravel like a fish that's been yanked from deep water and left on rocks to die.

I run to Danny, grab his arm. "Enough, Danny. You're going to kill him."

But he shoves me away and levels a finger at me in an accusation that I can't deny. Then he turns back to Ray McAllen and stomps his hand again and again until the hand is shattered and McAllen's wedding ring is buried deep in his bloody fingers.

A horrible roar echoes in my head, and for a second, I think it's coming from Danny, but I blink sweat from my eyes and see that Elmore has reared on his hind legs. The smell of blood or violence has riled him, and he has his head turned to the darkening sky, his mouth open, his teeth bared, and he no longer resembles a mangy dog or anything else but a bear.

"Danny," I say. "Danny, please."

I know it's useless. Things have gone so far that whatever is going to happen is going to happen, and nothing I say can change that. It's been too late for that for a long, long time. The best thing for me to do is walk back to my truck and leave Danny to whatever fate is going to find him. It seems like a petty, cowardly thought, but why should it? There's nothing I can do to help him now, nothing I can accomplish but get myself thrown into jail as an accessory.

Before I can turn away, Danny kicks McAllen in the ribs again, and this time the older man's breath goes out in a whoosh and frothy blood runs from his mouth. He jerks a couple of times and then falls still. It doesn't take a doctor to know that he's dead. Maybe a rib punctured his heart or maybe something else got him. That will be for the coroner to figure it, but it doesn't really matter. Dead is dead.

"Danny," I say.

He stands over McAllen, panting, his thumbs hooked into the belt loops of his jeans. "He had it coming. He got what he deserved."

The words sound tough, but his voice is high and quivering, and when he looks at me, his bottom lip is trembling. He looks like a terrified but proud five year old who is trying hard to not cry in the face of a spanking. Leave him, I think. I have to leave him. There's nothing else I can do. But I can't walk away from him, and that's so funny I have to stop myself from laughing aloud. The one time in my life when I can't do the easy thing and walk away is likely to get me locked in a state prison as an accessory to murder.

"Come on, son," I say. "We need to get out of here."

He's bending on his knee beside McAllen as if he intends to give him mouth-to-mouth resuscitation or check to make sure the man is really dead, but when he stands up he has something in his hand. My heart stutters a little because I latch onto the idea that it's a gun and my son means to kill me, too, so he'll leave no witnesses, but I know that's ridiculous. Then I see that Danny's holding a key ring in his hand.

We've gone three, maybe four miles when the sirens begin to wail. My heart races and I'm drenched with sweat. Every time I glance into the rearview mirror and see Elmore chained to the roll bar, the wind whipping his fur, I flinch and yank the wheel. I want to run, pick up the West Kentucky Parkway in Greenview and head south. Mexico seems like the best option, but I know that's a daydream. How far can you get with maybe four hundred dollars between you and a stolen bear? Then when the old brick buildings and glowing streetlights of Greenview are in sight, I turn right onto a gravel road and follow it for a half mile until it gives way into the old Sugar Creek Mines.

Danny's calmer now. He roots around under the seat until he finds five loose cans of Busch beer that have been rolling around under there since I went fishing last week, and now he's talking as if he didn't just leave a man lying dead on bloodstained gravel outside a roadhouse. He has a plan. We're going to release the bear out here, so he can grow fat and healthy off a diet of wild hogs and whitetail deer. The abandoned strip mines with their thousands of square acres of overgrown fields, pine thickets, slews and coal pits will be a paradise for a bear, Danny says, but when I start to pull over, he tells me to go further. He wants to find a just-right place to release the bear. I could tell him that here by the road or deep in the mines won't make a difference. Tonight, maybe tomorrow, the bear will make its way back to the bar because when you're lost and hungry and alone, you always return home, but I figure in the near future neither one of us has a lot of good days coming, so I listen to the stories my son wants to tell.

"You came through," he says. "I wasn't sure, you know? But you did."

I nod and leave it at that. There's no point in saying anything else. Danny's a dreamer, and tonight he's holding onto his illusions as hard as he can, but he isn't a fool. Besides I like the fact that in his eyes, at least for the moment, I've made some sort of amends.

When the haul road crests a hill that drops off to thickets and hollows, Danny says this is the place and jumps out of the cab before the truck has completely stopped. By the time I kill the ignition, Danny has scrambled into the truck bed and is unchaining the bear.

"Go!" he tells it when they're back on the ground.

Elmore grunts and sits on his haunches. Danny slaps his shoulder and tells him to run, and the bear lurches up, grunts again, takes a couple of steps and turns its muzzle into the air, sniffing. Danny picks up a handful of gravel and pitches it at Elmore.

"Run, you son of a buck," he says. "You're free. Don't you get it?'

Elmore whimpers and hangs back. Then Danny hits it with a clump of dirt, and suddenly, Elmore seems to remember that he's a bear. He rears on his hind legs and growls a deep, rumbling growl that makes me shudder and flashes his teeth at us before dropping to all fours and scrambling down the side of the hill into the pine thicket.

Danny hands me one of the warm beers and raises his in a toast. "Here's to Elmore," he says.

I open the beer and drink with him because how can you argue with an eternal optimist, a man certain that the next ticket he buys will win the lottery and that he will find true love and divine guidance in a dive bar and that each day holds the chance to start over no matter what you did the day before? This is my son: a murderer, a knight errant to lost girls, a rescuer of maltreated bears, a grown man who has almost forgiven his wayward father.

The sirens have grown louder, and I know it's just a matter of time until they come for us - most likely tonight, no later than in the morning. We must have passed a half dozen cars on our way out here, and who isn't likely to notice a truck that's carrying a wrestling bear? Soon, the blue lights will find us, and whatever future is coming our way we'll face it on our own, but for now the only light comes from the moon bluing the pines, the only sound the chirping of crickets and Elmore's fading growls.

For now, neither of us is alone.

Where You Find Yourself

When they set out to score Oxycontin in the aftermath of the winter's worst snowstorm, Lacy made sure to bring Baby Ty's heaviest blanket. Recently she'd determined to spite everyone by becoming a responsible mother, and the blanket was one of those small things she would have overlooked just a few days before. It pleased her that she'd remembered it now.

"You want to help throw some blocks in the back?" Bryson asked before she even had the baby's car seat buckled in.

"I'm busy in case you ain't noticed."

He made a hangdog face. "My arm's sore."

When she didn't answer, he muttered "Well, hell," grabbed a concrete block and threw it in the truck bed where it landed with a wallop that showered snow and rust from the tailgate. Baby Ty started squalling, and Lacy gritted her teeth and counted to five. She hadn't slept more than three or four hours in the last couple of days, and her natural inclination was to scream in his scrunched up face or pinch a hunk on his fat thigh. Instead, she dug a bottle from a diaper bag.

After the baby worked up a good suck, she wrapped him in the blanket, then climbed into the truck and fastened her seatbelt. She smiled down at Baby Ty. She didn't like taking him along, but her mother was working a double shift at Wal-Mart. Besides she'd decided to not rely on her momma so often. Her mother was always shaking her head when Lacy let the baby's diaper go a little too long or didn't bother with warming the bottle. Her momma liked to point out that *she* had breastfed both Lacy and her brother, and Lacy always said, "Well, that was you, wasn't it?" There didn't seem any reason to state the obvious. She'd stayed clean for most of her pregnancy but had gone back to using as soon as she left the hospital. If she had breastfed the way her momma wanted her to, Ty would have already been hooked on Oxy, Methadone and Codeine and would have had the THC level of a Jamaican Reggae star.

Now Lacy cracked her window and lit a Marlboro. She knew she shouldn't be smoking around the baby, but then again maybe people exaggerated the dangers of secondhand smoke.

She didn't know for sure. When Lacy was a little girl, her mother had chain smoked Salem Lights and never even bothered to roll down a window. Of course to hear her momma tell it, she'd never smoked a cigarette around Lacy in her life. When Bryson got into the truck, he looked down at Baby Ty and grunted.

"Give me one of those cigarettes," Bryson said.

"What happened to yours?"

"Smoked them." He took her next to last from her hand. "We'll stop up at the store."

He pulled his cell from his pocket, squinted through the smoke while he punched buttons. It was a three-hundred-dollar phone, one his daddy, who owned a huge, appliance warehouse over in Paducah, had bought him for Christmas. His daddy had been to the tiny shotgun house they were renting and knew that the kitchen stove only had one working burner and that the front window was covered with cardboard and that they kept it about sixty degrees in the house because they couldn't afford the gas bill. She would have thought the man had sense enough to give them a new oven from his warehouse or some furniture for the baby's room or just three hundred dollars to pay on the heating bill.

"What are you doing?" she asked.

He grinned. "Hold on."

He pushed the send button, waited and then turned the phone for her to see. He'd updated his Facebook page: *Searching for the pot of gold at the end of the rainbow*. He thought it made him slick to post things that most people didn't get but that his buddies knew referred to drugs. Now Bryson started the engine and goosed the gas. The truck jerked and shuddered, finally got traction and bounced over the rutted drive. The shaking made Lacy's stomach feel the way it had in the first trimester of her pregnancy. It didn't help that Bryson was whooping and laughing and that Baby Ty was gurgling happily to his bottle. Boys, she thought, and thinking it pleased her because it seemed like a womanly thing to think. She studied Bryson with something like affection. Since the baby, there'd been desire on occasion, resentment and anger more often, but she hadn't looked upon him with true fondness since those nights when they'd sat in the basement at his momma's house, and he'd talked about how beautiful she was and how he didn't know exactly where he was going or what he wanted, but how he knew he'd never be like his daddy. It all seemed so romantic. Perhaps, it should have been a warning that there were always plastic baggies with a kaleidoscope of pills and bottles of Boones Farm to wash them down, but she was just a kid then.

Now, she cupped Baby Ty's booted foot and watched Bryson wrestle the wheel. The seatbelt was broken on the driver's side, and he bounced in the seat, leaning like a bull rider with each lurch of the truck. For a moment she could imagine them many years from now living a better life, one where they had a nice house with flowers in the yard and a bright, warm kitchen where Ty would sit in the afternoons and do his homework. She could see them going to little league games in the summer and junior pro basketball games in the fall. No Oxy, no late night parties from which she woke feeling thick and hopeless, no shouting matches over who'd scarfed the last of the pills or smoked up the weed. She wasn't sure how they were going to get there from here, but as the Nissan smoothed out on the snow-packed pavement of Briar Creek Road, she was sure they would. Suddenly, she wanted to hold Bryson and feel his breath against her skin. The urge for it was so strong her eyes watered and stung with tears.

"Hey, it's okay. You're feeling jagged is all. We're going to score." Bryson said.

He was right. That was the worst of it. When she was coming down, her emotions were always balled up. It wasn't affection or hope she was feeling, but a frenzy of brain chemicals. A couple of pills or a few hits from a joint, and her head would be back to normal. She stung from the realization of her own stupidity. This wasn't the then they'd had and it wasn't the tomorrow she imagined.

She lit her last cigarette, thought about cracking the window and then figured it wasn't worth the cold air. "So where are we going?"

"Places." He took the turn onto Highway 70 without stopping and the rear end fishtailed, bouncing her against the door. "Share that. It's your last one."

"Yeah, it's *my* last one." She exhaled at the truck's roof and then tried to fan it away from Baby Ty's face when he started bawling. "Smoke follows beauty," she told him.

Their place was a little less than six miles outside of Greenview, and there was nothing but bare trees and strip-mined hills and flooded bottoms between here and town. The road was narrow, twisting, potholed. Sometimes, when she had insomnia and the baby was sleeping and Bryson had passed out, she logged onto Yahoo Chat and spent hours hunched over the old Dell she'd had since junior high, typing to people - men mainly - from all over the place. When she told them she was in Kentucky, they assumed either bluegrass or mountains, but the truth was Greenview was just a nowhere town in a south central part of the state that had been mined out thirty years ago. There were no mountains, just a few jagged hills and a thousand acres of abandoned mines, fenced off and forgotten.

But with the afternoon sun sparkling off the snow pack, it was easy to forget all that. The world looked like an illustration from one of the fairy tale books she'd loved when she was a girl. She spotted a herd of deer climbing an open hillside, a buck with ax-handle wide antlers leading the way. It was odd seeing them in the middle of the day, and she wondered why they were moving and what they might be searching for.

"When I was little I used to pretend they were unicorns," she said.

"What were?"

"Deer," she said. "Whenever I saw them, I imagined they were unicorns. Momma said I was silly, but Daddy would say if I wanted to see a whitetail as a unicorn there wasn't no damn law against it."

"What were you doing? Dipping your animal crackers in acid?"

She sighed and went back to looking out the window at the trees blurring by. He was right. Unicorns and elves and magic were cool to dream about, but this was real life: a drooling baby, a smart-ass boyfriend, a habit she had to feed. This was where you were when the dream ended, where you found yourself when you woke up.

Bryson turned onto a gravel road that was as nearly as rutted as their drive, and she realized they were heading for his Uncle Curtis's house. She knew Bryson was watching, waiting to see if she was going to complain the way she usually did when he dragged her to his ex-con uncle's house.

"I hope he's holding," she said.

* * *

Lacy had never been sure why Curtis had gone to prison. She'd heard stories of a drug deal that ended with murder, but she wasn't sure how much was true and how much was just a story that people liked to tell. One thing she knew for certain, she wasn't going to ask him. He called her honey and darling and seemed nice enough, but his eyes were pale blue and hooded, and he scared her awfully bad.

Now Curtis sat at his kitchen table and watched Bryson pace around the room, eating cheese puffs from an opened bag and pilfering through the refrigerator for a Pepsi. Curtis hadn't bothered to put on a shirt, and the muscles in his chest and arms were thick and pale and scrawled with tattoos. The kitchen, like the rest of the house, was neat and orderly, with gleaming counters and not a single dirty dish stacked in the sink. No matter what shape Curtis was in, the place always seemed to be freshly cleaned and smelled of lemon Pledge.

"You ever seen so much snow?" Bryson said. "They were saying on the Weather Channel this morning that we got another big one heading our way. Momma says we're going into another ice age."

"You can keep babbling about the weather all day," Curtis said. "But it's not going to change the fact that I got nothing to give you."

Bryson leaned against the sink and stared at Curtis. "You ain't got nothing?"

"Nothing to *share*. Day before the storm hit Nunley raided about half the dealers in town. I reckon he wanted to show folks they did the right thing electing him Sheriff." He stubbed his cigarette and glanced at Lacy who leaned in the doorway between the living room and the kitchen, bouncing Baby Ty on her hip. "He's kin to you, ain't he?"

"Some kin on my daddy's side," she said.

"Why don't you and the little man sit down." He nodded at an empty chair, and it was as much of a command as an invitation. "Nunley's a pretty good old boy. We ran together in school."

She sat at the table and stuck a pacifier in Baby Ty's mouth. Bryson said goddamn it, surely Curtis had a little something he could spare.

"You need to get a hold of yourself, boy. This ain't no kind of life. You ought to take some classes or get yourself a job."

"I got a job."

"Stealing lawnmowers and bicycles and tool sets isn't a job. It's just a dumb ass thing that's going to get you thrown in jail."

Lacy studied the two of them. Outside of the blondish hair and fair skin, it was hard to see the relation. Bryson was thin, willowy with delicate features and full lips. His momma's younger brother was broad-shouldered, thick necked, powerful. His face was wide and hard-boned, and he had a lot of scars. He reminded her of the washed up wrestlers her daddy used to drag her and her momma to see at the National Guard Armory. Her momma had complained a lot, but Lacy had never minded. Going anywhere with her daddy was all right with her. But then he'd run his truck into

Cyprus Creek, and her life had changed altogether. Now she wondered who Ty would resemble when he got older. His daddy or hers or some distant relative that seemed vaguely familiar when you saw a picture in a family album?

It got quiet in the kitchen with only the sound of their breathing and Baby Ty's sucking and voices from a television set drifting in from the bedroom to fill the emptiness. Lacy felt like crying or shouting or beating her head on the table.

"Look here," Bryson said. "We're about to crawl out of our skin."

Curtis scratched his bicep and yawned. He seemed different today, less here, as if his mind were chasing itself in circles.

"What are you planning on doing?" he asked. "Driving around all day in this mess looking to score?"

"If we have to."

"And you're going right along with him?" Curtis asked Lacy. He sighed and rubbed his hand over his face and turned his head towards the living room. "Shelby, bring three or four of them Oxy out here, won't you?"

A scrawny redhead wearing a man's sweatshirt and sky blue panties came in from the back bedroom and blinked at them as if she weren't sure who they were or if they were real. Lacy remembered her from junior high. Back then Shelby Markwell had been one of the well-off but geeky girls, the kind who made the honor roll and joined the Beta Club and always ended up playing the clarinet or the piccolo in the concert band. Now, she put four pills in front of Curtis and sat on his lap and lay her head against his shoulder.

"Grab a cup from the cabinet and one of them little straws from that second drawer," Curtis told Bryson.

When Bryson handed him the cup, he mashed the pills, careful not to scatter any of the powder. Bryson and his buddies snorted Oxy sometimes, but she'd never tried it. The idea scared her a little. It seemed like something a junkie would do, but her head was still pounding and her stomach sour, and her nerves felt like a million tiny razor blades beneath her skin.

Shelby took the straw and bent towards the table. Lacy felt a flash of anger when she saw how much the girl was snorting. She wanted to slap her or yank out a handful of her hair, but then finally Shelby finished. She offered Lacy the straw, but Bryson snatched it from her hand. He took as much as he could, the greedy son of a bitch, and let out his breath in a rush

Tim L. Williams

and said damn didn't that hit the spot.

"You go ahead," Curtis told Lacy. "I'm all right for now."

She shifted Ty on her lap and leaned towards the table. The powder burned her nose and watered her eyes. It felt weird and unpleasant, and she had to squeeze her nostrils to stop from sneezing. When she looked at Baby Ty, he was watching her, his lips moving on the pacifier, his chubby hands reaching for the straw. When she pulled it away, he tugged at the front of her V-neck sweater. She snatched it back up, but Curtis had gotten an eye full and was smiling his appreciation. Baby Ty took advantage of the distraction and grabbed the straw.

"He wants his turn," Bryson said.

Curtis eased Shelby off his lap. "Grab one of those paper bags," he told her. "Sack up a couple six packs from the cases in the utility room."

Lacy shifted the baby again, started to say that snorting the Oxy had been a waste but then the rush hit her. Suddenly, her head felt too heavy for her neck. Her body was warm all over, the blood pulsing through her veins as airy and sweet as cotton candy.

When Shelby came back with the beer, Curtis handed it to Bryson. "It ought to be enough to keep the edge off until the weather gets better."

"Thanks," Bryson said. "I appreciate it Curtis. You always did right by me."

"Uh huh," Curtis said. "You listen to me and get on back home. I don't want to have to put on a suit and tie and sit at Tucker's Funeral Home listening to my sister cry over your sorry ass."

Then Lacy was following Bryson out the door, tugging on her coat as she went, Baby Ty slipping in her arms. Once or twice Curtis told her to be careful before she dropped the baby, but she couldn't think of what might happen or why it would matter if she did.

* * *

Four hours later, the sun was setting and the Oxy buzz a distant memory. Still they kept driving. No one was holding or if they were, they weren't going to share.

Now, they pulled into the parking lot of a little Baptist Church on the outskirts of town. When Bryson got out to take a leak, Lacy touched Baby Ty's face. His skin felt as cold and damp as the glass in the window.

"We'll get you home soon," she whispered.

His lips puckered and sucked, a

pantomime of hunger. When he realized that no bottle was coming his way, he wailed in frustration. His face reddened and he thrashed wildly, working himself into a tantrum. She grabbed his thigh but stopped herself before she pinched him. She tried a pacifier, but he spat it out and bawled even louder. She jammed it back into his mouth, and he flailed his arms and legs, screeching until his face turned purple and blotchy.

"Jesus Christ," Bryson said, climbing back into the truck. "What'd you do to him?"

"I dragged him around looking for drugs with his asshole daddy."

He reached into the floorboard for another beer, opened it and drank deep. Belching, he set the can on the dash and pitched his phone in her lap.

"Check for an update."

"It's not going to do any good."

Still, she squinted at the phone and tried to ignore the baby's wailing and the overpowering urge to walk away into the cold and say goodbye forever. When Bryson's Facebook page finally loaded, there was only one new comment. His friend Chuck Whitaker had posted, "Dude, call me if you find the leprechaun!"

Bryson chugged the rest of his beer and put

the empty can in the baby's hands, and that quieted him to sniffles as he shook the can and rolled it on his belly and snatched it up again. Like father like son, she thought.

Bryson stared out into the dark for a second. "How many more beers have we got?"

"Four."

"Give me another one."

She rolled her eyes. "The baby's hungry and I'm freezing. Let's just go home."

"Give me the beer and quit bitching," he said.

She took a can from the floorboard and passed it his way. "Nobody's got nothing," she said. "How many times do you have to hear it before you understand?"

"He's a lying sack."

"Who?"

"Uncle Curtis. He ain't been caught without in his entire life, no matter how many drug busts have gone down. Three or four Oxy my ass end. I bet he's got a hundred of them stashed somewhere."

The truck spun and bounced out into the road, skidded on a patch of ice and veered toward the edge of the blacktop. Lacy nearly screamed, but Bryson manhandled the truck back on the road, giggling like a little boy playing bumper cars.

"We aren't going back over there are we?" she asked.

"I don't see where else we can go."

"Home."

"We ain't got no Oxy at home." He winked at her. Have a little faith. I can be persuasive when I want to be. Course you're going to have to play along."

"With what?"

He shrugged, suddenly coy, smiling. "With whatever. You want to get high, don't you?"

She didn't want to give him the satisfaction of saying yes, but it was pointless to lie. She thought about the rush she'd gotten when she'd snorted the Oxy and knew she had to have it again or else go crazy from the wanting. But it didn't matter what she said. He was already heading that way.

* * *

A Johnny Cash album was playing on the stereo, and it struck her as funny, like something her granddaddy would have listened to. She said she thought her granddaddy might have had this very record. Curtis winked at her through a cloud of marijuana smoke and said well your granddaddy must have known good music when he heard it.

"I still can't believe you ain't got Ne-Yo or Common," Bryson said. "Not even Usher?"

Curtis gave him a look. "You don't like my music, boy, you can always take yourself on up the road."

Bryson frowned and shifted in the recliner. "You don't got to get surly, Curtis. I was just saying ... "

"That's the problem. One of these days, you might want to learn to keep your mouth shut."

Lacy looked down at Baby Ty sleeping in his car seat carrier. She wished he was awake, so he could see how small and cowardly his daddy looked when Curtis spoke harsh to him. But she felt bad nearly as soon she thought it. Ty would have a lifetime to realize what a disappointment his father was.

When she reached forward to take the joint from between Curtis's fingers, she noticed how his eyes went down the front of her shirt. It wasn't much of a compliment. His little girlfriend had gone back home, and he was probably just horny, but she figured she might as well be friendly so she took her time about blocking his view. Besides, she wanted Bryson to notice. She liked the idea of him being jealous and angry but with nothing he could do. But the next time Curtis went to the bathroom Bryson moved over to sit beside her.

"You see the way he's been looking at you. He's dying to get you in bed."

"You act surprised anyone would want to."

"Naw, I ain't surprised." He took her beer from her hand and drank it. "But I know how we can score."

She sat up a little straighter and blinked at him. "You what?"

"He don't give nothing away for free."

Her face felt numb and hot at the same time, and she glanced in the direction of the bathroom door. "You want me to sleep with him? With your uncle?"

"Don't be looking at me like that. I'm not some kind of pervert. You don't want to go home with nothing but this pot buzz, do you? Besides it ain't like you're a virgin."

She couldn't decide if she wanted to giggle or slap him or run outside to cry. Bryson was watching her, waiting for an answer. She almost told him to go to hell but then thought better of it. Curtis was pretty old, but he wasn't exactly ugly, not her type but not ugly. Do it for me, Bryson whispered, but she didn't pay that any attention at all. It was the Oxy she was thinking about.

"All right," she said. "But make sure he's got something. I'm not doing it for free."

Bryson kissed her cheek and whispered

that he loved her. It didn't matter one way or the other. Love didn't change anything at all.

"Hey Uncle Curt, come on in the kitchen a minute. I want to talk to you," Bryson said.

She shut her eyes and tried to think about the deer she'd seen earlier. She wondered if they were bedded down for the night, all of them together. Then she wondered why she was thinking about deer when she was on the verge of whoring herself for drugs, something she'd always believed only a skank or an imbecile would do.

"Who are we?" she whispered to the baby.

But he was still sleeping, and he wouldn't have had the answer anyway. Not yet, maybe, if he was lucky not for a long time.

"I'm going to wait in the truck," Bryson said, unable or unwilling to look at her. He hesitated at the door. "I can take the baby."

"He'll be all right," she said. "He'll sleep right through it."

Curtis came from the kitchen and leaned against the wall, watching her. She tried for a smile that was flirty and playful and unconcerned, but that didn't feel right, so she just pulled off her sweater and tossed her hair back into place and waited.

He sat on the couch. He didn't say anything, and she felt clumsy and silly in the silence. She wished he would speak, maybe order her to do something or that Baby Ty would wake and begin screaming.

"Put your clothes back on," Curtis said after some time.

"You don't want to? With me, I mean?"

He didn't answer, just lit a cigarette and sat back on the couch, so she pulled on her sweater. She felt herself on the verge of screaming. She thought that once she started, she might not be able to stop. Then Curtis slipped three white pills into her hand.

"Take these," he said. "I gave him a dozen, but he'll probably try to hold out on you, so we'll just let these be our secret."

She slipped them into the front pocket of her jeans. She waited for him to say something, but he seemed content to just stare at her, so she said,

"Are you sure? That you don't want to, I mean."

He stubbed his cigarette and said it wasn't that at all. "You're a pretty girl, Lord knows."

"I don't mind," she said and realized that she meant it.

He looked toward the window as if studying on the darkness. "You ever wonder what's on the other side?" he asked.

"Of the window?"

"No, well hell, maybe." He set his beer down and ran his hands through his hair. "I killed a boy once, named Billy Lawson. You know about that, don't you?"

"I heard some things."

"I told myself I didn't have no other choice, but I probably did."

She put her hand on his shoulder. "You think about it a lot?"

"Not till here recently." He picked up his beer and then set it back down. "I got cancer in the lungs. You wouldn't know it to look at me, would you? It's pretty far gone. They keep talking about surgery and chemotherapy, but I can't wrap my head around any of that shit. I keep thinking about that boy, wondering if he's going to be waiting for me when I cross over, what I'll say to him if he is."

She touched his face, felt the hard bones beneath his skin. She moved her hand to his chest and felt his heart beat against her fingertips. She wanted to kiss him, but he took her hand and squeezed it.

"There's some things a man shouldn't ever have on his conscience."

"Maybe you ought to listen to what the doctor says."

"You sit here and rest. We'll just leave Prince Charming out there in the cold. Might do him good to freeze his butt off for a little while."

She took out one of the pills and washed it down with a swallow of beer. She straightened her legs and closed her eyes. The house was warm, and she nodded off for a little while. When Curtis woke her, she was dreaming about a huge stag that watched her and her daddy from across a tranquil, summer lake.

"I'd let you all stay over," Curtis told her. "But that little son of a buck would probably try to rob me, and I'd end up killing him. That's one more thing I don't want on my head."

She tucked Baby Ty's blanket around him and picked up the carrier. Shivering from the wind, she hurried towards the truck and then stopped and looked back at Curtis. He was standing on the threshold watching after her, and it struck her that she didn't really understand anyone, herself most of all. She went back to him and kissed his cheek, and then he turned back inside as if that had been what he was waiting for.

"Well ain't that sweet," Bryson said when she climbed into the truck. "You sure don't look like you had a bad time."

"You know what they say," she said, fitting the car seat in between them. "The older the ram ... "

She thought she would enjoy seeing his hurt, but when she looked at him, he was just shaking his head. Stricken. It was a word she barely knew, but it was the one she thought of when he leaned forward to start the ignition.

"Mission accomplished," she said.

"What?"

"We came looking for a score," she said. "So I reckon this is the end of the rainbow." She picked up his cell phone. "Want to tell your buddies about it?"

He didn't say anything, just shifted the truck into drive. In silence, they headed into the dark and snow.

The truck bounced and jolted, but she barely noticed. She drifted off, lost somewhere between sleep and the Oxy buzz. She felt like a ghost haunting her own life. At some point Bryson began talking, his words a drone of nonsense in the darkness. With her eyes closed, she saw herself and her daddy walking down a country road, a herd of deer standing in an open field watching them. She thought about Curtis and felt his arms around her, his breath warm against her skin as he whispered that she was beautiful, a possible past that hadn't quite happened, but then she saw herself looking down at him in a cold, white hospital room where all the machines had fallen silent.

Suddenly the truck jerked and slewed and Bryson said, "Goddamn it," and Baby Ty woke up bawling. She didn't bother to open her eyes to find out why, but she imagined that the big buck she'd seen earlier had darted in front of them, that Bryson had panicked and yanked the wheel too hard, imagined the truck lying upside down at the bottom of a gully, the three of them dead, silent and without hunger forever. Then it was only Bryson that she imagined dead. She clearly saw him pitched from the truck, lying crumpled and broken on dark snow while she and Baby Ty walked away into an imagined future where her house was clean and warm, and he did his homework at the kitchen table and his father was just a fond memory that couldn't hurt or betray or disappoint anyone. But she knew that future was a lie. Even if Bryson were dead, who was going to protect Baby Ty from his mother? Maybe she could do it. It would start with her kicking her habit. Who knew? Maybe Bryson would join her. If not, she could always leave him. Either way she could start right now by throwing away the pills Curtis had given her.

She jammed her hand into her pocket, but she didn't pull it back out. This was a big decision, and she was tired. For now the pills were fine. As long as they stayed in her pocket they wouldn't hurt anyone.

The truck bounced through a rut, and her head banged against the window. Then nearly as soon as she became aware of the truck's movement, it stopped and the motor went silent. A hand grabbed her shoulder, shook her harder than was necessary.

"Wake up," a voice said. "We're home."

She kept her eyes closed. Opening them seemed like too much trouble, but the voice wouldn't let her be. Home, it said over and over. Wake up. We're here. Suddenly, she wasn't sure what home meant or where here might be, whether it was some new place that she'd always dreamed of or just somewhere else she'd already been.

Magic Act

The day they fished Sherri Waddell from the river, it stopped raining. It had been raining a long time, and the sight of the sun through the gray clouds put everyone in a good mood. For a while, it had seemed it would rain forever. Dark brown water stood in fields, washed over roads, seeped into basements. But the day they fished Sherri Waddell from the river, we knew the worst of it was over.

She had washed up in the flooded beech trees on Clarence Gilles' place, just a few houses down from my family's farm. The river had carried her for miles, spun her topsy-turvy, head over heels in a rush of dark water, and then wedged her here in the V between two Beech trees. Her body was bent, her clothes torn, her hair thick with mud and bits of garbage. Four men in gum rubbers and raincoats waded into the water. They pushed and pulled at her body, but the trees wouldn't let go. They wrenched and twisted her body, but the trees wouldn't let go. Dwayne Pendley cursed the trees and cursed the water and cursed the corpse. My father joked that Sherri Waddell had always been trouble.

That was the truth. I was only fourteen, but I knew that. She was twenty-one and she had two children and no husband. She wore mini-skirts, see-through blouses, short-shorts, and halters. She had a tattoo. She slept with old men and young boys and husbands. Most of the women in town, my mother included, called her "that Waddell whore." Most of the men in town didn't call her anything. At least not in public.

Now four men shoved and grunted and tugged at her body. Someone suggested chopping down the trees. Someone suggested chopping her in half since it was her hips that were wedged and causing the trouble.

The men talked. They nodded. They agreed. Dwayne Pendley stomped through the water and mud, cursing quietly, a Pall Mall burning to a stub in the corner of his mouth.

The ax didn't make a sound, at least not one that I remember. Then two men grabbed the torso and two men grabbed her legs, and Sherri Waddell made it to dry land.

"Jesus Christ," Dwayne Pendley said.

No one moved. They stood there. My father

seemed to realize that I was with him for the first time that morning. He put his thick hand on my shoulder.

"Maybe you should head home," he said.

I didn't move. I stood there. Charley Renfrow pulled a pint of Yellow Stone from his pocket, took a drink, and passed the bottle around. When it came to me, I drank and gagged at the taste of it. Then, when my father nodded, I took another drink and passed him the bottle.

"Sun's out," Charley Renfrow said and pitched a cigarette butt into the water.

We looked up. We saw the sun. We knew the worst of it was over.

Tick

Yeah, I know what people say, what they need to believe. But get this straight. I didn't get in the wrong line when God was bestowing souls on all the soon-to-be-borns. I wasn't engineered in a mad scientist's lab or promised to the Dark Lord Satan at conception. I came into the world just like every other glorified ape on this planet - shat out in blood and urine between my mother's thighs.

Keep that in mind.

* * *

The clothes kept going around, ticking as they went. It was a zipper or button clanging against metal, but I didn't believe it. I knew it was a clock, maybe God's own wristwatch, counting down to a disaster. When it stopped, I'd turn to discover that the world had disappeared into blackness or that a mushroom cloud was blooming in the sky or worst of all that my mother had left me here to wander the Suds and Stuff Laundromat forever.

Deserting me was bad. Dying was worse. Once I had that thought, I latched onto it and couldn't let go. The longer I stood there and stared at the tumbling clothes, the more certain I became that when the ticking ended, my mother's heart would quit.

The dryer's buzzer sounded. The clothes slowly stopped their tumbling. I wouldn't look away from them. As long as I didn't, I wouldn't have to see that my mother was dead.

"Ronny Wayne, get out of that woman's way so she can get her things."

My mother sat on one of the long tables, flanked by a pile of clothes, her legs hanging over the edge. Her yellow, V-neck T-shirt was soaked through, her hair frizzed, her eyes puffy, but I thought she glowed like an angel. I ran to her and hugged myself to her legs. Her thighs were sweat-slick and smelled of old perfume and grit, but I breathed her in as hard as I could, wanting to swallow her so that she'd always be with me, and we'd be safe together forever.

"Let go of me," she hissed. "It's too damn hot for this nonsense."

She pushed me away. Everyone in the

laundromat was looking. I wiped my snotty nose on the back of my arm.

A yellow-haired little girl in a pink T-shirt stared at me over the lip of an Orange Crush bottle. I took a few steps towards her, my heart stutter-beating, my skin tingling. She looked up at her momma, a fat lady with dyed, red hair. Her momma told her to go ahead and say hello.

"Hi," the girl said.

"Tell him your name, sweetie," her momma said.

"Trisha," she said. "Trisha Beth."

I slapped her. My hand caught her flush on the cheek, snapped her neck around. She squealed in surprise, and I yanked the bottle from her hand. I was thirsty, but I didn't want to drink it. I smashed it against the floor, sent glass shards flying and orange soda splashing. The fat woman scooped up her daughter, but I grabbed the girl's ankle and bit the back of her calf.

Then my mother had me. She grabbed my arm, yanked me away from the girl, and I went down on my knees so that she had to drag me out of there. Some of those glass shards cut into my shins, but that was okay. Even then, I liked sharp.

"I'm so sorry," my mother said.

"White trash little bastard," the fat woman

said.

A gray-haired woman with clicking dentures snorted. "What do you expect from the child of a whore?"

I kept my eyes on the girl. She was crying and rubbing her cheek, and there was blood on her leg.

"Please momma," I chanted over and over.

"Please what?" she asked when we were outside.

I pointed back at the little girl. "Can we take her home?"

* * *

We rented an old Fleetwood trailer on a patch of weeds in Beech Creek, Kentucky. A man named Jessup Browning owned the trailer and a half dozen others littered along similar patches of ground at the edge of an abandoned strip mine. My mother liked to say the place wasn't much to look at, but the rent wasn't bad. Fifty dollars a month and two bottles of Listerine, she'd say and laugh. I didn't get it until I was nine, opened our front door and found Mr. Browning putting his thing in her mouth. It didn't freak me out or anything. By then I'd pretty much figured out what the word whore meant and why everyone whispered it about my mother.

I sat on the porch until he came out, zipping his pants and headed across the yard. When I went inside, my mom was gargling at the kitchen sink. I got the joke.

* * *

I loved to wash her.

I can close my eyes and be there: a hanging fog of steam in the bathroom, the steady splatter of the shower against the tile, coconut shampoo foaming in her hair, water beads on her back.

"Scrub hard," she'd say. "I hate to get black heads on my shoulders."

Early on those showers were reserved for special occasions, like when we were going to the movies or one of her boyfriends was taking us to dinner, times when she didn't want to wait for our small, struggling water heater to warm another tank. Later, when she started sipping what she called Hillbilly Tea, Ale 8 and bourbon, just after breakfast and kept on until she passed out, it got to be more often.

"Get in here with me, Ronny," she'd slur. "I'm powerfully lonesome."

There wasn't nothing wrong with it. Sure, I got an erection a few times, but she didn't scream at me or slap me or make me put on a dress or any of the things you sometimes see in movies. She didn't do anything else either. She just ignored it or maybe said something like, "Goddamn men," every once in awhile. She wasn't exactly unfamiliar with erections.

* * *

My mother had a lot of "boyfriends," but only two of them tried to kill her. The first was a long-haul trucker named Red Vick. He liked me. I knew that because he always brought me a gift. Nothing much, just a pack of gum or a roll of Life Savers or something like that. I liked old Red, and my mother did, too - for a while. She was that way. Give her a man who treated the two of us like we were human beings, and she'd get bored. She never truly cared about anyone who didn't hurt her.

Red loved her. After she ran him off the first time, he kept coming back. He'd sit in our driveway playing country songs on the radio until he worked up enough heartbreak and courage to bang on our door. When she'd let him in, he'd bawl and tell her how much he needed her and how he couldn't let her go.

A few nights before Christmas, I woke to the glare of headlights and heard a motor

rumbling in our drive. I peeked out my window at a new Camaro, black and gleaming under the moonlight. Then a car door opened, and I heard my mother's laughter.

There were two of them with her, pretty young, grownups maybe but not that grownup. They clumped into our trailer, and there was a lot of laughing and the sound of bottles clanking and then a David Bowie album on the stereo. I got restless when things went quiet and slipped out of bed to see what was happening. The two guys sat on the couch, their jeans kicked into a corner, and my mother was on her knees in front of them, moving her mouth from one to the other. I watched until I got tired of it. Not long after I went back to bed, the Camaro's engine roared and the rear wheels peeled out when they caught gravel.

My mother was in the bathroom and had just flushed the toilet when there was thud at the door, followed by a roar like a seriously wounded animal rousing itself for a last stand. My mother came running into the hall.

"You no good, lousy whore!" Red screamed at her.

When I opened my bedroom door, Red had her by the hair and was slamming her head against the wall. He hit her in the stomach. While she was gagging and gasping for breath, he got a fist full of hair and slung her into the living room. He was kicking her in the ass, calling her a lousy bitch and a slut and a no-account whore when I ran in between them. Then the side of my head exploded in pain. My knees buckled. I fell backwards into the Christmas tree and sent it sprawling, and everything went black and spotty.

Next thing I knew Red was saying, "Look what I did. Look what you made me do, you worthless bitch."

He twisted her head around so he could look down at her, hawked and spit in her face. On his way out, he slammed the door so hard it bounced off the busted hinge. My mother crawled in the corner and sat there sniveling and spitting blood. His truck started, and I ran after him. Red was sitting behind the wheel with a gun pressed against his temple. He sat there a good while before he rolled down his window and pitched it into the yard and drove away. I ran out there and picked up the revolver. It was heavy and cool in my hand, and I liked the feel of it. I hid it in the rusted out gap in the underpinning at the back of our trailer.

My mother had dragged herself against the wall and she was trying to grin. I sat down beside her. She laid her head against my shoulder, and we stayed that way until morning.

We never saw Red again. But that doesn't really matter.

* * *

I was eleven when I first saw someone die. Reese Abel. He was ancient, seventy maybe, and he lived in a house about a quarter of a mile away from us. He was a nice old man, one who would give kids candy or even an ice cold Dr. Pepper when he was in the mood to share.

That day was in September, just after the hot weather broke. I took my bike by there because he was always happy to see me. He told me I looked a lot like his own son who'd died in a car wreck twenty-nine years ago. I went by that day and found him in his porch swing. He'd slumped down, his face twisted, his legs kicking at the wall, a chaw of tobacco sitting on his chin like a giant horsefly. I watched him for a long time and then his breath went out in a sour whoosh and his eyes rolled, and that was all for him.

That night I had my first wet dream.

Jeannie Sampson would show you her boobs for a dollar, let you play with them or kiss them whichever one you wanted, for three. She wasn't much to look at - dishwater-colored hair that fell limp against her shoulders, close-set green eyes that tended to cross when she tilted her head a certain way, lots of pimples. Still, I wanted a look at what she had to offer, so I stole seven dollars and a squashed-flat joint from one of my mother's "boyfriends" and went looking for Jeannie the very next day.

She was a couple of years older than me, lived with her mom, little brother and stepdad in a small block house a few places up from our trailer. It was mid-October, truly cool for the first time, and I took long, deep breaths and tilted my head towards the powder blue sky. She was sitting on a crumbling front porch, a magazine open in her lap.

Finally, I stuffed my hands in my back pocket and looked her way. "Hey," I said.

She squinted up at me. "Hey."

"You reading?"

She pitched the magazine on the porch. "I was."

"I got some money."

"Good for you."

I wanted to run. Maybe those boys had been lying. Maybe this whole thing was a joke they were playing on me, and Monday they'd all be laughing and hooting on the school bus.

Then she smiled and showed a lot of too small, yellowing teeth.

I pulled a wad of dollars from my pocket. "Come on. My money's as a good as anybody else's."

She shrugged her narrow shoulders, stood up and motioned for me to follow her. Their house backed up to a scrub woods, and she started down a twisty path without bothering to see if I was behind her.

"You going to show me or are we going to hike all day?"

"Shut up!" she hissed over her shoulder. "My daddy hears you I'll get blistered." She gave me her crinkly little smile. "You'll get an eyeful soon enough."

The Caney Creek Mines began just on the other side of the thicket. Fifteen years ago, it had been a booming strip mine, one of the largest in the state, but the coal veins had played out and the company had moved on, leaving behind a couple hundred unemployed miners, a few rusting coal shovels that looked like metal dinosaurs standing watch, and thousands of acres of overgrown fields, sandstone cliffs, deep water pits and twisting haul roads. Now Jeannie headed that way. As soon as she climbed over a sagging gate, she stopped, pulled a crumpled pack of Salem

Lights from her pocket.

She headed for a little wood hut about a hundred yards away. It had been a guard shack back when there had been something out here worth stealing.

"I want to get out of the wind," she said.

"It ain't that bad."

"Not if you get to keep your clothes on."

Boards creaked and buckled under our feet, sending field mice scurrying to the shadows. I pulled out a dollar.

She took the money, stuffed it in her pocket and then pulled her sweatshirt up over her head. She wasn't wearing a bra and her breasts were heavy and white, the only part of her that didn't have pimples. She posed for a second, hands on her hips.

"You want anything else?"

I took my wadded bills out. The joint fell to the shack's floor, and her eyes sparkled.

"Oh wow, hey," she said. "You smoke?" She licked her lips. "I tell you what? Give me two more dollars and share your doobie and I'll let you touch them and kiss them, too."

"Sure," I said.

Her skin tasted sour and slick, a little like milk that's sat too long outside the refrigerator but hasn't gone over yet. Her breasts rose and fell as she took a deep hit from the joint, held it and then exhaled.

"This isn't bad shit," she said.

I bit her. I'm not sure why, other than I suddenly wanted to bite. I sunk my teeth into her skin, tasted blood squirt into my mouth. Her yelp made it better so I bit again, harder this time and tore and then she shoved me away. She stood there for a second screaming at me with blood running down her chest, calling me crazy and a motherfucker and all kinds of other nasty names. Then she picked up her sweatshirt and ran out.

I didn't try to stop her or run after her to beg her not to tell. I didn't think she would because then her daddy would know what she'd been doing. But it didn't really matter, not at that moment. I was trembling and licking my lips and aching deep in the pit of my stomach. I'd tasted blood, and I wanted more.

* * *

I don't like to talk about the dogs. Understand. I'm not apologizing for what I did. They were necessary. They helped ease the hunger that gripped me after that day at the mines, and I used Red's old twenty-two on them so they didn't feel a lot of pain. Back then I didn't start cutting until after they were dead.

Still, I don't like to talk about them. That's all I'm saying.

* * *

Jimmy Lee Morris was the second boyfriend to try to kill my mother. He didn't do it because he loved her too much or because she took up with another man or even because he got drunk and lost control. He didn't need a reason. Jimmy Lee Morris was just mean, and sometimes that meanness got out of hand.

"Fetch me a beer, Queer Boy," he'd say.

If I didn't jump up right then, he'd strike a match and pitch it at me. My mother winced every time he did it, but she didn't say anything. Maybe it was because she was scared of him, or maybe she figured I was a teenager and should be standing up for myself. But I don't think either of those were true. For the first time in her life, she had fallen in love.

He was a handsome man. That's what everybody said about him. He was tall, thin but with lots of ropy muscles, dark-haired and blue eyed. He combed his hair back like a young Elvis and wore four hundred dollar cowboy boots, indigo jeans, and sleeveless T-shirts that showed off the ink on his arms. A few years younger than my mother, he'd grown up in

Greenview, moved south to work an oilrig and then spent eight years in prison in Mississippi for manslaughter after a barroom fight turned bad. He'd served max time and walked away a free man. "Parole is for pussies," he'd say and laugh. He'd been back in Kentucky maybe a week when my momma found him at the Yellow Rose.

I was in my bed that night, not sleeping, just lying there and remembering the last dog I'd found out at Caney Creek and getting worked up about it, when I heard them come in. At first it didn't sound like anything different. They were drunk and laughing and making those sounds I'd been hearing for as long as I could remember.

"Not out here," my mother said at one point. "Ronny's home, and I don't want to wake him."

"You telling me no?"

"Not exactly," my mother said in her teasing voice.

I'm not sure I heard the slap, but I did hear her shout and then the sound of bottles tumbling in the kitchen. She said please a few times, and he growled that she should shut her fucking mouth. There were stumbling sounds and another thud and then the sound of my mother pleading again, but not the hurt and surprised pleas she'd made earlier. I went to see what was happening.

Her face was pressed to the kitchen counter, her skirt pushed up, her panties down. Jimmy Lee was fucking her from behind. He had a fistful of hair in his hand, and every time he thrust into her he banged her head against the counter, and she was begging him not to stop, to give it to her harder. Then he turned his head and saw me watching. He gave me a wink, then thrust again, and my mother shouted his name.

* * *

"Fetch me a beer, Queer Boy," he'd say.

But sometimes there was a little less nasty tone in it. If he was in a particularly good mood, he'd tell me to help myself to one while I was at it. Then we'd sit on the couch, watching a ball game, laughing. Those were pretty good times. I just want you to understand. Despite the way things worked out, I didn't hate him. Hell, it wasn't really personal at all.

Nights when he was feeling playful, he'd start teasing my mother because her fried chicken was over cooked or she'd left one of his records out or she hadn't kissed him like she meant it. She'd stop whatever she was doing and peer into his face to determine his mood and when she saw he was teasing, she'd tell him if he didn't like it he could kiss her ass.

"Smart-mouthed aren't you, girl?" he'd say. "Could be you need a spanking to put you on the right track."

"Maybe I do."

He'd undo his belt, and she'd take him by the hand and lead him down to her bedroom. The cracking sounds of leather on skin would begin soon after. Sometimes, he'd get carried away, and her sobs would fill the trailer, but before it was over, she'd be calling his name again and again, begging him to never stop what he was doing.

* * *

He had a big, deer knife with a wooden handle with grips and an eight-inch, serrated blade. He carried it everywhere. Sometimes, he'd pull it out and hold it up and stare at me.

"You're lucky I don't gut you, boy," he'd say. "You're such a worthless piece of shit."

I didn't hate him but I didn't care that much about him either. But that knife? Let me tell you. I dreamed about that son of a bitch.

* * *

My mother was drinking her Hillbilly Iced Teas all day long by then. She'd drink even heavier during those times when Jimmy Lee walked out the door in the morning and didn't come back for two or three days.

"Get in here with me, Ronny," she'd slur when she was in the shower. "I'm powerfully lonesome."

That's when I noticed the cigarette burns on her neck and breasts. It didn't take long to figure out how they got there or why nearly every night when he was around, she'd cry and whimper just before she started making those squealing, pleading sounds.

"I miss him," she'd say. "Oh God, I miss him so bad."

* * *

She'd passed out on the sofa. Her worn out robe gaped open; her Hillbilly Iced Tea puddled on the floor. I meant to put her to bed, but instead, I stood over her, watching the rise and fall of her breathing. I put my hand on her chest and felt her heartbeat. I closed my eyes and moved my hand down a little and squeezed. She moaned in her sleep.

I pulled the robe open on her thigh and left it that way. Then I lit one of her Virginia Slims, took a deep drag so the tip glowed and sparked. I pressed it to the inside of her thigh. She bucked and moaned and mumbled the word "Please." I ground it into her thigh, and smiled that I'd left my mark on unmarked skin.

"Oh please, yes, baby," she mumbled.

But I felt shaky, so I stubbed the cigarette and went to bed. She didn't say anything the next morning, but her eyes were glassy when she looked at me, and she hugged me so hard I thought she was trying to crawl into my skin.

* * *

I found his pills in the medicine cabinet - a rainbow of colors. Through trial and error, I figured them out. Yellow meant going up; red would take you to the top of Mount Everest; blue brought you back safely to solid ground.

* * *

None of this was premeditated.

The last time he came back meaner than usual. For two days, he stomped through our trailer, mocked everything I said, did horrible things to my mother while I watched and she held tight to a smile that seemed on the verge of melting. That's why I slipped the blues into his whiskey, six of them - enough I figured to make him pass out no matter how many reds he'd been popping.

Trying to make him happy, my mother cooked a "special" dinner - porterhouses and baked potatoes and Caesar salad and shrimp cocktails for an appetizer. He bit into his steak, chewed as if it had insulted him and then spat into his napkin.

"Like rubber," he said. "How do you expect me to eat this shit?"

"It's okay," she said. "Mine's good. You want to trade?"

He glared at me. "How's yours?"

"Not bad."

He grabbed my plate, slammed it at the sink and then up-ended the table and stood with his fists balled, glaring at my mother. "You think I didn't notice those burn marks on your thighs? You think I don't know where they came from?"

"Jimmy ... " she said.

He hit her before she could finish, not a slap, but a right cross that knocked her out of her chair. Then he fell on her, kicking her in the stomach and back. He lifted her by her hair and bounced her off the refrigerator a couple of times before punching her again and again. She tried to run, but he grabbed her. His hand closed around her throat, choked her until she was gasping and slobbering. When he got tired of that, he slammed her against the floor while blood ran from her ears and burbled at her lips. He held her there a moment and glanced back at me and then pitched her into the living room.

I leaned against the refrigerator and watched, feeling my heart hammering in my chest while he kicked her and punched her. At some point, he pulled the knife and cut off her denim shorts. He spread her thighs and looked back at me.

"Have at it, boy?" I shook my head and he said, "Suit yourself."

It didn't take him long to finish. When he did, he pulled himself to his feet and dropped the knife and roared like a wounded animal.

"I'm done," he said. "I'm out of this madhouse."

He didn't get far. His foot caught on the bottom step. He fell and lay still, passed out in the yard.

My mother wasn't dead, not quite. I could smell blood and semen and anger, and it had me all worked up and trembling deep inside. When I shut my eyes I heard a ticking, the sound of metal ticking against metal as clothes tumbled around. I picked up his knife. I knew what to do with it.

"Oh please," she said.

Or at least that's what I heard. Once I started cutting, I didn't want to stop.

When I was done I took a dime-sized hunk from her thigh and put it in my mouth and swallowed it. I knew I'd have her with me no matter where I might go.

* * *

No one was surprised by what happened. Scared and disgusted, but not surprised. The Sherriff accepted what he saw: an ex-con with a bullet in his head and a .22 pistol in his hand; the town whore with her face pulverized, her throat cut, hunks of missing skin. *Murder Suicide Rocks the Area*! It was the most exciting headline the Beech Creek *Leader* ever ran.

They sent me to foster care in Alabama, far enough away that my tragic past wouldn't haunt me. I didn't have many friends, but that was all right. I spent a lot of time in the library, read a lot about sharks and tigers and other predators. When I turned eighteen I hit the road. Now, I work construction when I can find it, steal when I get the chance, beg when I have to. I'm not anyone you would notice. Hell, you've probably passed me or sat next to me at a bar if I was flush at the time.

But I sometimes hear you talking about me, hear the smooth-voiced bush league psychologists on the local news speculating about my motives. They point out that my victims are prostitutes or drug addicts or teenagers engaged in some backseat groping and assert I'm a religious fanatic, a punisher, a delusional maniac who believes he's acting on behalf of God. To tell you the truth, I could give a fuck what anyone does in their spare time. This is America. Live and let live, right?

It's so much simpler than that. When people are doing things they don't want anyone to know about, they tend to go off alone. They leave the herd. They're a wounded seal thrashing. They're a broken-winged moth caught in a web. That's just the way it works. I keep my knife sharp and wait, and they always come to me in the end.

Tick tock. Around and around. I close my eyes and I can still hear that ticking and know that clock is still counting down the moments. Sooner or later, I'll open my eyes and see that the world has disappeared to black, see that I've been left in darkness just like I thought I would be back in that laundromat all those years ago. But it doesn't scare me now.

I've got so many of you inside me. I'll never really be alone.

END

Acknowledgments

The following stories first appeared, in slightly different form, in the following publications: "Where the Morning Sun Goes Down," "Promissory Notes" and "The Last Wrestling Bear in West Kentucky" in *Ellery Queen's Mystery Magazine*; "Breaking Ground in Paradise" in *Plots with Guns* and *Esquire: Ukraine*; "Something About Teddy" in *Plots with Guns* and *Best American Mystery Stories 2004*; "Happily" and "Tick" in *Plots with Guns*; "And Ivy Leaves the Door Unlocked" in *Murdaland #1*; "We Will Find Each Other" and "Where You Find Yourself" in *New Madrid*; "The Last Day of Your Life" in *Lullwater Review*; "Little Bell, the Beasley Boys and a Long Road Home" in *Not One of Us*; and "Magic Act" in *Eureka Literary Magazine*.

I would like to thank Dale Ray Phillips, an extraordinary writer, professor and friend who taught me the importance of having a strong first line, a clean sentence and a willing accomplice. Thanks Dale for always listening, for working relentlessly to help me become a better writer and most of all for passing on your love of a story. Brad Younkin was a hell of a writer and a close friend. I just wish that he were around to realize how much I'm in his debt. You left too soon, Brad, and you're still missed after all these years.

I owe a special thanks to Jonathan Woods at New Pulp Press for believing in these stories and for making this book possible. Nothing is better than working with an editor who happens to be a writer you admire. I'd also like to thank the editors of the magazines and quarterlies where these stories first appeared. Anthony Neil Smith and Sean O'Kane at *Plots With Guns* have a special place in my heart for publishing so many of these stories. It was Anthony Neil Smith who accepted my first attempt at noir fiction and started all of this. I also owe a huge thanks to the incomparable Otto Penzler of the Mysterious Press for his encouragement and for the honor of being included in the Best American Mystery Stories Series.

One of the luckiest days of my writing life was the day I mailed a short story to *Ellery Queen's Mystery Magazine* and began a decade long working relationship with Janet Hutchings. She will always have my respect, admiration and affection for being a remarkable editor, a perceptive critic and a gracious friend.

None of these stories would have been written without my wife, Sherraine, who read and critiqued all of them with unique insight and, more or less, gentle honesty through draft after draft. Sherraine makes my work and my life better. There is no way to repay that debt. Finally, I'd like to thank Pops and Thumpy-Doo. There are a million reasons.

About the Author

Tim L. Williams

Tim's stories have appeared in a variety of literary quarterlies as well as "genre" magazines such as *Ellery Queen's Mystery Magazine, Plots with Guns, Not One of Us* and the now sadly defunct *Murdaland.* Two of his stories have been included in Houghton Mifflin's *Best American Mystery Stories* series, for 2004 and 2012. He won a 2012 Thriller Award from the International Thriller Writers in the short story category, received a 2014 Edgar Award nomination for "Where the Morning Sun Goes Down," and has twice been nominated for a Shamus Award for best short story. Tim is a native of Muhlenberg County, Kentucky, an area known for its coal mines, its production of meth and its yearly Everly Brothers Festival. After years of drifting around the middle of the country, working jobs that ranged from assistant produce manager to college professor, Tim returned to his hometown in Kentucky, where he lives with his wife and two children.

Thank you for reading.
Please write a review of this book. Reviews help
others find newpulppress.com and inspire us to
keep bringing you the best in crime fiction.

http://www.newpulppress.com/